FROM OSTRICH TO STANDING STONE

Betty J. McBee

AmErica House
Baltimore

First printing

ISBN: 1-58851-555-9
PUBLISHED BY AMERICA HOUSE BOOK PUBLISHERS
www.publishamerica.com
Baltimore

Printed in the United States of America

Dedicated
To The Memory of
Carlton Bump
A teacher, a mentor, a friend

CHAPTER 1

Where were those policies? Elizabeth had put them in that proverbial safe place. She had no idea what that safe place was. She had looked everywhere. One more time she pulled open the heavy file drawer and began to search through the files. Her eyes fell on a set of yellowed papers. The ink from the old duplicating process was fading badly.

Elizabeth had forgotten about writing this. It had been so many years ago, a time when she was testing her skill at creative writing by recording significant moments in her life. Elizabeth took the papers out and closed the drawer.

This is an interesting time for this to surface, she thought as she began to skim the pages she had found. The search for the policies could wait. Elizabeth was going to settle down with a mug of coffee and read the pages she had just rediscovered.

It had looked like a good fire. The papers had flamed and burned for several minutes. The blue tongue of fire had licked along the log and had even caught hold on the smaller pieces. But the taste of success was brief. The blue flames first, then the yellow receded into the red-orange glow of the coals. There was still hope in the glowing coals. She got up and taking a magazine fanned the fire until, once more, flames sprang forth. But this new promise was not without cost. The prolonged fanning had brought the smoke of the fire into the living room. The room was filled with a gray haze. She settled back into her chair, eyes stinging. Tears rolled easily from her eyes and down her cheeks losing momentum and moisture as they proceeded down their unsteady course until they stopped short of their goal and dried. These tears, not being rooted in emotion, ceased as her eyes adjusted to the smoke.

Once more, the promising flames proved fraudulent. Slowly (or suddenly, who can tell), they lost their fire and zeal and faded out leaving only the snapping of dying embers and the howling of the wind around the corner of the house to keep her company. This room, in which she had envisioned herself a solitary figure filled with the warmth and happiness symbolized in the crackling, cheery fire before her, took on an air of chilly bleakness. The solitary figure was there but without the drama. She was sitting aimlessly before the blackening ashes of a dead fire a fire that had gone out, having never really burned at all.

How much like her life this episode was. How often had the bright promises faded away? In fact, when had they not? It was this latter fact that at once both discouraged her and encouraged her. It was so much the story of her life that even when she was plunged into the depths of despair she knew, rather by a vague feeling than conscious thought, that life would return to normal. Moreover, that she would try the same thing again. Sometimes she almost wished that were not the case. Somehow, it made everything pointless to settle back into the normal routine of existence with the monstrous, devastating emotional upheavals of life only a nearly unreal memory. She sensed that one could get used to anything, and she hated that resiliency of man. It seemed to her to be infidelity although others might see it as strength of character.

The fire had failed before. She had not yet built a successful fire in that fireplace, but this time she had been sure of success. She had prepared more and knew the techniques better this time. She had waited for an evening when she was alone and when the weather raged outside, making home more of a sanctuary. This touch of the dramatic or the romantic she allowed herself to indulge in private. The fire had failed again, and failure left her feeling exposed and hopeless--exposed in her foolish little romantics.

When one succeeds, things are taken and accepted by the world as part of a normal, healthy life. When one fails, the foolishness of the action becomes its most obvious aspect. Even in private, one is painfully conscious of it. Even then, you have the sense of a vast sea of faces, some familiar and some unfamiliar, all turned toward you with mocking smiles on their lips or pity in their eyes. You want neither, and they offer nothing else. So, though alone she felt thus - exposed, foolish, and hopeless. One failure has the power to negate all previous triumphs and leave one feeling totally and hopelessly insufficient.

Well, the pleasant satisfaction of the evening was ruined; and although she had no intention of becoming morbid over such a little thing, she did allow herself to consider briefly the parallel of this simple incident to the twenty-seven years of her life. As if to prove a point, just when she had settled down to a melancholy analysis of her life, she was no longer alone. Her roommate and fiancé returned home. She was caught in the

living room unable to escape unnoticed to pursue her melancholy thoughts.
"Oh, a fire. How nice."

"Is that fireplace smoking again? I suppose the smoke all went upstairs to my room!"

There was nothing to do but to explain the charred logs and smoke filled room, to be the reasonably intelligent, friendly young woman they expected to find, to tell the story of the evening as a mock tale of woe. She was a clown. Even this simple event, as she told it, became another amusing adventure. Her friends settled comfortably on the couch and the talk moved on to other topics - politics, chemistry, and capital punishment. Her presence was desired; her views were requested and listened to with interest.

She had to forsake her earlier thoughts to be active in the present. She retreated behind the mask, the facade she presented to the world, the false front of humor and wit that hid the depth of her private loneliness and despair.

No, this was not altogether true. She did retreat. She did put her private emotions and personal needs aside. But this so-called facade was not a mask. It was another facet of herself. This bright outlook, this ability to meet life as something not to be taken too seriously, despite all odds, was as much a part of the real person as were the other aspects she had so recently been considering. It was a part of her which, although it may lack the depth of the other, brought a satisfaction and honest contentment that was lacking before.

At any rate, the time of privacy was over. The normal had descended again. In the back of her mind, she promised herself the next fire would succeed.

Elizabeth finished reading the faded pages. The memory of the thoughts and feelings of a younger Elizabeth interested her. How accurate were those perceptions? Could her life be defined as a series of flashes of bright flames that quickly dwindled and faded into dying embers?

Elizabeth went to the kitchen to make herself another mug of coffee and took it back to the table. The missing policies were forgotten as Elizabeth fingered the yellow pages her mind drifting back in time.

* * * * *

Summer nights could be unbearably hot in southern Iowa, and the old house was built more to keep out the cold than to let in the summer breezes. All the bedrooms were upstairs and each bedroom had one long narrow window strategically located to block any cross flow of air. Later, Elizabeth's father would put in a row of smaller windows at the back of the house to allow night air to come in. For now, too many other things had to be done to make the house livable for a growing family.

Elizabeth was happy enough with the move to this house on the outskirts of town. It had a barn and sheds to house the menagerie of farm animals her father raised to help the family budget. It had a storm cellar half under ground and half a cement dome covered with earth and grass, which provided a "mountain" to play on. There were rhubarb plants with huge leaves that could be pulled off and used as make believe umbrellas.

Railroad tracks ran along the backside of the pasture and along their neighbor's side yard. A small freight train with a passenger caboose came past every day about noon on its way to the station in town and returned in the afternoon. The train marked the time for them on a summer day. And often, when they heard the train whistle as it rounded the bend along Mr. Finney's cornfield, they would run into the neighbor's yard, hang on tightly to the spindly tree in the middle of the yard, and wave to the engineer and the conductor.

If you didn't hang onto something when the train went past, it would suck you under. Lois and Janet taught them that as soon as they moved in. So, there was always an element of flirting with danger when they ran to greet the train. Once, Elizabeth was alone exploring the no man's land between the tracks and their pasture when the whistle sounded. There had been no time to get to the tree. She wrapped her arms around the nearest fence post and hung on as tightly as she could not even daring to loosen her grip enough to wave. The train steamed by with earth shaking power but it didn't suck her under. After that, she only went exploring after the train's daily round trip.

Lois and Janet lived next door with their mother and her parents in the grandparent's home. They were nearer in age to Elizabeth's sister Arlene who was two and a half years older than Elizabeth. That put Elizabeth as a five-year-old in the unenviable position of sometimes being included and sometimes being considered an unwelcome tag-a-long and never quite sure of her place. This time, though, she was included in the planned adventure.

The idea was probably Arlene's. She was more imaginative than Lois and Janet, who were more on the tough side, and Arlene liked to read and books gave her ideas. *Raggedy Ann's Alphabet Book* must have planted the seed. The words were captivating and the pictures enticing to a creative heart.

> *E is for Elves, tiny creatures so small.*
> *Nearly all Elves are just two inches tall.*
> *F is for Fairies, they whisper advice*
> *To all kindly children and that's very nice.*

On the opposite page were two or three paragraphs telling about elves and fairies. They come out late at night after everyone is asleep and dance in the grass with lightning bugs as lanterns lighting their way.

That summer, when it was too hot to sleep up stairs, Elizabeth and Arlene were allowed to spread a sheet on the living room rug and sleep on the floor. It may not have been any cooler down stairs but at least the living room had windows on two walls and a full-length screen door on a third. Night had a magical, forbidden magnetism. Only a hook on the screen door stood between them and a magical adventure.

"Arlene! Arlene, are you awake?" Elizabeth's whisper cut through the gray silence of the steamy night.

"SHSSS, Shsssss!" Arlene's irritation silenced Elizabeth and they lay motionless. Both listening for sounds upstairs to alert them that Mother and Dad were still awake. Stillness filled the air. It was time for the adventure to begin.

Lois and Janet would meet them in the front yard. They would form a "fairy ring" in the moonlight and dance in their nightgowns barefoot in the dew. Maybe the Elves and Fairies would show themselves as well.

Very quietly, Arlene got up and motioned to Elizabeth to follow. The hook on the screen door was high, almost out of Arlene's reach. Every sound seemed magnified as Arlene eased the hook up-ward. Humidity caused the door to swell and the hook to tighten. It gave with click and a clunk that echoed in the stillness. They held their breaths waiting for the sound from above that would end their adventure before it began. No sound came.

The pattern continued as the door stuck then gave way with a thud and the clunking of the hook on wood but all was well. The hard part was over.

Elizabeth and Arlene were free.

They ran down the front steps and into the yard to meet their friends. The yard was empty and the house next door appeared settled for the night, but that was good. Elves and Fairies never came out until people were asleep.

"Meow" "Meow" "Meow" Arlene and Elizabeth crouched beside Lois and Janet's house under the living room window. They dared not call them by name and wake up their grandfather whose belief in corporal punishment included neighborhood children as well as his own grandchildren.

"MEOW" "MEOW" "MEOW" "MEOOOW" "MEOOOOW" There was no response. No one came. There was no way to rouse Lois and Janet. There was no way to form the Fairy ring. There wasn't even any dew on the grass to cool their bare feet. There would be no great adventure. The night was no longer magical and inviting. The two sisters hurried back to the comfortable safety of their living room and fell asleep exhausted from the excitement.

"What were you girls doing outside last night?" Arlene and Elizabeth had no answer. "That had better never happen again!" Arlene and Elizabeth knew it never would.

CHAPTER 2

The house on Harrison Street was not as large as it appeared from outside. The bedroom Elizabeth shared with Arlene had sloping ceilings making the space smaller than the dimensions of the floor would indicate. A double bed took up most of the room with the dresser they shared and a small drop front desk fitted against the wall under the sloping ceiling.

The room was directly above the dining room where the coal stove sat in the winter months since there was no central heating. Directly above the stove was a floor register about a foot square. The opening in the floor was covered by a wrought iron grate to allow the warm air to filter up to the second floor. Even so, in the winter a glass of water would freeze solid if left on the windowsill beside Elizabeth's bed. Staying warm meant either standing on the iron grate when the fire was burning in the stove below or staying in bed under the heavy blankets and comforters.

After they had been sent to bed, Elizabeth and Arlene sometimes lay on the floor with their ears against the iron grate listening to the adult conversation below. Even two small heads didn't fit well on the small register and it often caused a scuffle that resulted in "You girls get to bed!"

"Nightsayyourprayerssweetdreams!" Elizabeth settled under the covers.

Almost in unison came Arlene's "Nightsayyourprayerssweetdreams!"

"I said it first!"

"No, I did!"

"I did!" The sisterly good night had turned into a power struggle again.

Elizabeth didn't want to give in. Being younger was always a disadvantage. Now she too was in school. She too could read, but she could never catch up with Arlene. Arlene was always going on to some new experience that left Elizabeth behind. Sometimes Elizabeth felt very sad and lonely.

Tonight, she withdrew from the conflict and moved to the edge of the bed withdrawing physically as well. She closed her eyes. For no reason, the image of a wall plaque that hung on the dining room wall across from her place at the table floated through her mind. It was a not really attractive; it was simply three pieces of cardboard connected by faded blue ribbon. Each piece of cardboard had one statement printed on it. The plaque blended into the wall so that Elizabeth hardly noticed it anymore, but she had read it so often she knew the words by heart.

"Jesus Christ is the Head of this home."

"Jesus Christ is the unseen guest at every meal."

"Jesus Christ is the unseen listener of every conversation."

Just words, the kind of thing you would expect to see on the walls of a pastor's home. Tonight, for Elizabeth, they were not just words. Elizabeth began to cry as the words pierced her loneliness. God had always been real to Elizabeth, but always distant. Her tears remained but the sadness was gone. Elizabeth knew she was not alone and what she did mattered because Jesus was there to see it. She moved over to make room for her unseen companion, no longer needing to feel physically or emotionally isolated.

CHAPTER 3

"What ARE you doing?" Elizabeth was taken back by the irritated tone of her mother's voice.

"I'm putting the sugar bowl away," she responded.

"Why are you bending over like that? Stand up straight!"

Elizabeth had not consciously leaned over as she put the sugar bowl on the second shelf of the cupboard. Now, as she tried to do as her mother said, she found that she couldn't.

"I can't reach the shelf unless I lean over."

"When did that start?" her mother questioned.

"I don't know. I think after I hurt my shoulder when I tripped on the basement steps."

"Humph," her mother registered dissatisfaction with the situation but dropped the subject.

There were too many more important matters to attend to. The family had grown to five children. Marilyn was only a year and a half, and baby Louise was four months old. The older children had to share the work. Elizabeth was nine, which was old enough to be expected to take on a good bit of responsibility. A sore shoulder was not cause to be excused from her chores so, as long as she got them done, how was not that important.

Elizabeth's shoulder healed, but she still had trouble reaching up with her right arm. Dr. Montgomery didn't think there was anything to be concerned about but suggested that they consult a specialist at the University Hospital to make sure. Years earlier, Elizabeth's parents had accepted Dr. Montgomery's explanation of why Elizabeth could not smile or make the usual facial expressions. Dr. Montgomery thought Elizabeth had had a mild case of polio. So mild that it had not been diagnosed but it had left her face relatively immobile. Now, if he thought they should check with a specialist, they would take his advice.

The specialist was in Iowa City, an hour's drive from home, and there were long tedious hours spent in waiting rooms. Elizabeth hated being the cause of all the trouble. They were sent from one doctor's office to another and given follow-up appointments, which entailed more trips to Iowa City. The doctors were obviously very important people and were very busy. Elizabeth was haunted by the fear that in the end they would find that nothing was wrong with her and she had caused everyone all this trouble

13

for no reason.

One doctor put both hands on her head and lifted her off the ground. "There's nothing wrong with this child except lazy posture!" His tone was one of annoyance. Shame at his words replaced the physical pain he had just inflicted. Elizabeth's worst fear was coming true.

The doctors decided to admit Elizabeth to the hospital for final tests. She had never been in a hospital before. When her mother and father left, she felt very small and unsure of herself. In all the visits to the specialists, her mother had always been there. Now she was on her own under the authority of strangers. It was late afternoon by the time all the paper work was finished and she was settled in. No sooner had her parents left, than she was moved from the room they had settled her into first, to another down the hall.

Everything was white and empty. Elizabeth didn't know what to do with herself. She went to the door of her room and looked out. Down the hall was a boy about her age amusing himself by wheeling himself in a wheel chair. The nurses and orderlies seemed to know him well, stopping to chat a minute as they went by. Elizabeth took her cue from him and decided to explore. She wandered down the hall glancing into rooms and observing the carts sitting along the hall.

"What are you doing? Get back to your room!" An orderly grabbed her by her arm and began pulling her down the hall, but he was pulling her toward the wrong room. He was taking to the first room before they moved her.

"No. No. Not..." Elizabeth pulled back afraid. The situation was beyond her control. If she went with him, she would be wrong. If she refused, she was wrong.

"What is going on?" a nurse intervened.

"I caught her wandering around in the hall. I'm trying to get her to her room."

"She should be in 237 C," the nurse said, then turned to Elizabeth and scolded. "We don't need any trouble. You are to stay in your room!"

Elizabeth had never been known to be an outgoing child. Time after time her teachers would write in the comments on her report cards. "Elizabeth is extremely shy," "Elizabeth needs to learn to participate more freely," or "Elizabeth has much to contribute but her shyness is a problem." Her venture into the hall had been out of character and had been a mistake.

She thought that the best thing to do was sit on the bed and wait as the hospital routine went on around her.

The next morning, Elizabeth was scheduled for a spinal tap. It took three people to hold her still enough to insert the needle safely into her spine. She tried to remain curled forward and absolutely still as she was instructed to do, but every time she felt the prick on her back, she flinched. Everyone was getting very annoyed with her. It was a terrible ordeal. Elizabeth hated being considered such a baby and now she was beginning to feel smothered by all the bodies holding her in place. The spinal tap was finally successfully completed. Elizabeth was relieved to get back to her room.

However, the hospital room was not a sanctuary. Four men in white coats visited her in her room. One seemed to be in charge. He talked to the others about Elizabeth using a lot of words she didn't understand. Elizabeth felt very awkward being observed as though she as a person wasn't really there.

The doctor in charge took an envelope out of his pocket and dropped it on the floor. He said to Elizabeth "There's a five dollar bill in that envelope. Pick it up and you can have it." Obediently, Elizabeth bent down and picked up the envelope. It was empty. She felt shame at being tricked. She would have picked up the envelope. He didn't have to try to trick her.

"Do you like to ride bikes?" he asked.

"Yes."

"There's a bike in the hall. Run out there and you can ride it."

This time, Elizabeth hesitated. She didn't really think there was a bicycle in the hall or that the nurses would allow her to ride it if there was. But she knew she should trust and respect adults and be obedient.

"Go on! Run out to the hall," he encouraged her. Surely, he would not think her so stupid as to have to be tricked twice.

Elizabeth did as she was instructed and ran the few yards out into the hall. The hall was empty. Elizabeth flushed with shame. How foolish she must appear to the others in the room. *Why did the doctor treat her like that?*

Elizabeth returned to the room and the doctors continued their discussion for a few minutes then left to see their next case in another part of the hospital. Elizabeth was forgotten before they left her room.

When her parents came to take her home, Elizabeth was sound asleep. The call from the hospital to tell them to come for her had come in the night. No one seemed to know why it could not have waited until morning. No one seemed very pleased to have this disruption in the middle of the night. A groggy Elizabeth allowed herself to be dressed, her things gathered up and led down the hall to where her parents were waiting.

George McKievey, Elizabeth's father, never found it easy to stay awake while driving at night. Money was always scarce with a large family on a small income, but tonight Elizabeth was in for a treat. Half way home there was a small roadside cafe that stayed open all night. Elizabeth's father stopped for a cup of coffee to keep him awake. They all went in and sat down at a little table in the center of the room. When the waitress came, he ordered coffee for himself and a piece of pie for each of them. This would stretch their budget and could never have happened with the whole family along. Elizabeth was not particularly hungry but it was very special to have this private time with her parents. The lateness of the hour with the blackness of the night isolated them into a family unit where she felt truly a part. At that moment, Elizabeth was happy.

They made one last trip to Iowa City that summer to meet with the specialist. Elizabeth sat alone in the waiting room for what seemed like hours while the doctor met with her parents.

"Elizabeth, will you come in now?" the doctor opened the door for Elizabeth to come in and motioned for her to sit in the empty chair. Elizabeth felt like she had just been summoned to the principal's office for some unknown offense or shortcoming.

"Elizabeth, I've just been telling your parents you have something called muscular dystrophy. That is why you have a hard time reaching up and you can't smile."

Elizabeth felt a wave of relief. There was something wrong. She had not wasted everyone's time with all these trips. It was not her fault.

Elizabeth nodded. She had heard enough. Now they could go home and life could get back to normal. Now she had a reason for why she was as she was.

CHAPTER 4

Elizabeth wandered out to the barn; it was a sunny day and there was always something to do in the barn. The barn was connected to the garage by the chicken coup. The three made one structure, which sat well back on the property. The garage was positioned so that it was easily visible from the house but the barn was not. The garage was too far from the house to be practical as a place to park the car. It did serve well as a place to store boxes and barrels and various and sundry things making it fertile ground for exploring and a good place for mother cats to hide their newborn kittens. On the right side of the garage, a third of the area was portioned off to form a coal bin to hold the supply of coal needed to heat the house in the winter.

One of the chores for Elizabeth and Arlene (and later Basil, Marilyn and Louise) was to keep the coal buckets full in the winter. It was a daily task and getting the coal was a scary business. Boards were nailed across the door shaped opening of the coal bin to keep the coal from rolling out and keeping the inside of the bin invisible from the rest of the garage. It was a perfect place for the bad guys to hide out. Lois and Janet filled Elizabeth and Arlene's minds with stories about the bad guys that roamed about doing their bad deeds and always looking for a place to hide. This was obviously the kind of hiding place they would like.

The board stopped about a foot and a half at the bottom leaving an opening for shoveling the coal. Darkness came early in the winter and it was seldom possible on school days to get the coal buckets filled before dark. The garage was lit by a single bulb hanging from the ceiling over a cluttered workbench. The bulb provided adequate light for shoveling the coal but cast suspicious looking shadows all around the garage. Inside the bin, the coal was piled up like a mountain and, at certain points, shoveling would set off a small avalanche of coal sliding down toward the opening. The rolling coal could as easily be started by the movement of someone hiding out in the coal bin as from the shovel. Elizabeth always felt as if her heart froze when the avalanche began, but she would keep on shoveling. Going back to the safety and warmth of the house with the coal bucket half full was never allowed.

Today in the bright sunlight, the garage held no threat of danger. She used the route to the barn through the garage into the connecting door of the chicken coup and out the side door next to the barn door to arrive at the barn out of sight of the house. Elizabeth wasn't meaning to be deceptive but this route would avoid her mother's questioning "What were you doing in the barn?" Elizabeth didn't know what she would do in the barn. It was spring and she was simply enjoying the freedom to be outside again.

The barn was small by Iowa standards; but, then, this was just an acreage not a farm. It had all the essential components. The hayloft was reached by a ladder nailed flat against the wall just inside the door. The ladder went up into the hayloft through a hole cut out of the floor. The hole was never covered except when hay was being delivered and loaded through the loft door just above the barn door. The children were forbidden to play in the hayloft but sometimes the temptation was too much. The bales of hay could be dragged around to make tunnels to secret rooms or simply used to climb to the roof and look out through the spaces between the rough boards of the barn walls.

On the main level, the door opened into a lengthy area where feed was stored. It was essentially a walkway in front of the three stanchions for the cows. Elizabeth's father always kept two or three cows for milk and to produce calves for sale. When the cows came in morning and evening, they went right to the stanchions. Someone needed to move quickly to close the wooden bar at their neck and drop the hinged block of wood down to hold the bar in place. Elizabeth sometimes helped but it was a long reach up to the wooden block and a cow that didn't cooperate could be too much for a child's strength. The closed stanchion simply kept each cow in her place while leaving the cows free to eat the feed and hay in the stall in front of them. Iron kickers hung on the wall but were seldom needed. The McKievey's cows were usually very gentle.

Cows do not always respect the inside of a building. To provide for that, a narrow straw filled trough ran the width of the barn behind the cows as they stood in their stanchions. The trough was just wide enough for a shovel, and a window on the back wall provided an opening for tossing the scooped up soiled straw and manure onto the manure pile behind the barn. A wire fence surrounded the manure pile to keep the farm animals away.

Elizabeth let herself out the cattle door into the pasture. She was surprised to see that the manure pile was completely gone. The fenced in area looked invitingly clean and fresh with the sun shining warmly on the sprouts of weeds already pushing through the soil. Elizabeth had an idea.

She could plant a secret flower garden and surprise everyone when she brought bouquets for the table. It was a great idea.

Elizabeth's aimless stroll to the barn had suddenly taken on a purpose. She would need to get seeds but she could start now to prepare the ground. Gardening tools were kept in the garage so she retraced her route to the garage through the chicken coup. With a hoe, Elizabeth loosened up a rectangular space of ground back against the barn so it would be as much out of sight as possible. There were some old bricks piled haphazardly against the side of the garage. No one would miss them if she took a few to make a brick boundary around her little garden. Elizabeth could hardly wait. It was almost like Christmas, planning a surprise, figuring out how to make it work, and keeping all the preparations secret until the time was right.

On Saturday nights, almost everyone went to town. It was a time when grown-ups would run into friends or acquaintances and spend a few minutes in conversation before going on about their business. When the family went to town that Saturday, Elizabeth managed to leave her parents sight long enough to purchase three packets of seeds, choosing by the colors and pictures on the front of each packet. At five cents a packet, it taxed her meager allowance but Elizabeth didn't mind. Her secret garden was getting closer and closer to being a reality.

Once the seeds were planted, Elizabeth checked her garden daily. It got a lot of sun, so she had to carry water from the cow's tank in the pasture. It wasn't unusual, though, for Elizabeth to be seen at the cow's tank. Keeping it pumped full for the cattle was one of their summer chores. The flower seeds sprouted quickly, as did the weeds. Elizabeth did her best to figure out which was which and to pull the weeds to protect her flowers.

Usually, Elizabeth tended her secret garden in the morning. Today it was after lunch before she was able to slip away unnoticed to tend her garden. She rounded the corner of the barn and stopped in dismay. Her garden was covered with a thin layer of soiled straw and manure. Elizabeth's father had cleaned the barn. Her secret garden was ruined. No one knew it was there. She would not get to see it bloom and no one would get to enjoy her surprise.

Elizabeth felt a deep, intense disappointment, and at the same time, she felt embarrassed. *How could she not have realized that the absence of the manure pile was only temporary? Why had she so carefully planted her garden right under the window?* She could have known what would happen.

CHAPTER 5

"MY NAME IS MR. BUMP, B-U-M-P! EVERYONE LAUGH NOW AND GET IT OVER WITH!" In the silence that followed, there was not a sound, not even a nervous snicker.

Elizabeth was glad she had found a seat in the back row where she could, hopefully, be unnoticed by this gruff looking man standing at the teacher's desk at the front of the room. It was the first day of seventh grade. Everything was different. Locolyn Grade School had been a small spread out building surrounded by a large yard and playground. Each class had it's own teacher and it's own classroom where they spent the school day. The junior high school was a very old building. It stood two tall stories on a corner lot just two blocks from downtown. In junior high, the teachers had their own rooms but the students moved from room to room all day long.

As seventh graders, Elizabeth and her classmates felt lost and a little overwhelmed as they searched for the right room for the right class. To get from one floor to the other, they had to use the huge staircases at each end of the building. One staircase was for going down and the opposite staircase could only be used for going up. On the first day, it was easy to get confused and not know which direction to turn. Being caught going down the up staircase or up the down was cause for discipline.

The basement was half finished but held the bathrooms and two classrooms. The basement just had one staircase leading to the classroom area. Elizabeth and her classmates had descended these stairs cautiously in search of the art room. They located it to the left at the bottom of the stairs. It was a long, narrow windowless room crowded with desks. Pipes of various sizes ran across the low ceiling. Some were covered with insulated padding. Some were simply painted yellow to blend with the peeling paint on the ceiling. Art class was considered somewhat of a playtime, but this new art teacher had gotten their attention. No one moved.

Mr. Bump continued to talk. Elizabeth listened to what they would be doing in the art classes and what he expected of them when they were in his class. Despite his frightening beginning and his firm style, Elizabeth began to like him. When the bell rang, the seventh graders filed quietly out of the room. Still no one laughed.

"Art is going to be hard this year," someone said as they all climbed the basement stairs. There was general agreement.

"What do you think of Mr. Bump?" "I don't know!"

I think he will be okay, Elizabeth said to herself but not aloud because she wasn't sure that would be a popular opinion.

Elizabeth liked art; she liked to draw. When she was younger, she liked to make line drawings of cartoon characters. She would sit for hours working on an enlarged version of a character. She would spread a comic book out in front of her, carefully pencil the likeness of one of the characters onto her paper, then take crayons and cover the pencil lines with color. Elizabeth kept all the successes clipped between two pieces of construction paper carefully stored in the back of her closet.

Three or four times a year, Elizabeth's family would travel the hundred miles to her grandparents farm. Behind the house was the well. Typically, it was covered with a square of cement with a hand pump anchored in the middle of it. The land around the well was almost always damp and part of the ground was yellow clay. When it was wet, it could be molded like other clay. One visit she sat on the cement slab holding the pump and molded a set of little animal figures. She left them drying on the cement. Elizabeth was surprised when on their next visit to the farm she found her little animals sitting in her grandmother's curved front china cupboard. That unspoken compliment encouraged her.

Elizabeth's most recent and most significant encouragement came during evening church. Elizabeth and Arlene were old enough now, to be allowed to sit with the other girls their age. They often passed the sermon time doodling. A favorite thing for Elizabeth was to write a series of capital letters and turn them into cartoon like bugs, animals, and flowers. One night, Aunt Flo Montgomery was sitting two rows in front of them. Aunt Flo was the oldest person Elizabeth had ever known. She always wore her hair in a braided bun at the nape of her neck. Elizabeth began to make a line drawing of the figure before her. The girl beside her reached for the sketch, nodded her approval, and passed it on. The whole row of girls were nodding, giggling, and snatching at the scrap of paper.

Standing at the front of the small congregation, Elizabeth's father was quite aware of what was going on in the back row. As soon as they got home that night, Elizabeth was asked to explain her behavior at church. As the pastor's daughter, she was expected to set an example, not cause a disruption and her parents were angry with her. Even so, they acknowledged that the sketch had captured the likeness of Aunt Flo surprisingly well. Elizabeth carefully stored the sketch in the back of her closet.

As Elizabeth went to her locker to get ready for lunch, she was thinking about Mr. Bump, the new art teacher, there was something different about the way he had talked to her class last hour. He had seemed gruff at first, but then he had joked with the class and said some things that made her think. One comment stuck in her mind, and she didn't know why. Mr. Bump said, "If you don't have a sense of humor, you just as well be dead." Elizabeth knew his words had struck a cord in her somewhere and she knew she was looking forward to art class in junior high.

CHAPTER 6

In junior high, Elizabeth had made two real friends. Usually, Elizabeth had spent her time taking care of younger children. Elizabeth and Arlene were expected to take a lot of responsibility for their two little sisters. Arlene was not especially drawn to children, but Elizabeth started babysitting in her neighborhood when she was eleven. Parents trusted Elizabeth with their children because they knew her family, and the children often preferred Elizabeth to their other babysitters. Elizabeth was happy to baby-sit. It gave her a way to make money in a household where money was always scarce; but, even more, she loved children. She loved being a substitute mother. When she grew up, she planned to have five or maybe six children of her own. Hidden in a crevice above her top dresser drawer, so that no one would find it and laugh at her, was a little envelope she labeled *dreams*. Among what she had recorded and hidden away were the names she had chosen for her children, three girls and two, or maybe three, boys.

Having a friend her own age was new to Elizabeth. She had played with other children at school and when families visited with her family, but those were playmates. These two girls were not playmates. They were friends who talked together, exchanged ideas, and shared feelings. They were not a threesome; each friendship was separate. Each friend brought out something different in Elizabeth, but by the time she was in tenth grade, her friends were no longer around. Thelma's family moved out of town at the end of eighth grade. Now, Winnie's family had sent her to a boarding school for her last three years of high school. Elizabeth missed their friendship, but she was generally well liked at school and life went on.

"Elizabeth, do you know what you are going to write your paper on?" Sharon asked.

"No. I can't think of anything. What is yours on?" They had gotten down to lunch late and the line extended from the lunchroom all the way up the basement steps and down the hall. Actually, they didn't mind. Standing in the lunch line was a social time.

"Is Miss Moore assigning a research paper to your class too?" Sharon addressed her question to Donna as she joined them in line nodding affirmative but changing the subject. "Look what Joe is wearing. Do you believe it!"

Elizabeth seldom got caught up in typical teenage boy talk. She kept her crushes carefully protected from public knowledge. Her thoughts turned again to the research paper she needed to begin. She wanted her paper to be original, different from what everyone else would choose to write.

Why she got the idea to research and write about muscular dystrophy she didn't know, but the idea stuck. She decided she had found her topic. The doctor they had gone to when she was nine had given her enough information for her to answer most questions like "What's wrong with your face?" or "Why don't you take gym?" She had never been particularly curious to know more but now it might be useful as a topic. She could include a case history to add enough words to meet the length requirement.

Elizabeth was satisfied with her decision and went to work. The school library was too small. She needed to go to the public library to find resource material. Even at the public library, information was limited. She took the encyclopedia and two magazine articles to the table to begin her note cards.

The words she was reading and transferring onto the small cards gave her a sense of unreality. To Elizabeth, muscular dystrophy had always been a label, a reason. Never something that could affect her life. Now she was reading that muscular dystrophy was a progressive condition. She was reading that it was inherited, passed on from parent to child. She read, she copied the facts, and she wrote the required number of words.

Just as she had planned, Elizabeth used herself as a case history, explaining how her case was not typical. Her type of dystrophy, FSH, did not usually become evident until a person was in their early twenties. There was no history of muscular dystrophy in her family. She must be, as one of the articles said, *a mutation*. Elizabeth was careful to write matter-of-factly. It was important that no one know that she didn't already know all this before she started the research paper. She didn't want the shame of her ignorance known, and she didn't want anyone to know how it was affecting her.

This was God's plan for her life. Elizabeth accepted God's plan but she was stunned and confused. She needed to understand and get on with what God expected of her. Everything stemmed from one fact that she now knew. The fact that she was not a whole person. Her life had no value. Since she was not a whole person, she had no right to any emotions; and since she was not a whole person, the sole purpose for her life was to make life easier for the whole people around her.

Once Elizabeth had figured this out, it was easier. She stood in the lunch line again as her classmates laughed and pushed each other, jockeying for place in line. Everything was the same but everything was different. She acted like one of the group, but the real Elizabeth was somewhere else watching and thinking, *you are not a teenager, this is middle age for you.*

As soon as lunch was finished, Elizabeth went to the empty art room. She knew that Mr. Bump would not be there. He was only working half days since his recovery from a serious heart attack. She really didn't want him to be there. She wouldn't have talked to him but she needed the comfort of being alone in this room that reflected so much of his strength and character. She needed time with his unspoken support to adjust to life again.

CHAPTER 7

October 17th marked a milestone in Elizabeth's life. This was the day she was scheduled to have her senior pictures taken by a professional photographer downtown. Two years earlier, Arlene had passed through the same milestone. Now Arlene's picture was standing on the piano in the living room and Arlene was away at college. Whatever Arlene was doing was always a step ahead of Elizabeth and seemed to be more important in her parent's eyes. This year, however, Elizabeth would be graduating; and, even though she wasn't the first to graduate, she knew it was a significant time for her and for her family. Every school activity took on a new importance. It was starting out as a good year. Elizabeth was editor of the school paper, vice president of the Art Service Club, and on the editorial staff of the school yearbook. Now she was about to have her senior pictures taken.

Elizabeth hurried straight from school to the studio. It wasn't a long walk, but Elizabeth wanted to get there early. She was nervous about how the pictures would turn out. She had chosen the photographer her parents had used for Christmas card family pictures. He would know that she couldn't smile. She wouldn't have to dread the inadvertent "Okay, now smile," followed by an apology after which everyone felt awkward. In the family pictures, he managed to capture her at her best. This picture that would stand beside Arlene's on the piano as an official record of Elizabeth's passage into adulthood, needed to be right. In the waiting room, Elizabeth wandered restlessly about looking at photographs displayed on the wall and worrying, "Does my hair look alright? Should I have my sweater tinted blue or green? Would a profile look better than half view?"

The door to the street opened and Elizabeth's mother walked into the waiting room.

"Are you ready to go?" her tone was abrupt and almost critical.

"Not yet. I haven't even gotten in yet. He's behind schedule."

"Well then, I'll be back in a half hour," and she turned and left the studio.

Elizabeth was a little annoyed by her mother's intrusion. She wondered briefly why her mother had driven down to get her and why she had been crying. *What had Elizabeth's brother, Basil, done now to upset*

29

her? It was embarrassing that her mother would come down town when her eyes were still red and blotchy. "I hope when she comes back, she'll look more presentable." Elizabeth thought to herself.

Elizabeth turned back to the photographs on the wall and the problem at hand. "I don't want to look scared. I wonder which kind of folder I should order?"

"Elizabeth, will you come in now?" The voice of the photographer interrupted her thoughts. She followed him into the studio while he put her at ease with casual conversation.

"How are your mother and father?"

"Oh, Dad hasn't been feeling well. He had the flu, I guess. Anyway, he went back to the hospital yesterday for his check-up."

Mr. Bakehouse talked and the camera flashed. Some of her tension had been anticipation. Now Elizabeth could just followed his instructions.

"Turn your head just a little bit more. Hold it - that should be a good one. Oh, hello, Mrs. McKievey; how are you?"

Elizabeth's mother was standing in the doorway. Mr. Bakehouse finished the last two poses keeping up a polite conversation with her mother. Once more, her mother was intruding. Elizabeth was not a child. She did not need her mother standing in the doorway while she had her senior pictures taken.

They left the studio and crossed the nearly deserted street to where the family car was parked. Neither spoke. Despite her annoyance with her mother's intrusion, Elizabeth was eager to talk about her experience; yet, something in her mother's manner silenced her.

"The hospital called," her mother said.

"Oh?"

"They said your father is in critical condition." Her voice broke.

Elizabeth wanted to say something to comfort her, but she could think of nothing to say.

"The Howells are going to take me to Iowa City in a few minutes. Will you call Ray and let him know? I got some hamburger you can cook for supper..."

She went on talking, giving Elizabeth instructions; but Elizabeth was only half listening. She was struck by the realization that her mother was completely alone in this crisis. For the first time, she could not turn to Elizabeth's father for support and Elizabeth could do nothing.

The Howells came and they drove away with her mother; now Elizabeth was alone. She began to straighten the living room and get supper for the younger children. They ate in silent uneasiness. Basil was in junior high school. He understood; but Marilyn and Louise were still in grade school. They didn't.

"Will he die?" asked Marilyn.

"No, of course not, it only means that he is very, very sick."

"But why is Mother crying then?" Louise wanted to know.

"Because she doesn't want him to be sick. Eat your supper!"

As Elizabeth tucked her little sisters into bed that night, she said, "When you say your prayers, pray that Daddy will get well."

They began to cry a little out of fright. Not afraid that their Daddy might die, but from the fear of the new situation, from the fear they sensed in Elizabeth.

Elizabeth spent a restless evening. She could not concentrate. She picked up her literature book, tossed it aside, turned on the radio, then wandered into the kitchen, and began putting the dishes away. Basil followed her into the kitchen.

"If Dad dies, do you think Mother will get married again?" Basil asked.

"I have no idea! Why are you even thinking about that now!" Elizabeth was not even angry with Basil for his inappropriate question. It was his way of voicing the fear and insecurity they were both feeling.

"Basil, I've decided that I'm going to the hospital with Mother tomorrow. It's senior court day at school. I can miss that. I don't care what she says. I am going. IF Mother comes home tonight."

Basil said nothing and they went back to the table where their homework was spread out. Minutes ticked by slowly. They didn't know whether to go to bed or to wait up. It was a relief to hear the car drive up.

"How's Dad?" Elizabeth asked as soon as her mother came in. She seemed more composed.

"He's about the same as he was when I left him yesterday. They're just giving him oxygen to ease his breathing."

Elizabeth and Basil breathed a sigh of relief. Just as Elizabeth had thought, it was really nothing to get too worried about. Her mother got upset so easily. Still, she would go along tomorrow.

"Mother, I'm going to Iowa City with you tomorrow." Elizabeth paused

31

for a breath before giving her arguments to convince her mother to let her skip school.

"Okay, we will have to leave as soon as the kids leave for school."

Elizabeth could hardly believe her mother had not uttered a word of protest. As she prepared for bed, Elizabeth began to plan what she would say to her father. She would be quite cheerful. She would tell him all about getting her pictures taken. She would even wear the same sweater and necklace she had worn then, so he would know just how she had looked.

CHAPTER 8

The bright sunshine gave promise of a perfect October day. The air was crisp and cold. The fall leaves had reached their peak of color and one by one had begun to filter to the ground. The drive through the Iowa countryside on the way to Iowa City would be enjoyable. Elizabeth and her mother started out as soon as Marilyn and Louise left for school.

As they turned onto the highway, Elizabeth's mother said, "I don't know what I'll do if anything happens."

"There's no sense talking like that; nothing is going to happen!" Elizabeth hated it when her mother over-reacted to things. She was not going to allow that today.

The hour's drive to Iowa City passed quickly. Mother and daughter kept up a steady conversation about what was going on at school and what needed to be done to the house. Elizabeth was determined to keep the day light and cheerful; but as they rounded the last corner and the huge red brick structure of the Veteran's Hospital came into view, her mood changed. Standing there at the top of the hill, towering over all the surrounding buildings, the hospital gave Elizabeth the impression that once you were inside its walls, nothing bad could happen.

This is the building that is going to make my daddy well, she told herself. As though by reverting to such childish thinking, she could somehow regain the security of childhood.

Elizabeth's father's room was on the sixth floor. They stepped off the elevator and her mother lead the way down a long corridor to the last door on the right. As she entered the room, the last of Elizabeth's resolve of the night before, to be cheerful and chatty, vanished.

All she could manage to say was, "Hi, Dad. We were just having court day at school today, so I decided to come see you instead."

Her father gave her the weak half-smile that Elizabeth thought always made him look so much like an elf. It seemed to take too much energy for him to talk, so no one tried to make conversation. Once, Elizabeth put her hand on the bed. Her father put his big hand over hers and squeezed it slightly, a small gesture that said so much. He was her father. She was his child.

Elizabeth walked out into the hall and stood looking out of the window at the end of the hall. The sun was shining on the parked cars in the lot below. She watched a little girl run across the lawn and up the cement steps to the road. She noted that the grass was still green even though the trees had turned to reds and yellows. She turned and looked back into the hospital room. Her father was lying on his back with the head of the bed raised halfway up. The whiteness of the bedclothes accented his pale face. Lying there with his eyes closed, he looked like a marble statue. His profile was sharp and clean cut.

Dad is really distinguished looking, Elizabeth thought to herself. *His hair is beginning to gray at the temples and just last week he proudly told us that he had lost the last pound in his quota. Life is just beginning anew for him. He likes teaching so much better than last year and with the extra money, he and Mom are beginning to be able to fix up the house like they've wanted it.*

As often happened, when she saw a sight that moved her, Elizabeth felt an urge to draw the scene before her with the sculptured figure lying in the bare hospital room. Immediately, she squelched the urge with, *No, Elizabeth! You don't want your last picture of Dad to be like this!* Elizabeth was shocked that such a thought had surfaced in her mind. She dismissed it angrily. *Dad is not going to die! Not when life's finally beginning to hold promises.* How could she have indulged in silly girlish dramatics at a time like this!

She went back into her father's room. His bare feet were sticking up out of the covers at the foot of the bed. "Are your feet cold?" she asked.

"No," was the weak answer.

As she spoke, she touched his feet. Her heart froze. His feet were stiff and cold--his ankles swollen. Her chest felt suddenly cold and empty. The room was quiet except for the constant monotonous rasping of the oxygen tank as it forced a continuous stream of oxygen into her father's lungs.

At noon, Elizabeth and her mother decided to find the hospital cafeteria and get some lunch. As they walked down the hall, her mother pointed to an empty room. "Last night there was a man in there under an oxygen tent. He must have passed away."

Elizabeth tried to push the thought from her mind but couldn't. Instead, she started imagining herself as young woman saying, "My father died when I was a senior in high school." And the listener would say, "Oh, I'm terribly sorry." Elizabeth hated herself for having such thoughts. *Why*

34

would something like that slip into her mind? She began to talk just to keep from thinking.

In the cafeteria, they were surprised to meet a friend of her father. They were surprised to learn that he was now employed at the hospital. He was sorry he hadn't known her father was in the hospital so that he could have visited him before. He would make plans to come up later. Elizabeth and her mother ate a quick lunch and returned to the sixth floor feeling a little better for having talked to someone they knew from everyday life.

The doctor was waiting to talk to her mother, and Elizabeth chose to go into the office with her. The doctor was very nice and reassuring. He explained the situation.

"Mr. McKievey is in a state of heart failure. In such cases, nothing is certain. He may go any minute, or he may get over this episode and lead a relatively normal life. I don't think there is any great cause for alarm right now in your husband's case. It is a good morale booster for him to have the two of you here, though."

"Is he aware of his condition?" questioned her mother.

"He knows that he is sicker than he has ever been before, but I don't think he knows just how sick" replied the doctor.

When they got back to his room, they were pleased to find her father asleep. It was the first sleep he had had for two days. In a few minutes, he opened his eyes.

"You know, George, I think I'll call the superintendent and tell him to get you a substitute for a month," Elizabeth's mother began.

"Let's just take it a week at a time," her father broke in, and her mother let the subject drop.

After his nap, Elizabeth's father could not seem to get comfortable. He sat on the edge of the bed; he climbed out into the chair then back into bed again. Each move was followed by a period of exhaustion. He got out into the chair and sat for almost ten minutes. Then with a sigh, he sat on the edge of the bed again. Elizabeth was standing at the window in his room looking out when she heard a groan. She turned to see that her father had fallen onto the pillows again, his head nearly off the bed.

"Hey, Dad, you don't..." she began teasingly. Then she realized that something was wrong.

"Ring for the doctor! Hurry!" Her mother ran around the bed and held his head in her arms trying to make him comfortable.

There was no call bell to the nurse's station. The staff had disconnected the buzzer when they turned on the oxygen. Instead, there was a small desk bell. Elizabeth banged on the little bell with all her might, but no one came. *How could they hear that little dinging so far away!* Elizabeth was nearly frantic as the seconds dragged by. The only sounds in the room were the rasp of the oxygen pump and the harsh, desperate clanging of the bell. *Why didn't someone come!*

She bolted out the door to get the doctor herself. A young orderly was ambling down the corridor toward her father's room.

"My Dad! Hurry!"

It seemed like he would not hurry. When he got to the door, he said, "I'll get a nurse."

They waited for the nurse. There was nothing Elizabeth and her mother could do. Elizabeth's mother still held her husband's head. Elizabeth tried to lift his leg onto the bed, but she couldn't move it. The oxygen tank pumped on.

The nurse came in with an air of efficiency. "We'll take care of him. Wait outside, please!"

Elizabeth and her mother stood in the hall, not talking just watching the activity. Now everyone was rushing in and out. Silently, desperately Elizabeth prayed. "God, please don't let Daddy die! Please, God, please!" Over and over, she prayed the same prayer, desperately as though if she stopped praying, he might die.

"You'd better stay all night, Mom. I'll find a way home."

Down the hall was a woman in a candy striper's uniform from their hometown. Elizabeth ran down the hall to see if she could get a ride back home with her so that Elizabeth's mother could stay with her father. The ride was arranged and Elizabeth turned in time to see her mother following the doctor. The doctor was just closing the door when Elizabeth caught up and slipped inside.

"Sit down," he said gently. "Mrs. McKievey, your husband just passed away."

Her mother began to cry quietly. Elizabeth walked over, stood behind her mother, and put her hand on her shoulder in a gesture of support. The doctor wanted consent to do an autopsy. Less than two hours ago, this doctor had told them not to be too concerned. Now he was telling them it was too late.

Words Elizabeth could hardly take in. She had never allowed herself to entertain the thoughts that there was a chance that her father might not live, and now he was gone. She wanted to run out of the room, to go back to her father's room, to say *good-bye,* if nothing else. She couldn't leave him just like that. All her plans and resolutions of the night before came flooding back. She was going to be so cheerful. She was going to tell him all about having her senior pictures taken. But she hadn't; she hadn't said anything. Now her father would never know even that little part of her graduation and she wanted desperately for him to know. She wanted to run away to be alone, but the voice of the doctor droned on and on. He was sorry. He had not thought this likely. He was taken by surprise. Then the endless details to be taken care of, already the funeral arrangements. He took them to the Red Cross room where they left a message for the lady Elizabeth had talked to. She would not need a ride home.

A nurse took them to a small drab room. The man behind the desk began to outline the funeral benefits available to them as part of the veteran's benefits. *Which did they want?* He began to talk to Elizabeth, rather than her mother who was crying. Elizabeth was not crying. She was trying to be strong for her mother. The man was explaining to Elizabeth slowly and completely. Did she understand? *Yes, she understood. But why? Why, when they still could not believe, could not understand, must all this detail be forced on them?*

Outside the room, sun was streaming into the corridor. It seemed strange that the sun was still, shining. Elizabeth's father's friend was waiting for them as they left the barren office. He stood there with tears in his eyes. His tears broke through Elizabeth's emotional control. The sight of this man crying brought grief too close to the surface. She ran into a nearby restroom away from the sight of grief and forced herself to stop her emotions. She had to allow her mother to cry. She had to be responsible. She had to get hold of herself. In a few seconds, Elizabeth was able to return to the hall again, under control.

Elizabeth did not have a driver's license and her mother was not really up to the long drive home. One of the Red Cross workers offered to drive them home. Gratefully, her mother accepted the offer. Once more, they took refuge in conversation. Grateful again to this stranger whose presence allowed them to keep their minds on surface issues and put off facing the reality of what was happening.

The drive was uneventful. They came to the familiar streets that led to home. Everything was the same. Life was going on as usual. Only they had changed--only Elizabeth and her mother.

Robot like, Elizabeth and her mother began to do what needed to be done. People had to be notified. The McKieveys did not have any family in the area, but one of the Elders from the church came over immediately and took over until the nearest relatives could be located. Elizabeth was responsible for the younger children. She did her best to explain to Marilyn and Louise what had happened and to keep them calm. They were confused and frightened and so was she. Focusing on their needs and household chores kept Elizabeth's own emotions at bay.

The day was finally over. Elizabeth turned off the light and settled into bed. Now there was no way to keep the tears away. They came uninvited. They burst upon her like water through a floodgate. These were not silent tears; and as her sobs grew stronger, Elizabeth began to fear that her mother would hear her. She didn't want her mother to know, but she could not stop. She felt completely out of control and was beginning to panic. She didn't even know how to pray or how to approach God in the face of this grief. God was so far away right now. Her father was far away, God was far away, and she was adrift in this sea of emotion.

"The Lord is my Shepherd. I'll not want. He makes me down to lie. In pastures green He leadeth me the quiet waters by." Elizabeth found herself singing in her head the familiar words of Psalm 23.

"My soul He doth restore again and me to walk doth make within the paths of righteousness even for His own name's sake. Yea though I walk in death's dark vale, yet will I fear no ill for Thou art with me and Thy rod and staff me comfort still." As the words flowed on, her sobs began to subside.

"A table Thou hast furnished me in presence of my foe. My head Thou dost with oil anoint and my cup over flows. Goodness and mercy all my life shall surely follow me. And in God's house forever more my dwelling place shall be."

As she finished the last line, Elizabeth felt a strange sort of peace. Her mind was calm; she slept.

CHAPTER 9

Elizabeth walked up the steps of the old State Capitol Building and sat down beside one of the tall pillars. She looked around at the empty campus. It was Sunday noon. No classes were in session and no offices were open. The lawn that stretched out before her was still green in the late September sunshine. Sidewalks leading to the doors of the two legislature buildings, now being used as university classrooms, criss-crossed the lawn and converged to lead up to the Capitol Building steps where she now sat. Trees edged the sidewalk along Main Street at the front of the lawn. The scene before her was tranquil and inviting.

This is your school, your alma mater, Elizabeth told herself. *It has three years of your life and you will have its degree.* Elizabeth was aware that she was being a bit melodramatic but this was a change in attitude for her. For the first time, she was beginning to feel a part of this huge impersonal institution.

Elizabeth was starting her third year at the university. It would be her senior year. Her freshman year, she had gone to a small college in Pennsylvania. She was following her plan to attend the small college one year then transfer to the university to get a degree in Fine Arts which was not available at the Pennsylvania school. Elizabeth had thrived that year in Pennsylvania.

Originally, she had argued not to go to college at all, to remain home to care for her younger sisters, but her mother would not even consider it. Out of respect for Elizabeth's father, people in her town had set up a fund to pay for Elizabeth's education. Her mother would have felt disgraced if Elizabeth had not gone on to school. So, Elizabeth had had no choice but to join her sister, Arlene, and go off to college. There to her relief, Elizabeth found that she could do well in her classes. She made friends easily, and she was able to develop the fun loving side of herself. The sense of humor Mr. Bump had advocated became her trademark. Elizabeth was happy that year, and she longed to stay where she had found happiness.

Two things kept her from changing her plan and staying with her friends in Pennsylvania. One was the memory of standing at her father's desk after he died and seeing his Bible open and an unfinished sermon lying beside it. She had been overwhelmed with the fleetingness of life. Elizabeth had thought, *You live and you die in the middle of living, and it's as though you never lived.* She needed to know there would be some record of her existence. That need was still strong enough to pull her away from the place where she felt like she belonged, to pull her to a place where she felt like a misfit but where she might learn to be an artist. If someday she had a painting hanging in a museum, the world would know she had existed. The university offered that hope.

The second reason she could not change her plan to transfer to the school in Iowa City was the Veteran Administration Hospital. Elizabeth was haunted by the memory of being ushered out of her father's hospital room and not seeing him alive again. Something in her was compelling her to go back to that room. *Why?* She wasn't sure. She just knew she had to go back and she had to go back alone.

It had been early October of her first semester in Iowa City when Elizabeth set out on foot. The hospital could not be seen from Elizabeth's dormitory but she knew that she would reach the highway if she made her way down the hill to where the Iowa River cut the campus into two parts, and she still remembered the drive along the highway up to the hospital. The men's dorms and the sports facilities were on that side of the river. Elizabeth felt a little awkward to be headed across the main bridge toward the men's dorms. It felt like her private journey was on display. The foot bridge to the art building would have been less obvious but she hadn't known how to find the highway from there. She joined the flow of college men, wondering again, *What am I doing this for? What do I expect to find?* Elizabeth was at a loss to answer her own questions.

Once she had crossed the river, Elizabeth had known there was no turning back. The highway followed the river then turned up the hill toward the hospital. The closer she got to the hospital, the more Elizabeth had felt the pull, the compulsion to get to her father's room, perhaps to find her father. The hospital lobby was deserted as she had entered and had headed straight for the elevators. It had only been two years. She remembered exactly where to find the room. She had headed for the window at the end of the hall not looking to the left or the right. Her eyes focused on the window.

At the window, Elizabeth surveyed the parking lot for a brief time as she had done that day. Retracing her actions of two years before, she had turned again to look into her father's room. The memory of his sculptured form, clearly in her mind. This was the moment she had been compelled to relive. She looked into the room, her father's room. He was not there. The room was not empty. Someone entirely different, bearing no resemblance to her father, lay in that bed.

Suddenly, she had felt like an intruder into someone else's life, into someone else's story. There was nothing for her there. She had hurriedly returned to the lobby and found a place to sit and rest for the long walk back to her dormitory room. Elizabeth had felt no sense of satisfaction. The need to return to her father's hospital room was now completely gone, just as her father was completely gone. Perhaps she had accomplished what she had had to do.

Two more years had passed and now Elizabeth was nearing another milestone in her life. She would graduate in the spring with a Bachelor of Fine Arts degree from this university. It was time to allow herself to belong; it would not be disloyal to her Pennsylvania school and friends. As she sat on the steps of the old Capital Building, Elizabeth told herself things would be different this year.

Her first year at the university had been overwhelming. Dormitory life was very different from dorm life on the small friendly campus of her freshman year. She had liked her studio art courses but her sheltered background had not equipped her to enter the Bohemian atmosphere of the university art department. Her academic courses went well except for Spanish where she had tested into the advanced class having never taken a course in any foreign language before. Elizabeth's reserve had been misinterpreted as arrogance causing the instructor to dislike her. Even so, she had managed to complete her foreign language requirement.

Junior year for Elizabeth had been more comfortable. She had moved into the new dormitory along with her roommate but in this dorm, there were three to a room. Elizabeth found a friend in the new roommate. She also knew better what to expect of her art courses and fellow art students. Still, Elizabeth had longed to be back where she had fit in so well.

Now, it was too late to go back and to her surprise, Elizabeth was finding herself ready to go forward. This would be her senior year and she would allow it to be a meaningful year. Elizabeth looked at her watch. Sunday dinner would be over if she didn't get to the cafeteria soon. Elizabeth stood up and started down the familiar sidewalks heading home.

CHAPTER 10

The house had character. It was an old home on a street of old homes in what had once been a good part of Philadelphia. The neighborhood had become lower middle class but it was still a respectable place to live and also accessible to buses and to Philadelphia's elevated subway line. The apartment was a furnished two-room efficiency. The tiny rooms were crowded with odds and ends of furniture. The bed was a pull out sofa bed in the larger of the two rooms. When the bed was opened, it nearly blocked the doorway to the closet size bathroom. The walk-in closet doubled for a pantry. The kitchen was one unit holding sink, stove, and refrigerator. Kitchen and bedroom were combined, and the small front room served as living room.

Loretta had found the apartment for them and was already settled in. Loretta was Elizabeth's first roommate; they had roomed together in the dorm as college freshmen. They had gotten along well, almost like sisters. When Elizabeth decided to go to graduate school in Philadelphia, Loretta decided to find a job in Philadelphia and they had made plans to share an apartment. Loretta had been on her own for the last two years while Elizabeth was still in school. Elizabeth had never imagined she would be living in a big city. She felt like she was on the verge of an exciting adventure and she was glad she had the advantage of Loretta's experience while she adjusted to city life.

"I got a transit map, Loretta; what route should I use to get to the university to register tomorrow?" Elizabeth spread the map out on the day bed in the living room.

Loretta picked up the map and studied it a few minutes. "It looks pretty simple. Just walk down to the El station I showed you. Take a westbound train and get off here. You'll have to walk down to here."

"How long do you think it will take?" Elizabeth worried.

"I don't know. You have all day, don't you?"

Elizabeth did have all morning to get to the university by 1:30 when she was scheduled to register. Loretta had been right. The trip went smoothly. Elizabeth was glad she had come alone. Here she was, finding her own way around the city relying on her map and her own ingenuity. Even the crowded subway was great. She felt like she was a real part of the life of a busy, important city. Elizabeth gathered the registration materials and sat down to study them and fill out all the forms.

The university was just starting their Fine Arts Department. The course offerings were not as flexible as they would be as the program developed in the next few years. Studio courses required a lot of studio hours per credit hours. Elizabeth decided she would only take eight credits. She was satisfied with her choices. She found a place in line and followed the registration process table by table getting all the required forms signed or initialed.

The end was in sight. Elizabeth handed her paper work to the clerk at the last table and received her bill in return. "Pay at the window across the hall."

Elizabeth slipped into an empty seat at a nearby table and took out her checkbook for the final step. She looked at the figures on the sheet before her, disbelief slowly rising up within her. *The bill was outrageous! There was no way she could spend that much of her meager bank account on one semester's tuition.* Her mind was reeling. *What was she going to do? How could this happen?*

"How?" Elizabeth could immediately see was pretty obvious. In all the brochures, all the catalogs and application forms she had poured over last year, she had never read anything about tuition. What embarrassed her now was that she had never asked about the tuition. She had assumed she would pay about the same as she had paid at the University of Iowa. Clearly, that was foolish of her. This was not a state institution, nor would she have the advantage of in-state tuition, as had been the case at Iowa. Her naiveté was painfully obvious to her now.

"What?" was a more complicated and more important question. Elizabeth's quick calculations told her that as things stood she could only afford two credits of graduate work each of the next two semesters. Tuition was not the only costs she needed to consider. Art supplies and transportation would have to be budgeted as well. Resolutely, Elizabeth chose two one-credit courses and returned to the registration process to reregister as a part-time student.

Loretta was not home from work yet when Elizabeth entered the apartment. That was good. Elizabeth sat down in the only chair in the tiny living room and put her feet up on the mismatched footstool. She needed to think. The walls of the room had been painted red, perhaps more correctly maroon. Three doors and three windows broke up what little wall space there was. The largest piece of furniture in the room was green plaid. Elizabeth's thoughts were as jumbled and uncoordinated as her surroundings.

She had come to Philadelphia to become a graduate student in art. Two credit hours hardly qualified her as a legitimate graduate student. In a way, she wasn't particularly disappointed. She lacked the confidence, which sometimes seemed to her as arrogance, and the drive of the serious fine arts student. Her talent and interest did not lie in the demanding field of commercial art. Further more, she didn't fit in the art world. At Iowa, graduate students and under graduates were in the same classes. Elizabeth knew that there was a level on which most graduate students viewed their work as a social statement. Elizabeth had no such vision for her work. *Was she really suited to be an artist? Was graduate work in art really what she should be doing?*

From the time Elizabeth had learned about muscular dystrophy, she had stopped planning for a future. She had told herself then that she had no future; and she believed that with a kind of passive aggressive acceptance. But here she was and she had to do something with her time and she had to figure out a way to pay her bills. To remain a full time student, with a small monthly check from her father's social security, would have been much safer. *What was she to give up? What was she to accept? What was she to do?*

CHAPTER 11

Elizabeth was on her way to Temple University to register for night school. She was satisfied with the solution she had come up with. As she saw it, her options were limited. Looking for a job as a waitress was out. She couldn't handle the physical demands of waiting tables. Secretarial jobs were out. She could never type efficiently. Likewise, the nursing field was not a consideration. Teaching was something Elizabeth knew she could do. The last three summers she had spent teaching Vacation Bible School in the Ozark Mountains. Her students had responded well to her and she had enjoyed working with them.

Tuition at Temple was much more reasonable and she needed to supplement her BFA degree with the courses required for a teaching certification. She could scrape through this year with her summer savings and her small income and look for a teaching job for next year. Elizabeth told herself she was not giving up her art. She was just being more realistic.

Elizabeth arrived at the registration area early and already a crowd had gathered pushing against the ropes that held them back. When the ropes were unhooked, the crowd burst through like water breaking through a broken dam. Elizabeth was carried along and deposited, bewildered, in the center of the room as everyone rushed to the tables set up around the perimeter of the room. She got her bearings and located the starting point where she picked up the forms needed to begin the registration process.

"You will have to get the instructor to initial your class card before I can file it." The young clerk from the registrar's office looked up as she spoke and recognized the confused expression of a first time registrant as Elizabeth took the papers back but didn't move on. "They are sitting at those tables against the wall," she added.

"You are registering as an education major? Have you been officially accepted into the Education Department?" the instructor asked.

"No, how do I do that?"

"Fill this out and get the signature of the dean. Then come back with your class cards."

Elizabeth was getting annoyed. *How many more lines was she going to have to stand in?* Impatiently she filled in the information requested and took her place in the line waiting to see the Dean of the Department of Education.

The dean scanned her form. "You have muscular dystrophy?"

"Yes." The dean seemed to expect a verbal response even though he was reading Elizabeth's own answer to the question *Do you have any illnesses or disabilities?*

"If you have muscular dystrophy, we can't admit you to the School of Education."

"I don't understand. Why not?" Elizabeth was taken by surprise by the dean's words.

"Our school has a good reputation. We can only graduate quality teachers."

Elizabeth had never faced this before. Her capability as a student had always been her strong point. The dean's words stunned her and stung her, but she could not let him dismiss her this way. There was too much at stake for Elizabeth to just gather up her things and leave.

"Muscular dystrophy has never been a problem for me in taking care of children or in my academic work," Elizabeth replied as she handed him the transcript of her grades for her under graduate courses. "I know what I can handle. You don't know me."

"Your grades are very good. You would be the kind of person we are looking for but. . ." he paused, shaking his head. "I tell you what. If you are willing to see the doctor at Student Health, we will let him make the evaluation. If he signs an authorization form, I will accept you."

" Don't I have to register tonight?" Elizabeth asked.

"Go ahead and register as a non major. We can transfer the credits later."

That had been a close call. Elizabeth finished registering, caught the subway and transferred to the Frankfort Elevated Train where it intersected with the subway under City Hall. She had only been in Philadelphia two weeks but already she was using public transportation with confidence. Tomorrow she would call and make the appointment with the doctor. The sooner she got through the red tape, the better.

Two days later, Elizabeth was on her way to Temple again. She had studied her transit map and decided to take the slower bus route because it would let her off nearer to the Student Health facility than the subway would. She was feeling apologetic to be taking up their time for such a trivial matter, but it wasn't her fault.

The wait was not too long. Things were going well. She might get an early start home and beat the stormy weather that was being predicted. The examination was routine. Elizabeth answered the familiar background questions and obediently followed the doctor's instructions as he did a simple strength evaluation.

"All I need is your signature on this form so I can declare an education major." Elizabeth knew that he knew that but it was something to say.

"Well, Miss McKievey, I'm sorry but I can't do that. I can't say you are capable of handling a classroom of children." The doctor's words had the tone of finality to them.

Elizabeth looked at him in disbelief. This was a doctor. He should know better. This should have been a simple routine visit to satisfy the red tape requirements.

"Why would you think I couldn't handle a classroom? I've worked with children all my life."

"In the classroom, you are responsible for the safety of the children. What if there was a fire? You wouldn't be able to get all the children out."

"I would get them out by not panicking and taking control. My mind is not weak." Elizabeth did not know how to counter such narrow-minded thinking. In the end, she couldn't.

"My decision is made. I will not be responsible for putting you in a classroom. I'm not going to discuss this further."

The doctor closed his file and walked out of the examining room. Elizabeth sat dazed. *What was the next step?* It began to sink in that there was no next step. The door had been slammed shut and there was nothing Elizabeth could do. She began to feel a need to get out. To leave this place where the doctor's words still echoed off the walls.

Elizabeth was glad to get back on the bus and sit down. She chose a seat near the back for the long ride home. All around her, people were coming and going in the normal pursuit of life. Their very normality made Elizabeth's chaotic emotions intensify. She wanted to be invisible. She was reeling from the shame of being judged inadequate. She was sinking under the weight of powerlessness. She didn't fit yet she had to live. *What did God expect of her? What was He doing?*

The bus turned onto Frankfort Avenue and a blast of wind hit rocking the heavy vehicle. The weather was changing. Philadelphia was getting the effects of the major hurricane that was hitting the eastern coast. The sound of the elevated trains over head blended with the roar of the wind gusts. The wind was gusting steadily now and tiny beads of rain were beginning to dot the windows of the bus. As the bus rocked, Elizabeth began to shiver at the raw power of nature. Fear gripped her but could not wipe out the inner turmoil instead it highlighted her impossible situation.

CHAPTER 12

"We have Miss McKievey today! She's Tough!" The two boys did not realize they were within earshot of Elizabeth. She was standing in the hall outside her classroom. This was the third time she had substituted at this middle school; and she was beginning to feel somewhat comfortable here.

The boy's comment was encouraging to Elizabeth. Immediately she thought, *I wish that doctor at Temple could hear that! I can control a class.* The painful experience at Temple was still with her and still affected her trust in how the world viewed her. But she had learned something.

Yes, Elizabeth thought, she had learned from that painful experience. Once she had gotten through the worst of the emotional devastation, Elizabeth had had to again face the question of what she was to do with her life. Almost by default one afternoon, she found herself in the vicinity of the Board of Education Building. She made a snap decision. She would go in and see if she could register as a substitute teacher. Substitute teachers were not required to be certified. They just had to have a Bachelor's degree. She had a Bachelor's degree. She could apply.

The receptionist had handed her the application without question. "If you want to fill that out now, Mr. Johnston could interview you at two o'clock."

Elizabeth took the form to the waiting area and began the task of answering the same questions she had answered on form after form. She stopped when she came to the question "Do you have any illness or disability?" Here it was again. *Now what?* Slowly, Elizabeth printed "NONE" and finished filling out the application. She still carried her college transcripts in her purse so she could stay for an interview at two o'clock.

While Mr. Johnston read through the information Elizabeth had written on the application, she tried to appear confident and relaxed. *What would she say when he asked her about her disability?* He would know; it was obvious when you looked at her that Elizabeth's facial muscles did not function. Her answer was a lie. Elizabeth waited apprehensively.

The interview went well. Mr. Johnston was very low key. He asked a few questions. Elizabeth answered easily. He completely ignored the question about disability and authorized Elizabeth to substitute in grades

K through 12. All she had to do was register in the school district in the area where she was living. She walked out of the building hardly believing what had just happened.

Elizabeth had told the truth on her application at Temple and met with disaster. She had been brazenly untruthful on this application and things had gone smoothly. *Wasn't there a lesson in this?*

The lesson, as Elizabeth understood it, was that God had given her a good mind. She could use that mind to control how much information she gave out and when. As long as people didn't know exactly what her situation was, they were less apt to reject her. She could live with the disability God gave her. She could not live with the attitude people had toward her when they knew.

She needed to sidestep the attitude. Elizabeth needed to learn from the ostrich. The ostrich, she told herself, met danger by hiding its head in the sand and if the danger got too close, the ostrich would deliver a powerful kick to fend the danger off. She had the mental dexterity to do that. She just needed to stay alert.

All that had been months ago. This was the beginning of her second fall in Philadelphia. Elizabeth and Loretta now with a third roommate, Jenn, had moved to a newer bigger apartment in a slightly better section of the city. For Elizabeth, that meant registering in a different school district. This time she stated her preference to be called for junior and senior high school openings.

When Elizabeth first registered in District #7 last school year, she was still wary and unsure of herself. She had thought little children would be less threatening to a substitute. To avoid further rejection, she had asked to be assigned to the elementary grades. A second lesson Elizabeth learned last year, as she went from school to school, was that she preferred the challenge of and interaction with the older students more. That had surprised her. It pleased her as well, because it revealed a growing strength to risk facing a sometimes-hostile world to be what she wanted to be.

Elizabeth walked back into her classroom following the two boys from the hall. The class settled down to do their assignment. Elizabeth was still thinking about the comment she had overheard. It was not really that she was *tough*. It was just that Elizabeth refused to tolerate disrespect. Elizabeth owed it to herself and owed it to her students to require respect or have the administration find someone the students would respect.

Elizabeth was finding out surprising things about herself through this job of substitute teaching.

CHAPTER 13

Stretched out before her as far as she could see were used cars, acres and acres of used cars of every make, size, and color. Elizabeth had come to this field of used cars with her co-worker, Sharon, and Sharon's husband, Ned. Ned was going to help Elizabeth buy a car today. Ned would have to make all the important decisions for her. Ned knew cars and liked to tinker with motors. Elizabeth knew nothing about cars and wouldn't even be able to test drive the car he would choose. She wasn't even sure she'd be able to get a driver's license. First she would buy the car; then she would find out.

Elizabeth was not as confident as she wanted Ned and Sharon to believe, but driving seemed to be the best solution to her current needs. So, she had to try. Ten years ago, Elizabeth had taken driver's training in high school, but she had been too young to get a license when the course ended. Elizabeth couldn't even remember now what had kept her from going ahead to get a license right after her birthday. Somehow, driving had lost its importance until now; and now, she wondered if she had lost her nerve.

"How much money are you going to spend?" Ned asked again.

"I have $600 and that's really all I have." When she had first mentioned her idea, Ned had lectured her on the cost of owning a car, and Elizabeth was quite aware that her money would barely stretch to cover everything.

"The salesman said that the cars are grouped according to the price. I'll start over there. You and Sharon wait here. I'll signal if I see anything interesting."

Sharon and Elizabeth watched while Ned moved further and further away bobbing up and down as he checked a tire or looked into an engine. They were glad that the sky was overcast keeping the acres of asphalt from radiating the stifling heat typical of a late July day. Ned was standing beside a black Corvair when he signaled for them to come.

"This one looks good. The mileage is good for its age and the engine sounds alright."

Elizabeth didn't dare voice her first thoughts. The seats were quite worn and a black car would be her last choice. Ned would explode over such frivolous objections. Ned took the car to the test drive area and came back pleased with how the Corvair handled and how it sounded. The decision was made. Elizabeth would buy the black Corvair.

Elizabeth had moved into another new era of her life. She marveled briefly, at how quickly an idea can turn into a reality; then she plunged ahead with the next step. Elizabeth dreaded the ordeal of proving herself to be deserving of a learner's permit. She knew that in this matter she could not resort to the protection of her ostrich style. Probably this dreaded ordeal was the main reason she bought the car first giving herself tangible incentive to enter the battle.

Her car sat in the parking area of her friends' apartment building. It would stay there until Elizabeth got a learner's permit. In the mean time, Ned was checking it over and making sure it was in good running order. Sometimes after work, Elizabeth went home with Sharon; and Ned would drive her to an empty parking lot where she began to practice driving her car.

Elizabeth surprised herself. Driving felt good. She could hardly wait to take the car out on her own. That, of course, had to wait; and while she waited, Ned loaned her Corvair to a friend who lived out of state. Reed was kind of a mutual friend. Elizabeth had first met him when she visited her college friends in New England. Their paths crossed again when she met Ned and Sharon who did not know Elizabeth's friends but were also Reed's good friends. Reed was in the process of moving from New England to West Virginia when he had an accident. He needed a car and Elizabeth's Corvair was mostly sitting idle.

In a way, Elizabeth didn't mind loaning Reed her car. She missed having it available for driving lessons; but she still didn't have a learner's permit. Elizabeth was beginning to admit to herself that she also had a personal interest in Reed's welfare. This was causing her a great deal of inner turmoil. Years ago, Elizabeth had dealt with her hopes and dreams for a personal relationship, home, and family. She had accepted the death of her dreams, but now, Reed's presence in her life was stirring it all up again.

No one knew the emotional turmoil she was in. Elizabeth dared not tell anyone and feel their sympathy, their pity, or perhaps worst of all their encouragement. Reed gave her a taste of relationship that was not available to her; and she could not will her emotions to stop. Reed would come and go. While he was there, she had a form of what she longed for; and as shallow as it was, she wanted that to last.

After Reed would leave, she was overwhelmed with feelings of inadequacy and unhappiness. Feelings that came partly because there was no one else that she related to so personally and when he left she felt that void. The feelings came from a second reason as well. Reed had an image of her that was not really accurate. Reed wanted her to be a very intellectual, free spirited artist and he related to her as though she was. Elizabeth did not want to fail to be what he admired and what he thought she was, but she knew he didn't really know her. If he discovered that, he would withdraw. There was no room in Reed's life for an Iowa farm girl. She hated those days after a visit from Reed when her inability to rise above her emotions dominated her life.

Reed returned her car with newly installed back-up lights and new, though drab, gray and white seat covers. Two days later her learner's permit arrived in the mail. It was now late September. The endless red tape had taken two months; but at last, she could actually drive her car on the road. Elizabeth drove at every opportunity. Her confidence grew. By mid October, she was ready to try for a license. Ned thought she needed three or four more weeks of practice, but Elizabeth had waited too long already.

Ned was away for the weekend and Elizabeth persuaded Sharon to take her to the licensing center. Elizabeth got her license that day. The long process was finished. Elizabeth could finally explore this new independence.

Elizabeth drove alone for the first time a few days later. She set out on the twenty-minute drive from Ned and Sharon's apartment about ten o'clock at night. She felt very much alone and unsure of herself as she got into the cold empty car; but there would be no freedom if she didn't face her fears and conquer them. Elizabeth was glad it was dark. She somehow felt safer enveloped in the blackness with only the tunnel of road ahead of her to concentrate on. Her tension increased as tiny flecks of snow danced in her headlights. The wind sifted and swirled it across the road.

There was no going back. She drove on, recognizing the turns as she came to them. Elizabeth breathed a sigh of relief as she parked the Corvair in front of Loretta's car outside their apartment. She also felt elated, exhilarated. The lights were on in the living room. Elizabeth was glad that Loretta was still up.

Elizabeth's driving confidence and skill had increased rapidly. Loretta was gone for the weekend and it was a beautiful Indian summer afternoon. Elizabeth made a thermos of coffee, gathered up a writing tablet, her latest letter from Reed, and her diary and set out on Sunday afternoon drive into the country. On another occasion, she had discovered two crumbling old silos sitting incongruously in a grove of trees above the river. It was a special place reminding her of her farm roots. She headed there today to think, to write, and to enjoy God's creation in privacy and solitude.

Reed was settled in West Virginia. Elizabeth eagerly awaited each letter, phone call, or visit. She was still overwhelmed with feelings of inadequacy after each visit and was still struggling to force herself to be realistic. She enjoyed Reed's company and she knew the feeling was mutual to some extent.

Sharon sometimes shared letters Reed wrote to her and Ned with Elizabeth. One of those letters had started with, "Sharon, thanks for the information on MD." The words had hit Elizabeth like a sledgehammer to the chest. Reed and Elizabeth had never spoken about muscular dystrophy. She didn't even know that he knew the diagnosis. For a while after that, she had watched for signs of Reed withdrawing but things seemed to go on the same as before and the subject was never brought up.

Life went on in a kind of erratic sameness. The winter was mild. Elizabeth told her friends that, "Independence is a car key and a snow-free highway." She had both this winter and the months passed quickly. Elizabeth spent less time doing things with Loretta and more time with Sharon, Ned and, when possible, Reed.

As a professor, Reed had summers free to spend with his parents in Oregon. He suggested that Elizabeth fly to Oregon for her vacation and he would show her the Pacific Northwest. Elizabeth had always traveled by bus or train. Flying across the country was something she had never ever pictured herself doing; but this would be a real vacation. Elizabeth had never taken a real vacation. The only cost would be the airfare. She could swing it.

Oregon was beautiful. It was early summer. Snow still closed some of the mountain passes and the desert was a bloom with flowers. Waterfowl were abundant in the marshlands. Elizabeth and Reed had no commitments except to see what there was to see. They relaxed and enjoyed the time.

Late one overcast afternoon as they watched the wild life around Warner Lakes their conversation turned serious. Reed said that early in their friendship he had realized that he was becoming emotionally involved. So, he had stopped it before it was too late. Elizabeth understood now why he had not withdrawn before. Reed could just stop his emotions and go on with things the same as ever. Elizabeth could not stop her emotions. As things went on, they had just gotten more and more involved. Reed dealt in philosophy and logic. Elizabeth dealt with relationships and emotions.

The task Elizabeth faced now was how to go back. She had never intended to let down her guard. She knew that an intimate relationship with a man was not her lot in life. She had let herself be blinded by a hope that wouldn't die no matter how often she struck it a deadly blow. She was filled with the shame of failure; failure to be desirable and failure to remain emotionally detached.

CHAPTER 14

Sleep would not come. Elizabeth could not shut her mind off. Her life was going nowhere. *Was it God's will that she just plod along working at dead end jobs watching her friends get married, establish homes, and start families?* God had to know that sharing in her friend's lives as they moved forward emphasized more and more the loneliness of her own limitations. *What did God want from her?*

Elizabeth turned over again. Her thoughts still going in circles. She had worked for the insurance company for three years now and she was still a correspondence analyst. Elizabeth was good at her job; but it was a low pay clerical position. Her supervisors had recommended her for promotions but the company did not want to invest money in training her. Muscular dystrophy was seen as a liability to them. *Elizabeth's job was secure but was security enough?*

On one hand, Elizabeth was grateful just to have this job. After she decided that it was time for her to stop substitute teaching and get full-time year round employment, she had spent four long distressing months looking for a job. She had answered every possible want ad and gotten little response. She had registered at no less than twenty-three employment agencies. Every agency had a set of aptitude and ability tests routinely given to all applicants. Elizabeth had taken so many similar tests that she was getting such high scores that it would cause a stir in the office. Her test scores only reinforced the refrain that she was over qualified and under experienced for whatever they had at the moment. They would call if something came in. Calls seldom came.

Days had dragged into weeks and weeks into months. One day, Elizabeth's pastor had made an appointment for her with the personnel director of a mail order insurance company. He had driven Elizabeth to Valley Forge for the interview and pushed her to call back again and again when the company showed the usual reluctance to hire her. Finally, they offered her a position as a correspondence analyst and Elizabeth's long trial was ended. She owed the company something for taking a chance on her; but now she was feeling more and more that there was no way she could prove herself worthy of advancement. *Was she now stuck where she was?*

Elizabeth checked the clock. It was 2:00 a.m. She had to get to sleep;

but these questions had been gnawing at her for weeks. Now, in the darkness of the night they wouldn't be quieted. She turned over again.

Okay, she said to herself, *you have a lot of years ahead of you. What do you want to do with them?* That's what it boiled down to and she wouldn't sleep until she had begun to resolve that question.

Basically, she wanted to be involved with people, but how? There was social work. Elizabeth had always thought about being a social worker but she knew she couldn't manage the physical strain of being out in the field as a caseworker. Reed once suggested she should be a counselor. That idea was new and completely unrealistic. She didn't have a Masters degree, which was the minimum she would need.

Elizabeth's thoughts began to circle again. *I can't afford to quit. I can't get anywhere if I stay.*

This was getting her nowhere. *Stop the cycle! Could I get a Masters? Even if I did get another degree, could I get another job? What if I couldn't?*

Was she stuck where she was because she didn't have the courage to take risks? That is what Reed had accused her of. It was a judgement that was unfair. Elizabeth's life was much more complicated than that. But the fact remained that she had to make herself be content where she was or take a major risk to move on.

Elizabeth began to do calculations in her head. Maybe she could swing it financially if she budgeted very carefully. Some of the courses she had been taking at Temple night school the last few years were graduate credit courses. They might be usable toward a degree. Tomorrow she would work this out on paper and see if it really would work. As Elizabeth finally drifted off to sleep, she knew her decision had been made.

There was no time to lose if she wanted to put her plan into action. The fall semester was about to begin. Elizabeth spent an afternoon at Temple. She could apply her current credits to a Master's degree in guidance and counseling through the Graduate School of Education. To her surprise, there were no daytime graduate courses offered in this department. Elizabeth could continue to work and take courses evenings and Saturdays. She registered for eight hours, which was the maximum allowed for anyone working a forty-hour week.

Elizabeth and Loretta always lived frugally. Now Elizabeth tightened the belt even more. Loretta's younger sister moved in with them. The apartment was too small for three but a third person sharing expenses allowed Elizabeth to save more from each paycheck for future tuition. She estimated that she could save enough this semester to allow her to ask for part-time work next semester. If the company would allow her to work part-time, she could take a full course load at Temple and by taking in two summer school sessions be able to finish at the end of the summer.

Things were going surprisingly well. Elizabeth had very little time for anything except work and study, but she was staying focused and doing well. She often went to church with Ned and Sharon and looked forward to the times Reed would visit.

"Trudy Rossman is taking a leave of absence this year," Ned told Elizabeth one day. Elizabeth had taken some evening painting classes taught by Trudy at the Christian School near Ned and Sharon's.

"That's too bad, but I'm too busy to paint this year anyway," Elizabeth responded. "What are they doing for an art teacher at Piedmont? She would be really hard to replace."

"I don't know. Are you interested? It's only part-time."

"No. I don't have the energy, and it wouldn't pay enough."

Elizabeth brushed the idea aside but it stayed in her mind. Her job at the insurance company was changing. They had not yet given her an answer about being part-time. The possibility of doing something in art again appealed to Elizabeth. Mr. Bump's style and variety of projects would be an example to follow. As significant as Mr. Bump was to Elizabeth, she never communicated with him and this would be a form of connecting with him again.

Elizabeth decided to call the school and just ask about the position. The phone call was followed by an interview and the interview went very well. The only problem was money. Elizabeth knew how much she had to save to cover the remainder of tuition for her degree. Her plan was to save it all in the fall semester then go onto part-time. The school needed someone to start immediately.

They had left it that if the school didn't find someone soon that they wanted to hire, they would call her again and see if she would teach the second semester. Elizabeth was pleased when the call came. She agreed and signed a contract to teach seventh and eighth grade art and one high school class to include both studio work and art history. This was going to be a challenge with a full course load. Elizabeth welcomed the challenge.

CHAPTER 15

Spring was in the air. Elizabeth hurried down the steps and over to her parked car. As usual, she had allowed just enough time. She turned the Corvair around in the landlord's driveway, headed back to the corner, and out onto Lancaster Pike. She turned again two streets later to take the back roads she had discovered for her daily travels. The back roads allowed her to avoid some traffic but they also allowed her time to enjoy the beauty of nature. A feeling of happy freedom rose up in Elizabeth, as all around, her spring was restoring life after a long, dead winter.

She was almost at the fork in the road. *I can take the short cut that fords the little stream. It wouldn't be icy today,* she thought. *No! Wait! That will take me to the expressway. Am I going to Temple at this hour? Where am I going, to the insurance office, to Piedmont? What day is it anyway?*

Elizabeth appealed to the pile of books and supplies on the seat beside her for an answer. The car seemed to know where to go. The moment of confusion passed, but it left Elizabeth with a feeling she couldn't shake. For a moment, she had been out of control. She was going so many different directions. Good directions, but each had its own set of demands. She had to keep herself disciplined or everything would collapse into one confused heap.

Elizabeth's decision to teach at Piedmont had been a good decision. Teaching art combined her art interest and her people skills. She liked developing a plan to try to make art history interesting to her students. It challenged her mind in a way she had missed doing office work. The job change also gave her scheduling flexibility for classes and for study time.

The insurance company was allowing her to pick-up a few part-time hours in the Telephone WATTS Line Department finding or verifying phone numbers. Elizabeth hated telephone work but the extra money would allow her to slow down in the summer and just concentrate on school and the comprehensive exams.

At the end of the month Elizabeth, Loretta, and her sister Janette would be moving again. The trustees of their church had asked the three of them to move into the empty parsonage beside the church to house sit for a few months. Living in a house would be sheer luxury. They would be able to move without bumping into something. They would each have their own bedrooms. Elizabeth would have a small study with a huge desk to use. The windows in the living room and the dining room looked out on a wooded area giving the impression of country living despite the busy thoroughfare outside the front door.

Elizabeth and Loretta had usually lived in furnished apartments. Their last apartment was not furnished but it was so small that they only owned a few second hand items. This house was partially furnished so they could enjoy the comfort of a real home. The living room had a wood-burning fireplace in it. Elizabeth was already looking forward to the fall when they could sit by the fire in the evenings.

Actually, fall came too quickly. As long as Elizabeth was taking classes or studying for exams, the outcome was, to some extent at least, dependent on things within her control. Now, she had finished the last class and passed the comprehensive exams. She had earned her degree. And now, her success would be dependent on decisions made by strangers. Simple, hard work could not make it happen.

The principal at Piedmont had asked her to come back in the fall and even to expand the art history course. Elizabeth was pleased by his affirmation of her work, but she knew that accepting his offer would be running away, avoiding facing the reality of the job market. She had made her choice to risk security to move ahead. She had gotten the degree that she hoped would help. She must not lose courage at this point.

Elizabeth was registered with the Temple Placement Service, an advantage she had not had in her previous job search. She had good references from her professors and from Piedmont, and she had a job history and a degree. The last time, she had had none of those things to help.

September moved into October, and October gave way to November. Elizabeth did what she could to explore all job leads during the day. Late afternoons and nights, she was back at the insurance company calling delinquent policy owners on the WATTS line. Elizabeth was not good at this work but she was glad to have a way to support herself while she tried to find a job in her chosen field.

November was headed to December. None of her interviews or applications had led to a job offer. Elizabeth opened the new mailing from the placement service. She read through each position description, discarding those out of the area and those she wasn't qualified for. There was one she knew her employment counselor would expect her to pursue. The position did not interest Elizabeth; but the placement service expected their people to demonstrate their seriousness by applying for all positions that they did not have an approved reason for refusing.

Elizabeth got out a copy of her resume and carefully worded a cover letter. The opening was for a Resident Director of a women's residence. Elizabeth did not want a live-in position particularly not in center city Philadelphia. The reason Elizabeth felt that she would be expected to be interested was that it was for an art college. She had never fit with art students but outsiders wouldn't know that. They would just see her background in art and think this position would be just right for her.

Elizabeth was confident that God had guided her decision to get her degree. She was struggling to trust Him as the months went by with no answer to her prayers for a good job. Her friends were praying, too. *Where was God in this new wrinkle?*

She consulted her friend Everett, a seminary student. "What if this job is God's will for me? It's not what I want, but nothing else has come up. Why does God's will never seem to be my will?"

"You don't know that this is God's will. Remember, Elizabeth, you are not obligated to take the first job you are offered. Be patient. The right job will come along." Everett counseled.

It was without enthusiasm that Elizabeth followed through on the interview. Despite herself, the job interested her. If only it wasn't a live-in position, she would consider it. Two days after the interview, Mr. Stuart, Dean of Student Affairs, called and offered Elizabeth the position to begin January 1st. She had a week to make her decision. *Was this job better than no job? Did she have the courage to go on risking?*

On her break that night, Elizabeth called Everett again. "They offered me the job. I don't know what to do."

"Elizabeth that job is not for you! They need someone who is street wise and can be very tough. You would be all alone there without a support group. It's not a safe area. Don't take this job. When the right job comes, you will know it. You will feel at peace about it."

That was it! What Everett said was true. When the right job came, she would feel at peace about it. What Everett couldn't know was that she was feeling a peace about this job. What he also didn't know was that Elizabeth had a toughness and a solitary self-sufficiency that would equip her for this job. His negatives were true, but Elizabeth had strengths he didn't know. Now she was even more confused about the right choice.

The peace Elizabeth felt was tempered by her awareness that this was not the kind of job she had set out to look for. Everett's council had weight. Elizabeth called Mr. Stuart.

"Thank you for the offer, but I have decided that it is not the position for me."

"I am very sorry. We would really like to have you with us. May I ask your reasons?"

Elizabeth didn't expect his response. She could give him her reasons, but not Everett's. "I am not really interested in a live-in position. If I took it, I would only want to be committed to one semester, so that I can move on to something more suitable. You are asking for a longer commitment. The salary is actually too low. Those are the major reasons. Otherwise, I liked what I saw. I liked your approach to the operation of a dormitory."

"If we can adjust the salary, would you consider taking the position for one semester?"

"I would think about it."

When the right job comes you will feel at peace about it. How could this be the right job? But Elizabeth was definitely feeling at peace about this job. The council that was meant to direct her away from this job was drawing her to it. She knew that if Mr. Stuart called back, she would accept his offer. Mr. Stuart did call back. They had raised the salary a small amount and Elizabeth accepted the position.

CHAPTER 16

"Co-ed Attacked Outside Art College Dormitory." The newspaper headlines jolted Elizabeth. They came just the day after she had verbally accepted the Residence Director position. *What had she committed herself to? Was she really up to this?* She called Mr. Stuart to arrange for the necessary paper work for her employment and asked him about the incident.

The girl had been walking home alone after working late at the college. She fought off her attacker; and except for fifteen stitches in a gash on her scalp from falling against the fence in front of the dormitory, she was all right. Mr. Stuart assured Elizabeth that the school was taking steps to insure the safety of the girls when they had to walk the seven blocks from the college after dark. The attack highlighted the reality of life in the city and the responsibility she would be taking on. Elizabeth's peace became an uneasy peace.

Elizabeth spent Christmas with her family in Iowa and returned in time to move into the Residence Hall the day before the students were scheduled to return from their holiday break. The building was an old seven-story structure that had once been a maternity hospital. The neighborhood was a mixture of run down and newly renovated row houses on narrow one way streets. Her building stood strangely alone and exposed on a city block shared only with an elementary school. The front doors opened onto a sidewalk separated from the school's concrete playground by a high, heavy wire fence. The back doors opened into the fenced-in parking lot that belonged to the dormitory. Mr. Stuart had told her that the building and the elementary school were scheduled to be demolished in two years to make way for a city planning project.

Elizabeth's apartment was on the first floor. Its nine-foot windows looked out on the parking lot and across an alley to the jumbled backyards of a line of three story row houses. The apartment was small but tastefully furnished. Her living room door opened into the public lounge, and across the lounge, back in the farthest corner, was another tiny room that belonged to her as well. In that room, Elizabeth set up an easel, hung a painting shirt over it, laid out her paints and supplies, and stored her artwork. For the first time in her life, she had a private studio; and for the first time in her life, she was living by herself.

When the friends who helped her move left to drive back to the suburbs, Elizabeth finished putting the last of her few belongings away. Then she went out of her apartment and walked around the corner, past the front desk and around the partition to the elevator. Downstairs was a TV lounge, vending machines, and laundry facilities. With the students gone, all this was part of her home.

But Elizabeth was not headed down. She entered the elevator and pushed the button #8. She was headed to the roof. The building had a flat tar paper roof with a three foot wall around the perimeter. Walking out on the roof eight stories high, she was above all the surrounding buildings. To Elizabeth, the view was breathtaking. Looking to the east, she could see all the way to the river. Looking off toward the northwest, she could glimpse City Hall between the taller buildings. For a few minutes, Elizabeth savored the view. Then for some unknown reason, she began to feel vulnerable, cut off from security by the seven empty floors between her and the warmth of her apartment.

Elizabeth returned to the elevator. Back in her apartment, the settling sounds of the old building made her uneasy. She decided to close and lock her living room door. Elizabeth was relieved when the night watchman arrived. Just having someone else in the building made her feel a little less isolated and vulnerable. To her surprise, Elizabeth began to look forward to the students returning.

Elizabeth's predecessor had seen her roll as predominately one of rule enforcer. Elizabeth was glad for the rules that were already in place; but her style was different. She wanted to get to know the girls and she enjoyed seeing their class projects. Generally, the students appreciated the change. Elizabeth found that she had a knack for observation and timing that allowed her to surprise the troublemakers before major confrontation was necessary. Elizabeth was finding a sense of satisfaction in the job in ways she had not expected.

Spring came and Mr. Stuart asked Elizabeth to consider staying another year. Elizabeth had weathered several crises through that semester. She had learned things about herself. Another year would give her time to test what she had learned. Elizabeth admitted to herself that she wanted to stay. In fact, there was no good reason for her not to stay another year. It would be the final year for the old building. She decided to stay with the girls through its final year.

The college had a summer program for high school students interested in a career in art. They offered two three-week sessions, one in July and one in August. All students stayed in the dormitory. Elizabeth's decision to stay another year committed her to summer school as well. She would have preferred to have the summer off and escape the heat and noise of the city. Instead, she would be responsible for thirty-five teenagers loose in the big city. The girls would be housed on floors one and two, and the boys would stay on floors four and five with the empty third floor between them. It was hardly an ideal situation in Elizabeth's opinion.

Dorm rules were to be strictly adhered to and the night watchman was to report any infractions to Elizabeth. The first summer session was a difficult transition for Elizabeth. Her role had changed from counselor advisor to one of unpopular jailer. Elizabeth knew that her control over the dormitory was within a hair's breadth of collapsing daily.

"Have you been listening to the news? On the way over this morning everyone's talking about it." The housekeeper rushed to Elizabeth as soon as she stepped out of her apartment.

"Is it bad?" Elizabeth had not heard any news reports but she did know that there were signs that racial unrest in Philadelphia was about to explode.

"There's fires all over north Philly and the whole city's on alert!" Mrs. Dunphy was excitable and Elizabeth kept a calm exterior in an attempt to calm her down.

The students were all at the college. They had classes straight through until four o'clock. Until then, they were Mr. Stuart's responsibility, but it was Friday and after four o'clock today until eight o'clock on Monday morning, the safety of thirty-five teenagers would be Elizabeth's responsibility. She went back into her apartment and called Mr. Stuart.

"I'm concerned about this racial situation, especially with the weekend coming up." She told him. "It really worries me. We're on the border of south Philly, only a block away from a black area."

"What do you think we should do?" he asked. "The police don't think there will be trouble in this part of the city. This morning they asked permission to post men on our roof here at the college just in case; but it's just a precaution."

Elizabeth was not ready to tell Mr. Stuart how weak and inadequate she was feeling--how fragile her control was even without this new threat. In the end, they decided that the students should be told to go directly back to the dormitory when classes were over and not go out again until morning. The college would have the night watchman come early and he would lock the front door at five o'clock. He would stay at the door, unlock it, and allow only authorized people in and out. Elizabeth did not feel very reassured as she hung up the phone. This was going to be a long, tense weekend.

Mrs. Dunphy left at her usual time and Elizabeth took over the front desk. The students returned alone or in small groups. Some ignored her completely; some anxiously questioned her and some openly relished the excitement. The night watchman arrived and took up his position at the front door. He was another adult on the premises but not a real support to Elizabeth. Elizabeth always thought of him as backward and socially insecure. He was a man in his seventies who never made eye contact when he spoke and never initiated conversation. Elizabeth could not look to him for strength.

As darkness descended, Elizabeth brought her radio out to the desk to listen to the newscasts. She tuned in the news station. It was monitoring the riot situation and reporting every rumor. With each new account, Elizabeth's uneasiness grew and at the same time, she had to present a calm capable exterior. No one seemed able to concentrate and go on with life as usual. Students milled around the desk asking questions and worrying.

"We have just had a report of a roving gang of young men moving south on Fifteenth Street." The excited voice on the radio triggered panic in Elizabeth.

It was getting too close, and now her escape route was being cut off. If she hadn't had the students to consider, Elizabeth would have gone out to stay with Jannett who was still house sitting safely away from the turmoil of the inner city. *Now,* she thought, *it was too late!* Elizabeth shrunk from the idea of driving alone through the city streets not knowing what was ahead or around the next corner. There was no route to the western suburbs that wouldn't take her through potentially troubled areas.

The dormitory building offered her no sense of safety. Fire had always panicked her and the building with all its tall windows and glass doors offered easy targets for firebombs if the trouble moved this direction. There would be no place to hide.

Elizabeth left a student in charge of the front desk and returned to her apartment to call Mr. Stuart. She still could not let him know the depth of her fear. Mr. Stuart listened to her report and told her to keep him advised of the situation. Those were easy words for him to say. He was safe in his main line home away from the tensions she was caught up in. Elizabeth returned to her post feeling somewhat better just for having shared the responsibility for a few minutes.

The guard unlocked the door for a familiar visitor. "Hi, Miss McKievey. Do you know that Gary and his friends are on the roof yelling at people down on the street?"

"No, I didn't. Thank you. I'll take care of it."

Elizabeth asked a student to take charge of the front desk and headed for the elevator. Gary was the ringleader. She could have expected him to give trouble, but not so explosive as this could be. All over, the city people were looking for trouble and taunting words yelled at the wrong people could be just the spark to ignite the fire. Elizabeth was furious. Her anger energized her and she stormed out onto the roof. Gary was insolent as usual, but he complied with her demand and led his friends back to his room.

Elizabeth stood a few minutes on the roof to regain her composure and her strength. Anger so intense made her physically weak. She had won the battle, but not the war. She could not control Gary or any of the teenagers. This situation was too serious for these kind of games. Elizabeth felt like she was sitting on a powder keg.

The news reports had not changed, but Elizabeth was no longer willing to continue the wait and see approach. She went back to her apartment with resolve and called Mr. Stuart again. This time she was ready to be frank. Mr. Stuart was supportive. He respected Elizabeth's instincts. If she said she couldn't handle this, then he would consult the Dean of Students and they would decide what to do.

Elizabeth called a dorm meeting in the lounge. "The college has decided that we will close the dorm for the weekend. The situation in Philadelphia, as you know, is unstable and it will be best for everyone to take a break and spend the time with their own families. Please call your parents and make arrangements. Tell them we will close at noon tomorrow and reopen on Monday morning before class."

The announcement brought turmoil. Tensions that had been hidden now surfaced. The students called their parents and parents began to call Elizabeth. Just how much danger was their children in, they wanted to know. Some parents left home immediately, arriving at one or two in the morning to get their child. The orderly closing that Elizabeth and Mr. Stuart had envisioned was replaced by chaos, but by noon, the dorm was empty and Elizabeth was free to leave as well.

The panic that had seized Elizabeth loosened its grip as she put actual physical distance between herself and the dorm. She continued to listen to the continuous news coverage as she walked aimlessly around Jannett's living room. The trouble in Philadelphia seemed to have reached its peak and the situation was stabilizing. There were no incidents south of City Hall so the college and dormitory had never been in real danger. Elizabeth felt a little foolish to have panicked like she did. On the other hand, she knew that she had needed to get away to break the hold it had on her. Her courage had been severely tested and her confidence shaken.

The final week of the first summer session passed without further incidents. Racial tensions in Philadelphia returned to an uneasy normal. Elizabeth dreaded the beginning of the second summer session, but to her surprise the students were more mature and allowed her to be their friend rather than their jailer. Even so, Elizabeth found herself looking forward to the fall and winter. This summer had taught her a new respect for colder weather and the help of her student advisers in the regular school term.

CHAPTER 17

Elizabeth had made a mistake. No one could have convinced her beforehand that it would be a mistake and now she was caught by it. Actually, it had been Arlene's idea. In a rare moment of openness, Elizabeth told Arlene that she was having some difficulty walking in certain situations especially when she was outside. Stepping up onto curbs or into buildings took concentration and effort. To carry a cane did not fit Elizabeth's ostrich style and might not help anyway. Arlene had said, "What you need is something like a seeing eye dog." The idea intrigued Elizabeth. A tall dog trained to walk at her side might work as a cane and people would not know. The idea did have drawbacks. One was Elizabeth's living situation. A dormitory in the city was not a good place for a dog. But she wasn't going to live in a dorm indefinitely; and she was going to have trouble walking indefinitely.

The idea stuck in Elizabeth's mind and the possibility of a clever solution to her mobility problem snared her.

"Mr. Stuart, I've been thinking about getting a dog. I know that we have a rule about pets in the dorm, but maybe I could be an exception."

"Please, Elizabeth, call me Glenn!"

"Sorry, Glenn. I've been thinking. My situation is different from the girls, since this is really my home."

Elizabeth didn't know why it was so difficult for her to acknowledge a first name basis with Mr. Stuart. She knew that he had a hierarchical view of life and for him to suggest she call him Glenn was to acknowledge a colleague basis for their relationship. Elizabeth was flattered that he accepted her as a colleague but she couldn't quite see herself as a real colleague. The question of "Why not?" bothered her. However, now was not the time for her to analyze it.

"A dog would be a companion for me," Elizabeth continued.

"Let me think about this for a little while. I think it would probably be all right. It is your home. What kind of a dog are you thinking about, any particular breed?"

"I haven't gotten that far. I wanted to talk to you about the possibility before I thought about that. It would be a big dog, though."

After Glenn gave her an official okay, Elizabeth began her search.

Height was her primary concern. Great Danes were the tallest dogs she knew of; so Elizabeth was leaning toward a Great Dane. Elizabeth had no experience with dogs. The only pet she had ever owned was a turtle. The cats they had had growing up in Iowa were barn cats and not really pets. She was in over her head but the hope of a unique answer to her secret distress kept her forging on.

Elizabeth parked her car and got out wondering where to start. Someone had suggested to Elizabeth that she go to a local dog show and observe dogs of all breeds. Well, she was here. She just as well locate the Great Danes first. She hadn't expected it to be so crowded. She had to be careful not to get jostled and lose her balance as people milled around while others with dogs on leashes moved purposely from place to place.

The Great Danes were big dogs all right. Elizabeth was standing near the ring where they were being shown. A crowd was forming, closing-in around Elizabeth. In front of her was a woman with a Great Dane puppy on a leash. The puppy was about four months old and already more than half the size of a mature dog. The crowd shifted and the puppy stepped backward right on top of Elizabeth's foot. He was crushing her foot. In that moment, Elizabeth knew that Great Danes were not for her.

Elizabeth had been pretty sure she wanted a Great Dane. It was a little discouraging to eliminate that breed. She didn't have other choices in mind. Elizabeth moved on, watching dog handler's taking their dogs into the rings. At one point, Elizabeth stumbled slightly and automatically put her hand out to stabilize herself. Her hand landed on the back of a dog standing at her side. The dog did not shy away from her touch but calmly stood his ground.

The dog was very tall and pencil thin, with fairly long curly hair. Elizabeth was impressed. She had never seen a dog like this one. The breed, she found out, was commonly called Russian Wolfhound. Elizabeth drove home that day comfortable with the image of herself walking down the street with a Russian Wolfhound walking calmly at her side. This was a dog that would be unique and would draw the attention away from her faltering steps while providing her with her needed support.

By March, Elizabeth had an eight-week-old Russian Wolfhound puppy who she named Vronsky. She was told that a puppy was work but that the dog would form more of an attachment to her if she raised him herself. She decided on a male because the males grew taller than the females. He had personality from the beginning. The girls in the dormitory loved having him as a sort of a mascot.

The college was negotiating for the purchase of a fifteen-story apartment building just a block from the school to be used as a co-ed dormitory. This would be the first time the college had offered housing for their men students. Glenn asked Elizabeth to stay one more year to help with the transition. He gave her a tour of the building. It was an old building with a mixture of one-room efficiency apartments and one-bedroom apartments. The location was ideal for a dormitory. The building was not.

Elizabeth had registered again with the placement office at Temple and was beginning to think about what to do next. Life had changed a lot for Elizabeth in the year and a half that she had been at the college. The friends, who had counseled with her and prayed with her before she took the job, had all moved to other parts of the state or other parts of the country.

Elizabeth's sense of identity remained anchored in her church group. They gave her the rootedness that Elizabeth needed, but the demands of her job kept her from developing deeper relationships there. Her relationship with God was a refuge for Elizabeth from the turmoil around her: but at the same time, God seemed strangely more distant in her growing isolation.

Vronsky dominated her life. That was not what Elizabeth had intended. The dog was to be an aide to her but that was not happening. Elizabeth loved the dog. They had bonded, but it was on Vronsky's terms not Elizabeth's. He was very intelligent but along with that intelligence came a willful arrogance and a demandingness that never let up. Elizabeth knew Vronsky had to learn to obey and fought many battles of will with him. She did not let him win and her hands often showed teeth marks, which were her battle scars.

Whenever Elizabeth left the dormitory, Vronsky had to go along. She could not leave him barking and damaging her apartment door with his insistent scratching. He was partly responsible for her isolation and because of the isolation, their interdependence grew stronger. Vronsky was growing tall: but with his behavior style, tall was not going to be a help to Elizabeth.

Glenn was pressing Elizabeth for a decision about next year. Summer school was coming up. Elizabeth's contract committed her through summer school. The purchase of the apartment building was moving ahead and Elizabeth had already been working with Glenn in the planning stages of making the building into a workable student residence. The student advisers were expecting her to be at the new site. That thought seemed to give some security to the change. She was pleased that the girls supported her leadership. Mrs. Dunphy, the housekeeper, relied on Elizabeth.

Elizabeth's half-hearted attempts to find another position had not met with any success, and she was beginning to feel a growing obligation to stay. Elizabeth decided to give Glenn the answer he was hoping for. She would stay another year but no matter what that would be her final year.

Elizabeth was glad to have the decision made. Just making that decision removed two major stresses. She did not have to sell herself somewhere else: and she did not have to wrestle any more with the pros and cons of the new building. Whatever they were, she would live with them for a year. Elizabeth was worn down both physically and emotionally. Vronsky's constant demands wore her down and his presence interfered with her freedom to administer the dormitory in the style she wanted.

As Elizabeth thought about the change ahead of her, she had very mixed emotions. The situation had many negatives for Elizabeth. She was well aware of that and yet at the same time it was a challenge. To say she was looking forward to the challenge would not be correct. She was too worn down to be excited about a challenge. Perhaps for Elizabeth it was another personal testing ground. If so, it was a test that was fraught with possibilities for failure.

CHAPTER 18

Elizabeth turned away from the window. Even though she was on the fifteenth floor, there was no view. She could look out of her living room window into the living room window of an apartment in the building across the street. Her bedroom windows were no better. They provided more privacy but still looked out on rooftops backed against nondescript taller buildings. The benefit of being on the fifteenth floor was that she would get more daylight than the lower floors got. Elizabeth was grateful that Glenn had thought of that. Elizabeth would rather have had her apartment located where she was more accessible to the students as they came and went and where she could be more in touch with who was actually coming and going. There was no such place in this building.

The apartment building covered one corner of a city block. The glass front door opened into a small lobby that in its day would have been elegant, but was more suited for the elderly tenants who had been displaced by the sale of the building than it was for students. The front desk was situated in an alcove to the right out of sight of the front door. On the wall behind the desk were open mailboxes for the apartments. The front desk itself was actually an old fashion switchboard where the four telephone lines coming into the building needed to be connected to telephones in each apartment. Whoever covered the front desk also had to be telephone operator and mailman.

Two very old elevators were located near the desk area. One was a passenger elevator and one was a freight elevator. Both elevators required an operator to run. Elizabeth could manage the passenger elevator if she needed to. The heavy iron grate of the inner door swung shut easily but was not so easy for her to open. Stopping it level with the hall floor usually took a couple of tries, but wasn't physically difficult.

Both elevators connected the basement to an elevator maintenance area above the fifteenth floor. Elizabeth could take an elevator to the maintenance level, then climb a flight of steps to what was called the penthouse apartment. The apartment was merely two small rooms with a bath and a door onto the roof. A high fence enclosed a room size area of the flat roof. The view was not spectacular but at least on the roof she was above all the surrounding buildings. Elizabeth took Vronsky to the roof for a daily outing. The roof was the only place within miles where Vronsky could run.

Elizabeth missed the parking lot of the old dormitory. She had never before had to walk Vronsky on a leash every time they went outside the building. The new building was only a few blocks from the old site, but this building was surrounded by busy streets and concrete sidewalks. Every excursion with Vronsky was risky for Elizabeth.

Elizabeth could not wait any longer to begin obedience training. Classes were offered for dogs aged six months and older. Vronsky was only five months old. Elizabeth had to argue her case to get him enrolled but her need was urgent and she persisted until they gave in. Marge and Ed, married students who had become her friends, offered to go to the training classes with Vronsky and Elizabeth and help with his training.

"Vronsky, let's go to the roof and play. You need to work off some of your energy before your class tonight."

Elizabeth was a little apprehensive. It was the day of Vronsky's second class; and the first class had not gone well. Vronsky had refused to co-operate even when the trainer took him in hand.

Elizabeth got the leash, just in case; and they headed for the penthouse. The tarred roof absorbed the sun making a typical hot muggy summer day seem even more oppressive. Elizabeth went out onto the roof with Vronsky, grateful for the shadow cast by the building and the light breeze blowing. She tossed his toy a few times. Then went back inside. Vronsky could play by himself for a while. Elizabeth had brought a book to read.

A moment later, Vronsky dashed to the doorway, yelped, turned sharply and fell to the ground. Elizabeth knew immediately that something was very wrong. Vronsky lay on the roof his legs twitching at first wildly, then more slowly.

"He's dying! This can't be happening!" Elizabeth stood watching, powerless to do anything. As she watched, he gave one last involuntary movement; then lay motionless.

Elizabeth held on to the doorpost. Her legs had turned to rubber. As soon as she could, she made her way to the penthouse telephone, lifted the receiver, and signaled for Mrs. Dunphy at the switchboard.

"Could you send the maintenance man up to the penthouse. I think Vronsky just died." Elizabeth's voice was matter of fact.

"Miss McKievey, what happened?"

"I don't know he just fell over. I don't think he's breathing. Please! Send someone up." Elizabeth could see Vronsky as she talked. The gentle breeze ruffled the curly hair on his back, but that was the only movement in the still body.

The maintenance man confirmed what Elizabeth already knew. Overwhelmed and still feeling powerless, Elizabeth asked him to make whatever arrangements needed to be made. This was more than she could deal with. She did not have the strength.

Back in her apartment, Elizabeth felt disoriented, empty of any emotions. Not knowing what else to do she called the Office of Student Affairs and asked for Glenn.

"I'll come right over." Glenn responded when Elizabeth told him what happened.

"That's not necessary. I'm okay."

Glenn did come over and to her surprise, Elizabeth discovered that she was not all right. She was devastated. Vronsky had been her constant companion. Her daily routine centered around Vronsky's needs. Her life had just turned upside down and grief enveloped her. She had let herself love Vronsky and in his own way Vronsky had loved her in return.

Strangely, though, in the midst of her despair Elizabeth was aware of God's hand in this. Vronsky was too much for Elizabeth. She didn't have much physical stamina. Vronsky was draining her physically and emotionally; and Elizabeth would never have been able to let go of him. God had intervened and despite her grief, Elizabeth was grateful.

Glenn led the conversation into business matters. The first summer school session, the first real test of how this building would work as a dormitory, was about to begin. There were still many details to address.

Summer school did give them an opportunity to get familiar with the building, but they discovered that the fall semester was the real test. Part of Elizabeth's job was to evaluate how the building was functioning as a dormitory.

The building seemed to be shaping Elizabeth's job and was not shaping it the way she wanted it. Elizabeth felt disconnected from the heartbeat of life in the dorm. She was either in her apartment in the farthest corner of the fifteenth floor or sitting behind the front desk operating the switchboard. The building did not provide any way for Elizabeth to casually get to know the students. The job became more like that of an apartment manager. Elizabeth became someone to report problems to. She was the top administrator in a hierarchy of management with the student advisors doing the things Elizabeth wanted to be doing.

Elizabeth hated it. She hated always having to search for a parking space. Driving around and around the block was not only stressful; but it ate up many precious minutes. The stress of being on call twenty-four hours a day was becoming too much for her limited strength. She dreaded the ring of the house phone and the knock on the door, the heralds of yet another problem needing immediate attention. The demands on her time severely limited her personal life.

To provide a way to spend time away from the dorm, Elizabeth took a part-time job teaching art in a private school in the suburbs. To provide a way to relieve the loneliness, Elizabeth got Leda, a female Russian Wolfhound. To provide a solution to the intrusion on her personal life, she decided to have no personal life. Elizabeth's plans to counteract her growing unhappiness only added new stresses.

Elizabeth had relied on her observation skills and timing to keep things under control in the old dorm. In this building with both men and women, she had to alter her style. The student advisors were pressuring her to use disciplinary measures she thought would be a mistake. The advisors began to feel that Elizabeth was not supporting them.

One student advisor was located on each floor. The women students occupied the upper floors six through fifteen and the men students were located on the five lower floors. The only public area was the corner apartment on the fifth floor designated as a lounge. The out of the way location made the lounge useless to Elizabeth as a means of casually meeting the students and keeping touch with what was going on. Elizabeth had to depend more on the input of her student advisors than she thought was wise.

The day had just begun when almost simultaneously two advisors knocked on Elizabeth's door and Mrs. Dunphy rang her from the front desk. They all wanted to report the same problem. During the night, someone had written obscene graffiti on the walls of the lounge and the hall outside the lounge. With an inward sigh, Elizabeth gathered up her keys and followed the students to the elevator.

The scrawling letters and squiggles could be seen almost as soon as they got off the elevator, black paint making offensive statements all down the long white hallway. Mrs. Dunphy met them in the hall incensed, declaring her support of the maintenance staff's refusal to take on the added work of this clean up and launching into a tirade on the disrespect of *them kids*. The student advisors were equally upset, taking personal offense to the scrawled words.

Elizabeth, quite truthfully, could not share the intensity of their reactions. Graffiti like this was commonplace vandalism. It needed to be cleaned up and those responsible needed to be found and dealt with. Everyone seemed to be blowing this way out of proportion. Elizabeth called a special meeting with the student advisors to attempt to find out who was responsible.

For the advisors, this seemed to be some sort of a final straw. Elizabeth did not understand completely. What she did understand was that they were at the point where she was in danger of seriously damaging her working relationship with her student advisors if she did not honor their pleas to take the action they advised. With Glenn's approval and against her better judgement, Elizabeth conceded and grounded the entire dorm for the weekend or until the offender in question turned himself in or someone else turned him in. The entire dorm was in an uproar. Parents were furious. And her student advisors, to save face with their fellow students, disclaimed any support of the disciplinary action they had demanded.

Elizabeth was left on her own to defend a position she had never believed in. Elizabeth stood firm supporting the decision. Once made, there was no going back. After she finally closed her door to the last angry student and fielded a phone call from another upset parent, Elizabeth broke down. All the stress and tensions of the last few months caved in on her, and her emotions took over.

Before the weekend was over, some students came up with a compromise that Elizabeth could accept. The crisis passed and the normal routine returned to the dormitory, but Elizabeth was not the same. Outwardly she was. The only change was within her. Elizabeth could not regain her emotional balance. She felt like she was two people. In public, she was calm, confident, and efficient. In private, she felt weak and inadequate always on the verge of tears. There was no one she could talk to, no one she dared talk to, no one who would understand.

Christmas break finally came. Elizabeth and Leda flew to Iowa for two weeks away from all pressures and responsibilities. Leda had to fly with the baggage and Elizabeth worried that the baggage compartment would be too cold for Leda and that Leda's crate might get missed in the lay over in Chicago. Her concern was unnecessary. All went smoothly and Elizabeth was home where she was able to simply be a daughter and sister again and regain a sense of balance.

Elizabeth and Leda returned to an empty dormitory. As soon as they arrived, the concrete of the city seemed to close in on Elizabeth again and the pressure felt the same as though she had never been away. Elizabeth had expected God to work some kind of a miracle. She had expected that she would return with a new perspective free from the weight that she had felt when she left, revived and strong. That had not happened.

Nothing had changed; and nothing was going to change until Elizabeth moved out of the dormitory and found a different type of job. As that thought took shape in Elizabeth's mind, she began to recognize another truth. If she was going to get through this year emotionally and physically intact, she was going to have to change. Without realizing it was happening, she had slipped into a pattern of reacting to the problems of life in this building. She was just keeping her head above water waiting for God or someone to throw her a lifesaver before she drowned. That was what was defeating her.

The change was in attitude and approach rather than in definable actions. Elizabeth could begin to act rather than simply react. Her action needed to be directed toward taking what steps she could to reduce the stress. Marge was interested in taking one of her three days of teaching art in the elementary school. Elizabeth arranged for that change. She also began to look for openings for a new job. Glenn already knew she was leaving at the end of this academic year. Finally, Elizabeth determined to be happy in her current situation. She believed it was God's will that she be here this year; and she believed that God wants people to be happy doing His will. Happiness cannot always be legislated but at least she can focus on whatever joys there were.

The phone was ringing when Elizabeth came back from the penthouse with Leda. Leda was a much different dog than Vronsky. She was loving and anxious to please. She did not have the confident assertiveness of Vronsky, but she was both skittish and dependent by nature making her no easier to walk with than Vronsky had been. Elizabeth had long since given up her idea of a dog as a walking aide; but the companionship of her dogs now filled an emptiness in her life.

The voice on the other end of the phone was Glenn's. "Elizabeth, I'm working on next year's budget. I'm asking for an assistant in my office next year. If I can get it through, would you consider taking the job?"

"Yes, I would like to consider it. At this point, I'm not sure what I'm doing next."

"I should warn you, I've asked for this before and it has always been cut in the final budget cuts." Glenn went on to say, "This year I'm going to really insist. If they don't give me some help, I'm not sure I'm staying next year."

"Well, Glenn, I hope you get it the in budget, for your sake. I would like to hear more about what you have in mind."

They made an appointment to talk in more detail the next day. Elizabeth hung up the phone feeling like a burden had just been lifted. Glenn could not have said anything more encouraging to Elizabeth. The possibility of such an easy transition from dormitory work to student personnel was beyond what she could have hoped for. The details of the position were for Elizabeth immaterial. If the job was available, she wanted it.

The next two months were an emotional roller coaster for both Glenn and Elizabeth. One day, the budget negotiations looked good. The next day, the position would be cut and Glenn would have to fight for it again. Glenn was so discouraged that he told Elizabeth that she had better begin to interview at other schools. Elizabeth tried but she had no energy for it.

Finally, the budget passed and the new position was in it. Glenn had been forced to compromise on salary, but Elizabeth did not care. Glenn wanted the new dormitory administrator to start with summer school and Elizabeth's responsibilities would be over at the end of the spring semester.

CHAPTER 19

April brought a change in weather. Spring in Philadelphia was always beautiful. For Elizabeth, the light at the end of the tunnel was getting larger and brighter. Finally, Elizabeth could actually take action. Her first action was to let Corrie know that she would definitely be staying in the Philadelphia area next year. That meant they could make plans to rent something together.

Corrie had been a student at the art college when Elizabeth first took the position in the old girl's dorm. They had gotten to know each other pretty well. Corrie loved animals especially dogs. Elizabeth had counted on Corrie's advice and help when she got Vronsky and, later, Leda. They had maintained their relationship after Corrie graduated and returned to New Jersey. Now Corrie was planning to move back to Philadelphia and look for a job.

The newspapers were full of apartments for rent; but most ads had the clause *no pets allowed.* Elizabeth and Corrie had to find a landlord who would tolerate pets. Corrie had two dogs an Alaskan malamute named, Yaska, and a toy poodle named Cocoa. Elizabeth said, "absolutely no" to Corrie's cat, Snowball; but Snowball was coming anyway. The animals dictated their choices of places to live. Elizabeth began to look for a house to rent with a yard for the dogs, for a house away from the concrete city and nearer to the homes of her church friends.

On her days off, Elizabeth would take Leda and the latest classified ads, along with a map of the western suburbs, and drive out to look at neighborhoods and potential houses. On one of those trips, she found the house. The house was an older, two-story, three-bedroom home with a large front porch and an enclosed back porch. It was in a residential area but sat back from the road with an empty wooded lot beside it. Behind that was an empty grass lot belonging to the realtor office on the side street. The house offered privacy without isolation. The landlord was the realtor whose office provided both the extra yard space and an off street entrance to the driveway; and the landlord agreed to the dogs.

Elizabeth was going to have a long commute to the college from the house she had chosen. Somehow, that added to its attraction for Elizabeth. She liked to think of putting miles between her job and her home. For too long, Elizabeth's job had invaded her home. This year it would not. They could afford the rent because rent was lower this distance from Philadelphia. Corrie would be job hunting so location was not important to her at this stage.

"I've always wanted to travel around the country. I'm thinking about taking a camping trip west. Would you come along?" Corrie had come to see the house, sign the lease, and make plans.

"I don't think so. I'm not much of a camper. If you do that when will you move in?" Elizabeth was focused on getting out of the dorm and settled. "We need to figure out what we are going to do about furniture for the house."

"Come on, Miss McKievey! You have vacation coming. I don't want to travel alone."

"What about the dogs?"

"They'll come along. I'm getting a tent and Mom and Dad have some camping things I can borrow. The bus will hold a lot."

Corrie drove an older Volkswagen bus. Elizabeth's initial resistance was weakening. She was getting interested. The trip would put miles between herself and the source of her stress and take her back to the wide-open spaces under blue skies and fluffy clouds. It would be an adventure.

"I can't drive the bus, you know. I just wouldn't be much help."

"I know. I'd rather do all the driving anyway. I'll set up the tent and everything; and you can be responsible for the cooking."

Elizabeth and Corrie decided to leave in late June when Elizabeth's responsibilities at the dorm were finished and the new job was set up. Elizabeth could take three weeks. They mapped out an itinerary. Corrie was a sculptor. She wanted to see the Badlands, the Black Hills, and Mt. Rushmore of South Dakota. The northern route would make it convenient to go through Iowa and stop at Elizabeth's mother's home. From South Dakota, they planned to travel through Wyoming and on to Salt Lake City, Utah, going south from there to the Grand Canyon and returning to Pennsylvania by a slightly southern route.

The morning of their departure Corrie loaded the bus. Everything fit in; but there was no room to spare. Suitcases, supplies, and camping gear filled the back section. The middle section was taken up with the large cooler, jugs of water, the dogs' dishes and paraphernalia, and the three dogs. Snowball, the cat, was staying with Corrie's parents. Elizabeth climbed into the front seat and pulled the little footstool in after her. The step from the ground into the VW bus was too high for Elizabeth but not for the dogs. They jumped up eagerly and settled down for the ride.

Elizabeth and Corrie would not start camping until after they left Elizabeth's Iowa home. As they drove across Illinois, the engine began making strange sounds. Neither Corrie nor Elizabeth was knowledgeable about mechanical matters. They were glad that there itinerary took them to Elizabeth's hometown. They spent an extra day while the engine was being repaired. They were relieved when the local bank agreed to cash Corrie's out of state check because they trusted Elizabeth's family.

Corrie's spirits were dragging. The repairs cost more than anyone expected. Elizabeth blamed herself a little. She was older, more experienced. She should have made sure Corrie had had the bus overhauled before they started out. Volkswagen dealers were not numerous in the Midwest. They were fortunate that the problem came up while they could stay with her mother and had mechanics they could trust.

The repairs were completed and they set out heading west on Interstate 80. Elizabeth had made the trip from Philadelphia to Iowa often enough that it was familiar to her; now, she felt that they were really getting started. A good feature of the VW bus was the gas mileage Corrie got. They were well across the state before they needed to stop for gas. On this trip, there would be no quick stops for gas. The dogs were good travelers; but they had to get out at every stop. The old bus was not air conditioned so everyone needed a long cold drink whenever they had a chance.

Refreshed, Elizabeth climbed back into the bus. Corrie settled the dogs, slid the side door shut, and climbed in herself. Corrie turned the key and the engine gave a tired clunking sound. She turned it off and tried again with the same result. Elizabeth started to say something but the expression on Corrie's face stopped her. Without a word Corrie, got out and went into the service station. Elizabeth waited silently with the dogs. Corrie returned followed by a mechanic who began to poke around in the engine.

After several tries, the engine began to run. The mechanic came around to talk to Corrie as she sat at the wheel.

"Well, it's running; but you've got a problem. I can't fix it. You are going to have to take it to a dealer. The nearest dealer would be in Omaha. Just don't turn the engine off until you get there." He closed the door and headed back to his work inside.

It was four o'clock when they got to Omaha. The Volkswagen dealer was not too hard to find. Corrie got out and went inside. Elizabeth and the dogs waited in the bus with the engine running.

"They won't take it now. I have to bring it back at seven tomorrow morning." Corrie returned a few minutes later to report. "They told me where a KOA Campground is."

"How can we do that if we can't turn the engine off?"

"I explained everything. They said they could show me what to do to get it started in the morning." Corrie did not invite further conversation. She drove the bus around to the garage and turned off the engine.

Elizabeth's first night of camping was disappointing. Corrie set everything up silently, deep in her own personal distress. They ate, took care of the dogs, and went to bed. They got up very early to break camp, pack up, and be at the dealer's by seven in the morning. Breakfast had to wait.

Elizabeth was relieved to find courtesy coffee and sweet rolls in the waiting area at the dealership. The dogs could not stay in the bus while it was being worked on. Yaska and Leda stayed on leashes stretching out across the floor and chewing determinedly on their rawhide chips. Cocoa sat on Corrie's lap. People came and went, cautiously keeping out of reach of the big dogs.

Elizabeth and Corrie spent much of the time studying the maps to see how this delay would affect their schedule. In a rack of brochures, Elizabeth found a listing of Volkswagen dealers and of KOA Campgrounds, which she added to their pile of books and maps. Planning was too difficult. They decided that when the bus was done they would just drive, see what they could see and how far that would take them.

Elizabeth's second night of camping was also disappointing. It was late dusk when they stopped and darkness had descended by the time Elizabeth had the food ready. Again they ate and went to bed; but they had come far enough that tomorrow they would enter the Badlands. Tomorrow would be a fun day.

Driving through the Badlands the next day, the bus's engine began to give trouble again. Elizabeth and Corrie were able to enjoy the wonder of God's creation, but there was an underlying tension, as the car trouble was not improving. They decided to camp on the outskirts of the town where the next Volkswagen dealer was located. A pattern was emerging of a day on the road, a hurried camp, and a morning in the waiting area of the next VW dealer. For a while, the pattern seemed set.

"You know, Miss McKievey, I think they may have solved the problem this time. The old bus is doing fine. Maybe we could take a break and stop early this afternoon."

"I'm ready to have a leisurely evening." Elizabeth reached for the directory of campsites. "What about stopping by the lake. It's about an hour away."

They were checked in and camp was set up. Corrie was relaxing on a chase lawn chair with Cocoa on her lap. Elizabeth was cooking an early dinner looking forward to settling onto the other lounge chair. Without warning, there was a loud snarl followed by the sound of a vicious dog fight.

Elizabeth whirled around to see Yaska and Leda at each other's throats. They were both on long ropes tied to different trees but close enough to reach each other. Yaska and Leda had always gotten along. This was a total shock. Elizabeth and Corrie both yelled at their dog but the dogs paid no attention. Corrie ran into the fray to separate the dogs. When she tried to separate the dogs, Yaska turned and bit her. Corrie screamed in pain and retreated holding a bleeding hand.

Elizabeth was terrified. She hated violence of any kind. She had no experience with dogfights; and Yaska was part wolf. Corrie couldn't help. All these things tumbled through her mind almost incapacitating her. One thing, though, seemed clear to Elizabeth; she had to take some action. As it was, the dogs could not be separated with their ropes tangled together as they were. Gathering all her strength, she approached the dogs still locked into a hold on each other. She unfastened Yaska's rope and unsteadily retreated to safety.

The commotion had attracted the attention of the neighboring campers. One man ran in and with his foot gave Leda a solid blow to the ribs and ran back out. Stunned, Leda let go of her hold; and Elizabeth seized the moment.

"YASKA! COME!" Elizabeth used her most commanding voice.

Yaska was obedience trained and her training came through. She came to Elizabeth.

"Yaska, get in the car!" Yaska obediently jumped in the car and

91

Elizabeth closed the door.

Another camper was driving away with Corrie taking her to find a doctor to get her hand taken care of. Leda was lying on the ground breathing heavily and unresponsive to all Elizabeth's efforts to minister to her.

Elizabeth sat down at the picnic table beside the uneaten meal. It was cold, dried up, and unappetizing. She didn't feel like eating. She felt nothing and she felt overwhelmed at the same time. Here she was almost two thousand miles from home. *What if Corrie's hand was so injured, she couldn't drive? The VW bus had a manual gearshift.* There was no way Elizabeth could drive. *What if Leda was really injured? What if the dogs couldn't get along anymore? What if it got dark and Corrie wasn't back yet?* Elizabeth wished she were not alone.

The injury to Corrie's hand, though painful, was not as serious as it had first appeared. She could drive and the next day, they continued on toward Salt Lake City. Leda was herself again after a few days of stiffness; and the dogs showed no further signs of animosity. The bus slowed down crossing the beautiful Medicine Bow Mountains and the engine began to give trouble. The pattern returned.

In Salt Lake City, Elizabeth and Corrie took stock. Their traveler's checks were almost used up. It was difficult to get the dealers to accept personal checks for the repairs. The only credit card they had was Elizabeth's gas card. The wisest decision, and the most desirable decision under the circumstances, was to head straight home. They were hot, tired, and irritable. The adventure was over. They wanted to go home.

They drove across Colorado, staying north of Denver and not taking any scenic detours. The bus was running well until they were halfway across Nebraska. As soon as Elizabeth heard the noise, she knew this was a major problem. She was aware of Corrie's stony countenance beside her without even looking. Elizabeth had learned not to talk at times like this. She looked at the map. They were not too far from a small town. Silently, Elizabeth prayed that the engine would hold out until they reached the town

Elizabeth was relieved when they passed the city limits sign on the out skirts. By now, the bus was lurching slightly and the engine knocked loudly. Corrie drove silently, eyes straight ahead. They drove through the tiny business district.

"Don't you think we should stop at a service station?" Elizabeth ventured a comment. Her tension wouldn't let her remain silent.

Corrie did not answer. She kept on driving on past the scattered homes as they left the city limits and on down the open highway. Elizabeth sat quietly. She had no idea what was going on in Corrie's head. Asking would only direct anger toward her; so, Elizabeth chose to wait and pray.

The engine gave a final loud clunk and stopped completely. Corrie was able to guide the bus off to the side of the road as it came to a stop.

"Why didn't you stop at a service station back there?" Elizabeth asked. Corrie looked defeated.

"Because I didn't see any!" Corrie snapped.

"There weren't any on the main street but I saw one a block over."

"I didn't see it."

Elizabeth wished Corrie had talked to her while they still had some options. "What shall we do now?"

"I'll have to get help. You'll have to stay with the dogs."

Soon after that, a trucker pulled over and offered to drive Corrie to the next service area. Elizabeth watched as Corrie climbed into the high cab and the big truck pulled back onto the road. For the moment, she was glad to be away from Corrie. They were both feeling stressed but they couldn't seem to be together in it. Perhaps it was because of the confusion of their relationship. Elizabeth was still Miss McKievey, the dormitory administrator. While Corrie was still the age of the students under Elizabeth's authority. In the current situation, Corrie had more responsibility; but Elizabeth had more life experience. Roles were unclear.

Time moved slowly. Only a few cars passed. Elizabeth sat with the passenger door open hoping for a little breeze. The temperature was in the nineties. The grass in the fields that stretched as far as the eye could see was long since dead. There wasn't a tree in sight. One hour passed with no sign of Corrie. Elizabeth had questioned the wisdom of Corrie going off with a stranger, but Corrie said there was no choice. Elizabeth began to worry.

The heat was building in the bus. The dogs were panting and restless. Elizabeth managed to get some water into their water dishes. They drank and settled down but the panting still shook the bus. Elizabeth thought about trying to get them out of the bus. She decided against it. The roof at least protected them from the beating sun. There was nowhere to go. Elizabeth herself was beginning to feel sick. She found a can of warm coke in the cooler.

Corrie had been gone almost two hours when a pickup truck pulling an empty flat bed trailer pulled off the road ahead of the bus. The long wait was ended. Corrie got out along with two men wearing mechanic's uniforms. They went right to work loading the bus onto the trailer and strapping it down. The dogs would have to stay in the bus. Elizabeth and Corrie got into the pickup with the two men and slowly and carefully, the driver made his way back to the service station. Elizabeth could see the bus in the rear view mirror. The dogs were jumping back and forth causing the old bus to sway even more as they drove along. Elizabeth sat praying silently. Only the men talked with each other.

The nearest service station did not have a mechanic. They were taking the bus on to Grand Island where help was more accessible. Elizabeth's stress mounted as the miles slowly rolled by. The men threatened to put the dogs out if they didn't settle down. Finally, they turned off the highway and cautiously eased the truck and its trailer into the service area. Weary and relieved Elizabeth and Corrie climbed out of the truck. The dogs had to wait until the bus was unloaded from the trailer but they arrived safely. The engine was not repairable. It had to be replaced. Elizabeth, Corrie, and the dogs checked into an air-conditioned motel nearby. Elizabeth relished the luxury of air conditioning and a soft bed. The day had been hard on the dogs, too; but the air conditioning helped them revive.

Elizabeth was so relieved to be safe again that she had a difficult time supporting Corrie. Corrie was devastated. She had called her parents. They owned a prosperous business and were very willing to wire her the money for a rebuilt engine. To Elizabeth, that was an answer to prayer but it did not ease Corrie's tears. Elizabeth could not help her. Corrie did not want to talk.

When the bus was ready, they headed east again. Corrie drove long days stopping only to sleep overnight at Elizabeth's mother's home in Iowa and Arlene's home in western Pennsylvania. They had no heart for camping anymore even though the rebuilt engine was running perfectly. In spite of everything, Elizabeth had had a memorable trip. They had seen a lot of the USA and had experienced new things, but Elizabeth and Corrie were both glad to be home and back to ordinary life.

CHAPTER 20

"Up, two. Up, one. Up, three. Up, two." Elizabeth was climbing the stairs to the second floor of the college building. "Up, four. Up, three. Up, Five. Up, four."

Every day she invented a simple number game to put blinders on her mind and to keep focused as she worked her way upward, step by step. Today's game was a number series, one number for each step. She started with two, subtracted one, added two, subtracted one, and so on. The rule was that if she missed a number, she kept moving but started the series over again. Oddly, Elizabeth enjoyed this private mental challenge.

Elizabeth left her house early every morning to insure herself of a parking space in the small parking lot inside the college wall. The parking space she tried to get was the space beside a side door opening into this stairwell where iron steps wound upward from ground level to the third floor. Elizabeth's office on the second floor was up three sets of steps. Elizabeth's increasing difficulty with climbing stairs was complicated by a fear of heights. She did not dare leave her mind free for fears to creep in.

Elizabeth reached the door to the second floor hall having not progressed in the number series beyond the teens; but feeling successful none-the-less. The hall was long and narrow with closely spaced windows along the inner side looking out onto a courtyard, completely surrounded by the building. Elizabeth's office was directly across the courtyard but a long walk from where she now stood looking out.

The college had originally been built and operated as a prison; and from the back and sides, still had the appearance of a walled fortress. The front of the building was impressive. An expanse of steps led up to a pillared portico and massive front doors. This portion of the building had been declared a historical building and was only used for administrative offices not classrooms or studios. Glenn's office was in this front building but Elizabeth's office was on one of the side halls in what must have been a cell block area.

The layout of the building was an advantage to Elizabeth. She could camouflage her weakness by pausing to lean against a window pretending to be taking in the view of the courtyard as she was doing today. She moved on down the hall and rounded the corner into the front building. Here she paused to look at student work displayed on the walls and regain her energy then started down the last hall to her office.

A nameplate with Elizabeth's name and official title, *Assistant Director of Financial Aid and Housing*, had been mounted on the wall beside her office door while she was on vacation. The nameplate pleased her. For the first time, Elizabeth had a job that was not just a stopgap job and the nameplate was a tangible reminder every time Elizabeth unlocked her office door.

At nine-thirty, Glenn's secretary called to tell Elizabeth that he was ready to begin reviewing late financial aid applications in his office. It had been an easy transition from the dorm job to the office. Glenn and Elizabeth worked well together and generally had a similar outlook on life. Elizabeth locked her office door and walked back to Glenn's office. She was ready to get on with the work of the day and ready for some people contact.

"Glenn, I may need to leave a little early today? I might have to pick Leda up at the vet's."

"We don't have a lot of applications to finish. I'm sure we will finish early. How did it go this morning?"

When Elizabeth bought Leda as a puppy, she had signed an agreement to have Leda spayed and not allow her to breed. Leda was a pure breed Russian wolfhound but she had a defect, an overbite. It was a defect that kept her from being officially registered and made her genetically undesirable. Elizabeth had taken her to the veterinary hospital today on her way to work to fulfill her agreement.

"It was pretty upsetting. I had to practically drag her from the car into the office. I ended up yelling at her; and inside she was shaking and leaning on me. I hated to leave her like that after yelling at her. I couldn't even comfort her because she was making me late. It was bad."

"When can you get her?"

I have to call after 2:00 and they'll tell me then."

The morning passed quickly. Glenn and Elizabeth took a short break to eat their sack lunches and went right back to work. At two o'clock, Elizabeth went to her office to make the phone call.

"I won't need to leave early. They said Leda is doing fine but they are keeping her overnight." Elizabeth came back with her report and settled back in her place at the worktable. "I don't know if I will get her before I come in tomorrow or not."

The next morning, the veterinary's office suggested she wait to pick Leda up. Elizabeth was to call again early afternoon. In the afternoon, they wanted to keep Leda one more night for observation. Elizabeth was becoming concerned but they assured her there was no problem.

The next day was Saturday; and when Elizabeth got the same response to her morning call, she insisted on visiting Leda. The office was filled with people with their pets waiting to see the doctors. After a few minutes wait, Elizabeth was ushered into a small back room. Leda was carried in and laid on an examining table. Elizabeth was shocked. Leda was awake but totally unresponsive. She gave no indication of recognizing Elizabeth.

"She needs to get on her feet and walk around before we discharge her." The staff worker left Elizabeth with those words and went back to his other duties.

Elizabeth began to massage Leda's stiff legs and talk to her. She talked to her about going home, about Yaska, Cocoa, and Snowball, about anything that came to her mind. Minutes went by with no response at all, but Elizabeth kept on. Finally, Leda began to lift her head. After more massaging and talking, Leda tried to get up. Elizabeth was encouraged. Now Leda needed to be on the floor where it would be safe for her to get up; but Elizabeth couldn't lift her off the table. Elizabeth called for the young man who had brought Leda to her.

"She's trying to get up. Would you put her on the floor for me?"

"Sure." He picked Leda up; but instead of setting her down where they were, he carried her back into the kennel area where she had been.

Following, Elizabeth saw Leda stiffen when they walked through the door. When he laid her down, she was back to the zombie-like state she had been in when Elizabeth first saw her. Leda remained unresponsive to Elizabeth's efforts. Elizabeth was frantic. If Leda stayed here, she would never heal.

In tears, Elizabeth appealed to the veterinary staff to get Leda out of the kennel. If they would just carry her to the car, Elizabeth would take her home. Her appeals fell on deaf ears and, in the end, Elizabeth was ushered out a back door so that she wouldn't upset the other pet owners.

Corrie was home when Elizabeth came in. Elizabeth's emotions had intensified as she drove home. She was near to being hysterical as she poured out her story to Corrie.

"Leda is going to die if I don't get her out of there! She thinks she's been abandoned. She's given up."

Corrie called the veterinary office to see what the situation was. They assured Corrie that Leda was fine. She was just slower to shake off the anaesthetic and they couldn't, in good conscience, discharge her yet. They told Corrie that Elizabeth was simply over-reacting. That is why they don't let pet owners see their pets until the pets are ready. They promised Corrie that she could pick Leda up in the morning.

Corrie had been Elizabeth's last hope. She was not reassured but all she could do now was wait. The phone rang early the next morning before either of them was up. Elizabeth let Corrie answer it. Leda had died during the night. They were very sorry. There had been no indication of a problem. They didn't know what happened. Elizabeth knew. Leda died of a broken heart.

Elizabeth felt the loss keenly. Leda was Elizabeth's closest companion. She had given undemanding loyalty and affection. Elizabeth had learned about love through Leda. Elizabeth had loved Vronsky intensely. He was a unique dog. He had personality. Elizabeth knew there would never be another dog to equal Vronsky. She could never love another dog like she loved Vronsky. Then she got Leda, and Leda was a different personality. She did not have the arrogant charm and exhausting selfishness of Vronsky. Leda was more sensitive to Elizabeth's needs.

Elizabeth grew to love Leda; but it was a different love than the love she had for Vronsky. It was not Vronsky's love transferred. It was a special love for Leda, a gentle peaceful love, a love that did not drain her energy. It was a much better love for Elizabeth.

Elizabeth had loved Reed in the same way she loved Vronsky. Reed, too, had been a unique personality. Elizabeth had believed there could never be another person in her life to equal Reed; but there was in Reed a bit of that same arrogant charm and exhausting selfishness of Vronsky. There would never be another person like Reed, but Elizabeth now knew there could be another love, a love that would be much better for her.

Elizabeth had always bemoaned her ability to adjust to life. To be able to do this so often seemed, to Elizabeth, to belittle the pain of the emotional crises or be a blatant act of disloyalty. Now Elizabeth was beginning to understand that it is not. That to remain rigid to prove the depth of an emotion, now useless, is deadly. To Elizabeth, this made life seem so shallow that it magnified her need for God, for God who is the only stability in life, for God who is the complex aspect of our existence, for that part of God's love that is uniquely hers.

CHAPTER 21

Elizabeth could make the drive between her house and the college in forty minutes when traffic was good. The summer days gave her time to experiment with routes and to become familiar with the drive while daylight lasted longer and road conditions were better. To Elizabeth, forty minutes didn't seem too long as a trade off for living outside the city. City living had been exciting when Elizabeth first came to Philadelphia; but the newness had worn off and her country roots were surfacing.

As Elizabeth drove home, she was thinking about the evening ahead. Ed and Marge were coming to dinner. It was something to look forward to. Elizabeth felt the loss of Leda most at the end of the day when she came home to Corrie's dogs. Ed and Marge, like Corrie, were former art students; and they were some of the few friends Corrie and Elizabeth had in common. They lived on the opposite side of the city but still kept close contact.

Ed was playing with Yaska when Elizabeth got home and Marge was helping Corrie with last minute kitchen chores. Elizabeth entered the house thinking how nice it was to relax with friends after a busy day.

"Miss McKievey, are you going to get another dog?" Ed asked as they sat around the table relaxing with coffee and desert.

"No. I don't plan to. I get too attached."

"She'll give in. I'm working on her," Corrie interjected.

"I told Corrie that if I did get another dog it would not be a wolfhound; but I can't see me with any other dogs."

The conversation drifted from one topic to another for a while. Then Ed took charge of the conversation.

"We have something else we want to talk to you about, Miss McKievey."

An uneasiness came over Elizabeth as she waited for Ed to continue.

"We've been talking and we've decided that from now on we are going to call you 'Elizabeth'."

Ed stated it with finality. They were not asking Elizabeth for permission. Ed was stating a fact. Elizabeth gave no indication of her emotional response to the announcement. In fact, she didn't understand it herself. What she felt was resistance. Her friends were taking a step

101

forward in friendship. *Why didn't she feel grateful? Why hadn't she initiated this name change herself months ago? What was it about names?*

Elizabeth had always hated being *Miss McKievey*. Those years in the dormitory as Miss McKievey, she had been more of a figurehead than a person. There had been no home to go to where she could just be Elizabeth, the person. Ed, Marge, and Corrie were saying, "from now on, with us, you are just our friend Elizabeth."

This was what Elizabeth wanted; but her emotions were saying, *Wait. You're getting too close.*

The awkward moment passed as Elizabeth simply responded, "Oh, okay." The conversation moved on to other things and the evening ended pleasantly.

Elizabeth buried herself in work. Glenn had needed an assistant for a long time so there was plenty to do. Elizabeth found that she was drawn to routine tasks. She was emotionally burned out from the two and a half years in the dormitory and found herself impatient with student problems. It still felt really good to go home and leave it all behind.

The Philadelphia area was enjoying a few days of Indian summer. Elizabeth came home from a Saturday morning trip to the grocery store to find Corrie pouring over the classified ads.

"I think it's time for you to look for another dog, Elizabeth. What about a collie? There is a kennel with three month old pups for sale."

"Corrie, I really don't think I want another dog. Collies are nice, but they are so ordinary. After Vronsky and Leda, I don't want a Lassie."

"Why don't I just call? It would be a nice day for a ride anyway. We could just go look at the puppies."

"The only way I would even consider a collie is if it was one of the black and white ones, a female, and cost a whole lot less than I paid for the wolfhounds."

Corrie ignored Elizabeth's objections and left to make the phone call while Elizabeth continued to empty the bags of groceries she had carried in.

"I got the directions. It's the Carolann Kennel up in Bucks County. It will be a pretty drive into the country." Corrie was back with her report. "They don't have any black and white puppies in this litter; but they have another litter only a couple weeks old. It has three and they are all females. They're called 'tri-color' because they always have brown on their faces."

The directions were hard to follow once they left the main roads. They drove deep into the Pennsylvania countryside past farms with fields now sitting quietly, waiting for winter. The trees had mostly lost their leaves and stood out in black silhouette against the blue sky. The air was cool but the sun was warm. It was a great day to be in the country. Elizabeth was glad Corrie had insisted they visit the kennel.

The puppies that were for sale were roly-poly balls of fluff with pointed noses. When Corrie and Elizabeth came in, they tumbled over each other in their excitement to greet the visitors. Elizabeth was drawn by their warm enthusiastic welcome but she resisted the urge to give in. They were cute and they were lovable but she would stick to the requirements she had stated to Corrie. She was still not sure she wanted to risk letting another animal into her heart.

Corrie asked if they could see the tri-color puppies. Erma, the kennel owner, led them into the old farmhouse where the tri-color puppies were still nestled with their mother and their three siblings all with the standard collie coloring. They squirmed more than they bounced. Their short hair lay flat against their bodies and they still had the rounded noses of a new born. They didn't look like collies at all. Elizabeth tried to imagine what they would look like when they were ready to leave the kennel.

"Can we see the father?" Corrie was giving the impression that they were seriously interested in purchasing a puppy despite Elizabeth's stated reservations.

"I can show you his picture. We don't own the father. He is a beautiful dog, the national champion." Erma took a frame photo off the shelf beside the desk and handed it to Corrie. "We bred our champion female to him to start our own line of tri-color collies. We were really pleased to get three females."

"How long before these will be ready for sale?" Again, Corrie was pushing ahead too fast for Elizabeth. With a pedigree like that, Elizabeth knew she could never afford one of these puppies.

"Well..." Erma hesitated; then went on. "They aren't exactly for sale. We plan to keep the pick of the litter and contract the other two."

"What do you mean by contract?" Elizabeth asked.

"We would let them go to carefully chosen homes at no charge with a signed contract allowing us to breed the dog to a male of our choice. The litter of puppies would belong to us and the female dog would then legally belong to the family she was living with."

"If I decide I want one of the puppies, would I qualify?" Elizabeth knew the question had to be asked.

"I couldn't say at this point. My husband and I haven't worked out all the details. Think about it and call me in a few days if you are interested."

As they drove away from the kennel, Corrie said, "You can't do better than that, Elizabeth."

Elizabeth had said she would only consider a collie if it were a tri-color female that cost a lot less than the wolfhounds. The puppies inside the old farmhouse met every specification. Elizabeth wondered if it was a sign. At the very least, it was pushing her to make a decision about getting another dog, and she already knew what her decision would be.

Time flew by and days dragged while Elizabeth waited for the puppies to mature enough to leave their mother. Elizabeth and Corrie made several trips to the kennel to visit the puppies and work out details of the contract. Elizabeth had a favorite but Erma didn't want to choose her own pick of the litter too quickly. The puppies were almost ten weeks old when Erma finally made her decision. Elizabeth was allowed to take the puppy she liked best.

Elizabeth named her puppy "Shona", a Scottish name according to Glenn's Irish secretary. Officially, she was registered as *Carolann's Lady Shona.* The name seemed to fit her. Shona adapted to her new home quickly and just as quickly filled the empty hole in Elizabeth's heart. Elizabeth was grateful to Corrie for not allowing her to refuse to risk again.

"Shall we have Ed and Marge come over this week? They haven't seen Shona yet." Corrie asked.

"Okay; but not Tuesday. I'll be home late. I have to stop at Dr. Bendle's office on the way home."

"Who is Dr. Bendle?"

"She's my muscular dystrophy doctor. I check in about once a year."

"You don't have muscular dystrophy!" Corrie's words were almost an attack.

"Yes, I do." It was too late for Elizabeth to side step the truth now. Corrie had always accepted her disability, but they had never discussed it. Corrie had never shown any curiosity.

"You do not!"

"Yes, I do." Elizabeth couldn't believe she was arguing for something she seldom even let be known. Experience had taught her it was best left unsaid; but now Corrie would not let it go.

"You can't have muscular dystrophy. You never told me!"

"I assumed that you knew. Your best friend, Helen, knew. I just assumed the two of you had talked about it."

"You can't have muscular dystrophy. I've got to go to work." Corrie gathered up her things and stormed out of the house.

Elizabeth dropped into a chair to try to make sense of what had just happened. Shona hurried over taking that as an invitation to be petted. Elizabeth scratched Shona's ears and ran her hand across Shona's furry back. It was comforting to have the little dog so eager for her touch, so accepting of her inadequacies, so unconcerned about muscular dystrophy. Elizabeth regretted her carelessness in mentioning muscular dystrophy. She knew better. She had let her guard down. She had forgotten the ostrich.

Corrie kept a distance between them, busying herself with her work and her church activities. She no longer welcomed Elizabeth's involvement in her life. They got along all right but they had lost the sense of togetherness they had had.

In the spring when it neared the time to sign a new rent lease, Corrie told Elizabeth that she was getting married and would be moving out. The news was unexpected. Elizabeth had not anticipated another major change; but she could not afford to pay the rent for the house on her own. There would be changes.

CHAPTER 22

Elizabeth drove down the now familiar route for the last time. She would like to have savored the drama of a final drive, noting the landmarks and remembering significant moments; but Elizabeth had too much on her mind. She would only have about an hour to sort and pack the last of her things before the men from her church arrived to move her out of the house. Corrie had moved two weeks earlier, so the only "good-bye" would be to the house itself.

Shona was waiting on the enclosed back porch. She began to bark as soon as she heard Elizabeth's car drive up welcoming Elizabeth enthusiastically. Elizabeth hurried past her feeling a little guilty for not taking time to return Shona's welcome. She stepped into the kitchen and stopped. The kitchen was empty and beyond the kitchen, the dining room was empty.

The house had the feel of emptiness, that almost tangible change from a home to a house. Elizabeth picked up a piece of yellow paper lying on the counter. It was a note. *We moved everything this afternoon. Give the house one more check and come on over for supper.* Elizabeth tucked the note into her purse and began a room by room inspection. Everything was gone, even her trash. There was only Shona's water dish on the back porch to show that they had belonged here.

Elizabeth laid her set of house keys on the counter as she had previously arranged with the realtor, turned the lock on the back door and pulled it firmly closed behind her. It would have been easier to close this door behind her if she had really known where she was going. Temporarily Elizabeth and Shona would be staying at the parsonage again. They would be staying with the current pastor and his family. The Harpers had graciously offered her a place to stay until she could find something else.

Nine-year-old Zoe and seven-year-old Andrea were sitting in the front yard watching for Elizabeth. They spotted her car and ran into the house to announce Elizabeth's arrival and back out with little Vickie toddling along behind to hurry Elizabeth into the house. Inside, Elizabeth snapped the leash onto Shona's collar, settled her in the front hall, and went into the kitchen to see if she could help. Elizabeth was moved in. She was, for now, part of the household.

Henry Harper was not fond of dogs; but because he understood how important Shona was to Elizabeth, he welcomed her too, with reservations. Shona was used to being alone all day. She didn't mind staying in the garage in the daytime while Elizabeth was at work. Elizabeth's belongings were mostly in the basement which was ground level at the back of the house. Elizabeth and Shona spent a lot of time in the basement and back yard. This living arrangement gave the family a good bit of privacy and at the same time provided Elizabeth with a taste of family life again.

Elizabeth left for Iowa for her vacation a couple of weeks after she moved in. Soon after she returned from Iowa, the Harpers planned to leave for their three-week vacation and were counting on Elizabeth to house sit while they were away. Elizabeth could not begin to look for a place to rent until things got back to a normal routine.

Things did not settle back into a normal routine. When vacations were over, a new college year was about to begin. Glenn and Elizabeth were snowed under with housing and financial aid details. The college was granted some federal funds to begin a work study program. Elizabeth was assigned the responsibility of setting up and coordinating the program. Elizabeth liked this kind of challenge but it involved a lot of time and stress. Once the students returned and classes started, the office was even busier and Elizabeth and Glenn were forced to work on Saturdays.

Three months had gone by since Elizabeth had moved into the Harper's home. Everyone had expected Elizabeth to be ready to move out by now but she was no nearer to moving than the day she had come. Henry and Eva had said nothing to pressure her and the girls loved having Elizabeth around; but Elizabeth was becoming increasingly aware that it was time for her to leave. She had nowhere to go.

Life was overwhelming Elizabeth again. Once more, there seemed to be no options. She couldn't stay where she was. She couldn't get a break in the pressure at work to seriously look for another place. She could not afford to pay the rents she was seeing in the classified ads. She didn't know anyone to room with. Most places would not take dogs. Some places Elizabeth could not even consider because of her limited strength and energy, particularly since she had Shona to care for.

A familiar feeling of hopelessness was descending on Elizabeth. Her thoughts kept cycling, looking for some detail she had overlooked that would provide an answer. There had to be an answer. Elizabeth knew that

God had the answer; but Elizabeth did not understand God. Nothing ever seemed to work out. *This time, God had provided a fulfilling job but how could she work at the job if she had no place to live? He had provided a dog to ease her loneliness but the dog was a major problem in finding a place to live. What did God expect of her? Why did He make it so hard all the time?* Elizabeth felt powerless to make life work, to be the self-sufficient person she was expected to be.

"Glenn, I'm ready to give up. I can't impose on the Harpers any longer. I don't have time to find a place of my own. Even worse, I don't make enough to pay full rent anyway. I'm thinking I should just ask Arlene if I can move out to western Pennsylvania and live on their third floor."

"Maybe you could find another housemate."

"I don't think so. After what happened with Corrie, I think I'd better be on my own or with my family."

"Elizabeth, you can't just leave. I can't handle the work study program and everything else on my own. Can I do something to help? If I can get you more money, how much would you need?"

"I think I could manage on another hundred a month. I won't know until I find a place to live."

"Let me see what I can do. You know that I've argued with them before that your position doesn't pay nearly enough."

"Okay, Glenn. I really don't know what to do."

Elizabeth felt better for having had the conversation with Glenn. She turned back to the work at hand. That, at least, was something she could do.

Late that afternoon, Glenn walked into Elizabeth's office and with a sigh dropped into the chair in front of her desk.

"Well, I couldn't get the full hundred but they were willing to go up some. It works out to about eighty a month. Will that help?"

"I don't know, Glenn, but thanks. It gives me something to work with at least. I need to put in less overtime and do some serious house hunting."

Elizabeth decided to give herself three weeks to look into all possibilities no matter how unattractive they sounded. A few days later, she was standing in the Student Affairs Office when Emily Baxter came in. Emily had been a student advisor when Elizabeth was in the dormitory.

"Hi, Miss McKievey. How are you doing?"

"Fine. Thank you."

"Are you still living with Corrie?"

"No. Corrie got married. I'm actually looking for a place right now." Elizabeth's answer seemed to end the conversation; but as Elizabeth turned to leave the office, Emily spoke again.

"I don't know if you would be at all interested, but my mother is thinking about renting part of her house. It isn't really an apartment. It's what my dad used as his office."

Elizabeth knew that Emily's parents were divorced and that her father was a physician.

"You know I have a dog. Would that make a difference to your mother?"

"I don't think so. She doesn't have any pets now, but we always had animals when we were growing up."

"I might be interested. Can I just call her and tell her I talked to you?"

"Sure. I'll give you her number."

Elizabeth took the scrap of paper Emily gave her and returned to her own office. This did not sound ideal but it was something to investigate. Elizabeth dialed the number. She had to set something in motion for the sake of the Harpers.

Mrs. Baxter sounded hesitant. She had not definitely decided that she wanted a renter but they set up a time to get together the next evening to talk about it.

Elizabeth carefully followed the directions as she had written them down. It was early evening and dusk was descending quickly. She needed to locate the house soon before darkness made it more difficult. Elizabeth finally spotted an entrance along the row of high hedges that lined the road and turned in. The house, sitting at the back of an expansive well kept lawn, reminded Elizabeth of pictures in her history books of country homes of well to do early Americans. The house next door was just visible through a grove of trees. It looked to be of the same vintage and quality.

Elizabeth stopped the car and picked up the page of directions. She reviewed them step by step. As far as she could tell, she had followed every step. Satisfied that she was not going to embarrass herself, Elizabeth shifted into drive and continued up the driveway to the parking area.

Mrs. Baxter was not at all what Elizabeth expected. She was a small attractive lady, who tended to look a little older than her years. Her quiet reserve and dignity revealed an inner strength. Her home was furnished simply and artistically in the early American style consistent with the house. Elizabeth felt both out of her league and yet comfortable as they talked.

Mrs. Baxter led the way through her kitchen and a tiny pantry to a door connecting the main house to what she called the 'complex of rooms' she was thinking about renting. The door opened into a small entryway.

Elizabeth's attention was immediately drawn to a large antique lock on an outside door to the left. Simple white curtains hung on the window in the door and on a nearby window at the end of the entryway. Mrs. Baxter flipped the light switch near the door so Elizabeth could look out. Outside was a small stone porch and stone steps bordered by wood railings painted white. Three stepping stones led to a parking space behind the house. The light was only strong enough for Elizabeth to see as far as the shrubs that lined the other side of the drive.

"This was my husband's office so it does have a private entrance, but it only has a half bath." Mrs. Baxter said apologetically as she opened a door directly across from the front door. "You would need to use the full bath upstairs for bathing."

"This was the waiting room."

Elizabeth turned back to the room at the other end of the entryway. It was a small room with a huge stone fireplace on the outside wall. There was one window on the same wall. The thick stone walls of the house allowed for wide windowsills; that seemed to add depth to the small room. The floors were uncarpeted revealing the original wooden floor. This would be the living room.

Beyond that was a smaller room almost more of an area than a room. Mrs. Baxter assured Elizabeth that it was large enough for her double bed with little space left. Opening off this area was a large walk-in closet with a curtain covering the doorway. This had been the office dressing room and would both extend the bedroom space and provide privacy needed because of the two windows in the other room.

"This was the original front entrance to the house. It's pretty small but could be a kitchen area." Mrs. Baxter led the way across the little room to a door on the right. "Dr. Baxter had a sink in this corner. The plumbing is still here. I was thinking I could install a kitchen sink unit here; and a refrigerator fits nicely in this alcove where the door to my living room has been sealed off."

A 'complex of rooms' was a good name for what Mrs. Baxter had just shown Elizabeth; and, oddly enough, Elizabeth was drawn to this 'complex of rooms'. Each room had some feature that made it unique and seemed to diminish the definite drawbacks. The setting would be perfect for Shona and Mrs. Baxter even said she would welcome Shona's company in the house when she was alone all day.

Elizabeth left feeling encouraged. This would be a makeshift apartment but because it was makeshift, Mrs. Baxter would be asking for less in rent. It would be a short-term solution because Mrs. Baxter had to sell the house in a year or so as part of her divorce settlement. Elizabeth was thinking that she could live here for a year and enjoy the house and grounds while saving money for her next move.

Mrs. Baxter still needed time to think about it but Elizabeth had decided that if it was available, she would move in and make it work. This odd shaped collection of rooms was not what she had envisioned as God's provision for her, but maybe it was.

CHAPTER 23

It was moving day again. Mrs. Baxter had decided to go ahead with her plans to rent the rooms and Elizabeth had been pleased to be able to tell the Harpers that she had found a place of her own. Elizabeth had lived in the Philadelphia area about eight years and in those years, she had lived in nine different places. Mrs. Baxter's house would be another short-term situation. Elizabeth was a person who longed for permanence and security but her life seemed to be one of continual change.

Today, Elizabeth didn't have much to move. The new place was small. She was moving only what she needed or would use. Everything else she was storing in the Harper's garage. Elizabeth had been busy the last two weeks sorting, and repacking. Now she was anxious to get settled in her new home.

The sink in Elizabeth's little kitchen was not completely hooked up yet. Mrs. Baxter invited Elizabeth to have meals with her until the sink was ready. Elizabeth had purchased a two burner electric hotplate and a second hand rotisserie oven to equip her kitchen. Cooking was a creative outlet for Elizabeth. She wasn't sure how that would work out in this setting; but Mrs. Baxter had offered to allow Elizabeth to use the oven in her kitchen occasionally.

Supper was set for six o'clock. Elizabeth had gotten her things unpacked and was ready to take a break when she heard Mrs. Baxter's knock on the connecting door.

"Everything's ready, if you want to come on in. Bring Shona so we can start to get acquainted."

The meal was simple but good and although the conversation was that of two strangers, Elizabeth felt comfortable. Mrs. Baxter was able to be interested without being intrusive and open with discretion. Shona provided a neutral connection for them. Elizabeth was both pleased and relieved to see that Mrs. Baxter truly was looking forward to having Shona in the house.

Elizabeth's life was on track again. The overload of work at the college tapered off. The forty-five minute drive to and from the college became routine. Elizabeth put herself on a very strict budget and was finding pleasure in seeing the budget work and a small savings begin to appear.

For Shona, the move was definitely a change for the better. Up to now, she had spent long days on the enclosed back porch of the house and, after that, closed in a cluttered garage. Now, Elizabeth closed off the bedroom and kitchen area when she left for work in the morning and Shona spent her days in the comfort of the remaining space. At four o'clock every day Mrs. Baxter took her out to the yard to play, then kept Shona in the kitchen with her for company while she cooked her evening meal.

Mrs. Baxter wanted to take Shona jogging with her but Shona was not a jogger. Shona would simply sit down and refuse to move. Shona was a wanderer not a runner. Mrs. Baxter did take her along for company when she jogged on the track at the back of a nearby school yard and allowed Shona to wander while she jogged.

Shona was a good dog for Elizabeth. She was gentle, loyal, and eager to please. A close companionship had developed between them. But Shona would not officially become Elizabeth's dog until the terms of the contract were fulfilled. Shona was maturing. Now Elizabeth needed Corrie's help again. Corrie would know when to call the kennel to arrange to have Shona bred.

Corrie and her husband had purchased a small house in a Philadelphia suburb not far from where Elizabeth now lived. Corrie's husband worked the night shift, which meant that Corrie was free when Elizabeth got home from work and Elizabeth did not have to intrude on time Corrie and her husband had together. Elizabeth hated to be a nuisance and this way, she felt like less of a nuisance.

The kennel owners wanted to board Shona from the time she came in season until she was bred to avoid any mistakes. When Corrie determined that it was time, she and Elizabeth drove Shona out to the kennel in Bucks County. Elizabeth was glad to be relieved of the responsibility of a dog in heat; but she was finding it difficult to drive away without Shona in the car.

"Thanks for coming, Corrie. I'd hate to do this alone. At least they took her into the house instead of putting her into a pen. I feel better about that."

"Did you hear Erma say she thinks Shona is a better dog than the one they kept for show?"

"Yes, I did," Elizabeth responded. "It's kind of fun to think I have the pick of the litter. I chose a quality collie."

"Do you think you would like to have one of Shona's puppies?"

"Not this time but maybe I'll let her have a second litter,"

"Yaska really misses Shona. They used to play together so much. You know Yaska; she doesn't like other dogs all that well."

"I remember." Elizabeth was thinking of Corrie's friend who brought her dog along when she came for a visit. The poor little dog had gone home with eighteen stitches in his neck from Yaska's attack.

"When you get Shona back, why don't we plan to get together once a week. You could pick Shona up after work and come over. We could eat together while the dogs play in my back yard."

"Okay. That sounds good."

Elizabeth and Corrie were slowly re-establishing the friendship they had once had. This time, though, they were starting as equals. There was no longer any residue of Corrie being Elizabeth's student friend. For Elizabeth, this restoration of the friendship was like a weight being lifted but she was careful not to expect too much.

As far as Elizabeth could tell, Shona survived the separation better than she and Mrs. Baxter had. Shona had become so much a part of the routine of their lives that her absence made a significant hole. All three were glad when the two weeks were up and Shona was back home. In nine weeks, it would happen again. Erma wanted the puppies to be born at the kennel.

Elizabeth and Shona now spent every Tuesday evening with Corrie and Yaska. Corrie was glad to have someone to confide in and Elizabeth needed someone she could talk to as well. Their friendship seemed to be growing. It was as though the words "muscular dystrophy" had never been spoken.

"Corrie, I never really understood what happened between us when we were living together." Elizabeth had never meant to let this topic surface but the conversation this evening was of a depth that the statement just came out. "Things were going fine and it just all fell apart."

"When I was in high school, I used to baby-sit a boy who had muscular dystrophy and he died. When you said you had muscular dystrophy, I couldn't take it. I was too emotionally dependent on you. I thought you would die, and I couldn't take another loss."

"The type of dystrophy I have is not as severe as the type that young boys have. It's not really the same at all."

Elizabeth understood more than Corrie's words. They had talked before about Corrie's older sister. Corrie and her sister had been quite close. In their early teens, her sister was diagnosed with leukemia. The doctors could not help her. Corrie's family had never fully recovered from her death.

Corrie's reaction to Elizabeth made sense in this context. Knowing this was healing for the pain Elizabeth still felt from Corrie's earlier withdrawal. It allowed her to trust the friendship she and Corrie had now re-established. At the same time, the knowledge of how the facts of her disability affected her friends deepened her feeling of aloneness. Elizabeth needed to protect her friends from herself and that, in turn, would protect Elizabeth from some emotional pain as well.

The nine weeks passed quickly and Corrie and Elizabeth made the familiar trip with Shona to the Carolann Kennel where she would be staying for the next few months. After the puppies arrived, Corrie and Elizabeth planned to spend Tuesday nights visiting Shona and her puppies at the kennel. Erma promised to call as soon as the puppies came.

Elizabeth found that she could not wait for Erma's call. She called Erma every evening when she got home from work so that she could report to Mrs. Baxter. After five days, Shona had not delivered.

"If Shona doesn't have her puppies by tomorrow, I think we will have our veterinarian check her out."

"I hope that isn't necessary. I'll call tomorrow. Tell Shona I called."

Elizabeth hurried home from work the next night to call Erma. It was Tuesday. She was going to Corrie's but she wanted to call first.

"You can pick Shona up any time. The veterinarian checked her over and found that she's having a false pregnancy."

"Oh, no! What do we do now?"

"Nothing. Her system will settle down and we can try again next time."

Elizabeth was disappointed. She didn't want to go through all that again and she really had been looking forward to seeing Shona mother a litter of pups. On the other hand, Elizabeth was anxious to have Shona home. Corrie would go with her and to get Shona. She was glad it was Tuesday.

"We can pick her up tonight."

"She'll be glad to see you. She isn't used to having so many other dogs around."

Once again, life settled back into a comfortable routine. Vacations and holidays came and went. Elizabeth and Shona spent most of these times with family either in Iowa or Beaver Falls in western Pennsylvania. Mrs. Baxter decided to wait at least one more year before putting her house up for sale. Elizabeth's job was satisfying. It lacked excitement but she knew that she was making a contribution to people's lives. She was fulfilling the role God had assigned her. Elizabeth was happy.

CHAPTER 24

Glenn was a real suburbanite in ways Elizabeth could not quite understand. He and his wife, Alice, lived less than two miles from Mrs. Baxter's house but Elizabeth could seldom talk him into riding with her. He preferred to take the commuter train. The train was not faster but it was his way of unwinding on his way home. Elizabeth liked the independence and flexibility driving her own car provided.

This afternoon, Elizabeth and Glenn were leaving together. As she sometimes did, Elizabeth was dropping Glenn off at Penn Station downtown on her way home. Glenn wanted to finish the discussion they were having but he didn't want to miss his train.

Glenn held the heavy door open; and Elizabeth stepped into the stairwell. She put her hand on the top of the stair railing and stopped. For Elizabeth, the moment in time froze; she didn't know what to do. Physically, Elizabeth could not step down onto the first step. Glenn was waiting for her to go on down the stairs. She had to descend the steps or she couldn't get to her car. She had to move forward; but something was wrong. She was sure that if she put her first foot down on the step she would lose her balance completely. Glenn was waiting; Elizabeth had to do something.

"Glenn, I'm feeling a little dizzy. Would you just walk down the steps ahead of me."

"Alright. Do you want me to carry your bag for you?"

"No. Just walk ahead of me. I have a fear of heights. For some reason, I think, it just kicked in."

After the first two or three steps, Elizabeth knew that she was on safe footing again. Glenn was taking the steps slowly and carefully. When they reached the first landing, Elizabeth said "You can just go on down, Glenn, I'm fine now."

They drove out of the parking lot gate in silence. Then Glenn picked-up the conversation he had started in the office.

"I'm tired of the preferential treatment the business office gets. I don't know what Greg does. He's never in the office and when he is he never knows what's going on."

"I know. We are always straightening out their mistakes in some student's financial aid. A business office should be more precise."

"Well, I do know what Greg's salary is. I'm starting now to let it be known that at budget time I'm going to fight to have your salary brought in line with Greg's. My assistant is as valuable as the business manager's is."

"Greg has a family. He couldn't possibly be living on what I make."

"No way, he makes almost double what you make. It's insulting to me. I had to fight really hard just to get an assistant. I guess you know that."

"I remember!" Elizabeth pulled over to the curb. Glenn gathered his newspaper, located his brief case, and got out of the car.

"See you tomorrow."

Elizabeth had been through ups and downs with budget fights before. She knew that Glenn was going to have an uphill struggle; but, every time, he made some headway. She was a little hopeful as she drove home.

The incident at the top of the stairs bothered her. Elizabeth was embarrassed that Glenn had been there but she didn't know how she would have gotten down the steps if he hadn't been. She didn't want to think about it and allow herself to develop a fear of going down those stairs. Still, she couldn't shake an uneasiness.

Elizabeth couldn't wait to tell Corrie about her conversation with Glenn. She held off until she was settled on the reclining chair that had become her place for after dinner conversation.

"I had an interesting conversation with Glenn on the way home the other day."

"What was that?" Corrie settled into her place on the couch.

"He is planning to try to get me a major salary increase for next year."

"What brought this on?"

"I don't know. It's interesting, though. I think it's more about him than me. It's the position he is fighting for. I just happen to have the position."

"Do you think he will succeed?"

"I hope so. The timing would be good for me. I think Mrs. Baxter is really going to sell the house this summer, and I'll have to move again."

Elizabeth and Shona left a little early in order to miss the snow showers predicted for later that night. From all indications, Pennsylvania was in for a severe winter. Early winter had been bad enough that Elizabeth decided not to make the drive across the mountains for the Christmas holidays. When the day came, she knew she had made a wise decision.

It was the first time Elizabeth was alone on Christmas. Mrs. Baxter's daughters visited her on Christmas Day. She invited Elizabeth to join them for Christmas dinner; so, the day was not entirely without people and a touch of holiday. Nevertheless, it was a lonely day and Elizabeth was glad when it was over.

There was much to do at the college while the students were on break. This was budget time and in addition to the financial aid budget requests, Glenn was diligently pursuing the salary increase he had told Elizabeth he would ask for. Elizabeth was giving him whatever support and help she could, but she was less encouraged personally than she had been.

Elizabeth was in another, very private turmoil. She had experienced other difficult times at the top of the staircase. The times were rare but they were persistent. Sometimes it would be a brief sensation that she could push through with careful determination. A few times, she had been forced to ask the school nurse, whose office was nearby, to walk down the first part of the flight ahead of her. Elizabeth always blamed it on vertigo when she asked for help but she knew it was more than that.

Going up the stairs had been a problem from the beginning but going down had not. Elizabeth had to find a solution before the problem got worse. The college was expanding to a building with an elevator but the administrative offices were staying in the old building. Until she had an answer, she could not talk to anyone about this.

Elizabeth came to the only conclusion she could come to given her set of circumstances. Now she needed to talk it through, to get it out in the open so that she could accept it.

"Corrie, the steps at the college are getting to be too much for me. I'm going to have to quit." Elizabeth didn't know what kind of response she would get from Corrie; but to her relief, Corrie didn't react.

"Are you sure you can't work something out with Glenn?"

"I've gone round and round all this in my mind. There just isn't any way. I'd rather leave while I have the respect of the people at the college, before all they remember is what I couldn't do."

"What will you do?"

"I know that getting another job now will be really hard and maybe impossible. I think the time has come for me to be near family. I can't ask the church people to carry me through another job hunt. I'll move to Beaver Falls. I'm a little worried about Shona, though. Do you think I'll have trouble with the kennel?"

"I don't know, but they are concerned that Shona have a good home. They know she's happy with you. I don't think they would refuse to let her go."

"I can bring her back to be bred and to have the puppies."

"Elizabeth, are you really sure you have to quit? There must be another way. I don't want you to leave the area."

Elizabeth didn't want to leave either. She had built a life here and it was a life she valued. Elizabeth did not want to give it up; but a part of her had always known she was living on a borrowed reality. Like Cinderella, for Elizabeth the clock was striking twelve.

Elizabeth was not ready to talk to Glenn yet. She had to adjust to the decision herself first; and she had to plan ahead. She needed to be near family; but unless she went back to Iowa to live with her mother, she could not actually live with her family. For Elizabeth, a better option seemed to be Beaver Falls, but she would need to find a place to live that would be close to Arlene's. Arlene and Ralph owned their home. Marilyn who was now married and also living in Beaver Falls was renting so she was not permanently settled.

The necessity of making definite arrangements for life in Beaver Falls helped Elizabeth move on from decision to action. She wrote to Arlene about an idea she had. Arlene's home stood on the front right corner of a large double lot. Elizabeth asked if they would consider allowing her to put a small modular house on the back left corner of the double lot, behind their garage where Arlene had her garden.

Ralph thought that a better idea would be for Elizabeth to look into purchasing a doublewide mobile home that could be moved in intact and moved out in the future. He wanted to maintain ownership of the land, but Elizabeth was welcome to use it. Ralph would look into getting a zoning variance. Until that hurdle was behind them, Elizabeth could not be sure it would work.

Glenn was successful in his budget negotiations. Elizabeth decided to wait for the budget to be finalized before she told Glenn about her plans. Then, she let him revel in his success for a while. The truth was that Elizabeth didn't want to do something so final that there would be no going back; but, already, there was no going back. Elizabeth had to talk to Glenn.

"Glenn, do you have time to talk?" Elizabeth used the interoffice intercom from her office.

"Just give me five minutes and come on up,"

Elizabeth dreaded starting this conversation. "Glenn, I am going to have to resign at the end of the summer."

"Elizabeth, what brought this on?"

"I really like my job and I really like working with you. But the last several months I've had trouble off and on walking up and down the stairs. The problem isn't going away, so I have to resign." Elizabeth had never before spoken to Glenn about her disability.

"Maybe we could find an office on the first floor. That would only be one set of steps. Would that work?" Glenn did not press for details regarding the disability.

"I could do one set of steps, Glenn; but it wouldn't work. I don't want to do a half job. Your assistant's office needs to be near your office."

"The secretaries could carry work back and forth."

"No, Glenn, it just wouldn't be satisfactory for any of us."

Elizabeth was glad that she had had enough time to make her decision firm. She wanted more than anything to keep her job at the college and for life to go on as it was. She might have compromised. She might have hung onto something that would no longer work.

Elizabeth had set the wheels in motion. Now she had to put her resignation in writing so that Glenn could begin to search for her replacement. Elizabeth did not like to think of someone else doing her job. She had more or less created the position. It was important to Elizabeth that the right person be chosen to take her place.

CHAPTER 25

Glenn quickly read through the letter of resignation Elizabeth handed to him and laid it aside. "Elizabeth, I know you're planning to leave at the end of the summer, but it would really be better for the office if your replacement started late May when we review financial aid applications. That way you could do the training for me and the other person will be familiar with the process when the students come back in the fall. I'd rather your termination date be June 30th."

Glenn's words fell like weights on Elizabeth. For Glenn, he was simply stating a fact, but for Elizabeth his words were personal arrows. To Elizabeth, they clearly said that she was expendable, easily replaceable. Glenn was rushing ahead, pushing her out.

Elizabeth wanted the satisfaction of reviewing financial aid applications with Glenn one final time. Glenn just wanted to be sure she trained her replacement. Elizabeth had been a part of Glenn's campaign to get the salary increase. She had hoped to have two months of the new salary. If she left on Glenn's schedule, she would be leaving at the end of the current fiscal year. Glenn's concern for the smooth transition of the office didn't leave room for concern about Elizabeth's finances or her feelings.

"Well, Glenn, I'll need to think about this. Have you started to look for someone yet?" Elizabeth refocused the conversation to gain time to process her emotions.

"I need to talk to Stacie Trent before I advertise the position. I haven't got it done yet."

"No, Glenn!" Elizabeth caught herself and proceeded cautiously. "I don't think you would be happy working with her. You know how frustrated we've been over some of the things at the dorm."

Stacie Trent had been hired to administer the dormitory when Elizabeth became Glenn's assistant. Stacie's opinions and style changed after she was hired. Elizabeth resented the direction Stacie's leadership had taken the dormitory. She destroyed what Elizabeth had tried to build up in the dorm. Now was she going to follow her into this job that Elizabeth had been molding into shape?

"I know, but it's just a courtesy. Stacie won't be interested in this job."

Glenn passed off her concern.

"If you offer her the job, I'm sure she will jump at it."

"I don't think so, Elizabeth."

Elizabeth did not respond. Whoever Glenn hired would be his assistant; it was his job to do with as he pleased. What Elizabeth had to say was better said to Corrie. Elizabeth determined to keep her thoughts to herself for a few more hours.

Yaska and Shona had finished their romp in the yard and were now settled in the living room each contentedly chewing on their rawhide bones. Elizabeth and Corrie settled down as well.

"You can work as long as you want to. You don't have to go by Glenn's schedule."

"He does have a point. It gets pretty crazy when the fall semester starts. The trouble is that if I insist on staying through the summer, I'll ruin our good working relationship; and I won't enjoy it. I lose either way."

"Glenn isn't being very considerate of you."

"I'm really upset. At this point, I don't even care when I leave. Glenn doesn't give me any credit. As far as he is concerned, just anyone can take my place! My worst nightmare is coming true. Glenn is going to offer 'my' job to Stacie Trent!"

"That's never going to work. Is it?" Corrie knew Elizabeth's opinion of Stacie.

"No, it isn't. Stacie is aggressive and thoughtless and I don't think she has much integrity. The cohesiveness of the office will be gone and Glenn is never going to know why. That makes me mad. I know what I bring to the office. I like working with Glenn. I felt like we were a team, but he isn't that easy to work with. Bonnie will just do her own thing. He gives me no credit for who I am and it makes me really mad!"

"I just can't believe Glenn would want to work that closely with Stacie."

"Glenn thinks she won't want the job, but I know she's going to snap it up before he even gets the words out. I feel so personally belittled or something. Actually, I hardly know what I feel besides anger."

Elizabeth was glad to have Corrie to talk to. Corrie knew the college and the people involved. She understood the situation in a way Elizabeth's other friends could not.

Elizabeth told Glenn that she was willing to rewrite her letter of resignation giving her date of resignation as June 30st. Glenn told Stacie Trent that Elizabeth's position would be available if she wanted it. Stacie immediately accepted the offer and excitedly rushed down to Elizabeth's office to view the office through new eyes.

Spring break came at a good time. Elizabeth was driving to Beaver Falls. The long drive alone in her car was always a time for Elizabeth to think through whatever was happening in her life. Elizabeth needed that time right now. She needed to find a balance. She needed to figure out how to let go. She needed to connect with God.

Since Elizabeth had moved the date of her resignation forward, it was time to start making some solid plans for her future. Ralph had done some work for the owner of a trailer and mobile home dealership and had laid the groundwork for Elizabeth to visit his lot. Elizabeth's small savings, thanks to her time in Mrs. Baxter's home, gave her some confidence that she could buy a trailer home.

The weather was not inviting as Elizabeth and Marilyn set out to look for possibilities. The dealership was further away than they had expected. By the time they found it, the drizzle had changed to pellets of snow and a thin layer of ice was beginning to develop.

"What do you want to do?" Marilyn asked.

"We're here. We just as well go in and talk to the man. I'd like to know the price range of these homes. Maybe we could just get some brochures."

The salesman at the desk was busy on the phone when they walked in. He stopped his conversation and looked up inquiringly. The owner had gone out but would be back shortly. The sample homes on the lot were unlocked; he said they should go on out and look around.

Outside again, the wind swirled around them driving the biting snow into their faces. Elizabeth held on to Marilyn to keep her balance on the slippery ground. The sample homes were all sitting on pillars made of concrete blocks. Temporary metal steps provided an unstable access to the front doors making an impossible situation for Elizabeth.

The nearest home was a plain looking doublewide trailer. It was the obvious place to start. Marilyn and Elizabeth stopped at the steps while Elizabeth surveyed the situation feeling miserable and frustrated.

"You go in, Marilyn, and see what you think. I know I can't make it up these steps."

Marilyn hesitated, then went up the steps and disappeared into the trailer. Elizabeth turned her back to the wind and shoved her cold hands into her coat pockets.

"You need to see this." Marilyn was back at the door. "It has the things you are looking for but I can't tell. You'll have to see it."

"Oh, Marilyn! I can't get in."

"Sooner or later you will have to. You can't buy anything unless you see it." Marilyn's point sunk home.

"I can't walk in but I can probably get to the top step and sit in. I hate this public display!" The door of the trailer was in plain view of the highway and the parking lot.

"Forget it, let's just get you in."

Elizabeth sat down on the doorsill and Marilyn pulled her inside and shut the door. Together they got Elizabeth to her feet again. Inside, protected from the bitter weather outside, Elizabeth's spirits lifted. She was pleased with what she saw. The L-shaped living room and dinning room combination gave a feeling of space and openness. The dining room had a large sliding glass door that would give Shona a place to look outside. There were three bedrooms and space for a laundry area. The kitchen was small but open and conveniently arranged.

"I like it," Elizabeth told Marilyn. "It is simple but comfortable. I wonder what it costs."

"Shall we look at some others?"

"I guess, if we can get me in. Let's look at that one."

Elizabeth pointed to a singlewide trailer with an attractive exterior. The bad weather had kept people at home, so Elizabeth's unorthodox entrance was again accomplished in private. The interior of this trailer was done in rich looking Spanish décor with a fireplace in one corner.

"This is beautiful!"

"Yes, it is," Elizabeth agreed. "Let's look at the bedrooms."

"The bedrooms aren't as nice as the living quarters. But it's a really pretty trailer inside and out."

"I agree; but, you know, it just isn't me. It doesn't have the light and openness of the first one. I really liked the feel of that one. I'm not sure there is any reason to look at any more. Let's just go talk to Ralph's friend."

Elizabeth had not expected it to be so easy to find what she wanted.

128

The doublewide trailer was modestly priced. The living and dining rooms came with the furniture she had seen in the sample home. Elizabeth would have a choice of colors for the carpet and drapes. For a small extra charge, she could have a sink and tile floor put in a back bedroom to make it into a studio workroom.

Elizabeth returned to Philadelphia more at peace with the future. She had, in writing, all the information she would need to make the final arrangements from Philadelphia. Elizabeth was to call the dealer six weeks before she wanted delivery and give him her color choices and any other specifications. Ralph was going to arrange for the utility hook-ups and prepare the lot. Everything would be ready for her by the end of June.

The school year was winding down and the daily routine at the office was focused on that. Elizabeth had gotten beyond her anger with Glenn and they were working in harmony again. Elizabeth dreaded the time when the dorm would be empty and Stacie would join them to begin her training. That day came all too fast.

"How are things going with Stacie?" Corrie was making up a new pitcher of ice tea. The heat and humidity had been unseasonably high all week.

"Fine I guess. She is supposed to do the work. I just sit and watch. She's not one who welcomes instruction."

"Where is Glenn in all this?"

"He pretty much stays out of the way. I'm supposed to be doing the training. He knows how I feel about Stacie and her takeover style and he's beginning to see what's happening. Now he's saying things to emphasize that it's still my office until I move my things out. It's kind of like 'shutting the barn door after the horse is out', as the old saying goes. It's too late now."

"Changing the subject, what did Erma say when you called the kennel?"

"She was really good about it. I didn't actually ask permission to move Shona out of the area. I just told her I had to move but I would honor the terms of my contract. She didn't seem to be concerned at all."

"Erma always is pretty laid back. I'm glad you will have to bring Shona back. That way I know you have to come. You can stay in our extra bedroom."

"Thanks, Corrie. I'm glad I have a reason to come back, too. My life is here. I don't know what I'm going to do out there."

Elizabeth found less and less reason to be in the office. She was kind of a fifth wheel taking up space with no real purpose. Every morning, she stopped at the bottom of the three flights of stairs thinking, *this isn't worth all the effort.*

Then she would contemptuously say to herself, *Okay! Fine! Just tell Glenn you want to quit early and LET Stacie take your place right now!*

The strength of her emotions got her up the steps and through the days of the final week.

CHAPTER 26

Rain was relentless all across Pennsylvania. Day after day, the forecast was the same. Creeks and rivers were flooding in Philadelphia and across the state. It was Elizabeth's last week of driving to work. She had to keep tuned to the radio traffic reports and keep up on which bridges were closed and which were open to traffic.

Weather, so often, seemed to be a major factor in Elizabeth's life. Elizabeth's trailer home was ready at the factory but delivery was being delayed a week because of the torrential downpours. Elizabeth would like to have adjusted her arrangements for leaving Philadelphia to coincide with the delivery of her home, but that wasn't possible.

Elizabeth's youngest sister, Louise, and her husband were now living in Maryland outside of Washington D.C. They took Friday off from their jobs to help Elizabeth move over the weekend. It was still dark when they drove away from Mrs. Baxter's house for the last time. Elizabeth led the way to the turnpike. James followed in the rental truck they had loaded the night before, and Louise followed the truck in their car. Elizabeth set the pace.

At first, it was comforting to Elizabeth driving through the black tunnel of night to glance at the rearview mirror and see the truck's headlights following along. After a while, Elizabeth began to realize that the headlights were getting smaller each time she looked up. She slowed her speed and the distance between them lessened briefly, then it happened again. Elizabeth slowed to a crawl. She could barely see two dots of light; headlights no longer recognizable, that she hoped were the trucks.

The comfort Elizabeth had felt at first, gave way to a sense of loneliness and isolation. She was driving well below the speed limit and now the truck and Louise's car were completely out of sight; and she was alone inching down the highway not knowing what to do. They had not made plans for what to do if they got separated. *What if the truck had broken down somewhere behind her?* Elizabeth had all the paper work for the rental truck with her. They had intended to stay together.

Elizabeth pulled off onto the side of the road and stopped her car. She decided to wait with the engine running to see if the truck would appear. Minutes passed. Elizabeth felt uneasy sitting alone in the dark. A light fog began to settle around her. The turnpike seemed deserted. Elizabeth's imagination was beginning to run wild.

Finally, headlights appeared in her side mirror. Elizabeth watched, waiting to see if she could identify them as belonging to the truck. The vehicle seemed to take an inordinately long time getting to where Elizabeth sat watching and waiting. Finally, it was close enough for Elizabeth to recognize the lights of the rental truck. She forced herself to wait longer before pulling back onto the road just ahead of the truck.

This time, Elizabeth was careful to keep her speed low enough to keep the truck in sight all of the time. The day dawned hazy but without rain. Before they got to the mountains, Elizabeth led the way into a service plaza for a breakfast stop.

"I lost you guys there for a while. What happened?" Elizabeth snapped the leash onto Shona's collar and handed it to James.

"The truck has a cruise control locked in. It just won't be pushed. I'll put Shona back in the car as soon as I walk her. You and Lo go on in and I'll be right there."

Breakfast coffee helped bring Elizabeth out of the daze that had been descending. They needed to revise their plan. Elizabeth was going to have trouble staying together with Louise and James through the mountains at the speed the truck traveled. After some discussion, they decided that there was really no reason to stay together. The route was turnpike all the way to Beaver Falls. If James got lost finding Arlene's house after they got off, they could call for directions.

Elizabeth handed James the rental agreement for the truck and returned to her car. Shona was waiting anxiously aware of the stress Elizabeth had been feeling. "Okay, Shona, we're on our own. Let's go!"

Elizabeth felt released. Freed from being responsible. Freed from the loneliness and isolation that she had felt.

Being alone in her own world was less lonely for Elizabeth than trying to be part of something else. She didn't really want to be alone all the time but on one level, it brought less unhappiness.

The truck, followed by Louise in her car, took two hours longer to make the trip than it took Elizabeth. By the time they arrived, Elizabeth had started to worry again; but they had not had any trouble. Ralph and James unloaded the truck so that it could be turned in at the local agency. All of Elizabeth's boxes and furniture were crowded into Arlene's dining room completely filling the small room. This was going to be a major inconvenience for this family of seven. The house appeared large from the outside but the actual living space was limited.

The good news was that the rain had held off for three days and the factory had scheduled delivery of Elizabeth's home for the end of the next week. Elizabeth was restless waiting for the trucks pulling her house-on-wheels to arrive. It was coming in two sections each twenty-four feet wide by forty-eight feet long. Ralph said that they were not going to cut down the tall hedge along the back alley to get the trailer sections in place. Elizabeth could not imagine how they were going to get it behind the garage if they didn't.

Mid-afternoon, the truck pulling the first half of the house arrived and turned into the narrow alley beside Arlene's house. Fifteen minutes later, the second half arrived and was parked across the street. Excitement rose. Elizabeth sat on the back steps with Arlene's children to watch as the men backed the first big load past the garage into the backyard and made a big U-turn to swing it back into the space prepared for it. Elizabeth was amazed at the ease of the whole process.

Elizabeth and the children moved inside to watch from the windows. The men asked them to leave while they backed the second half into the yard. This time they would need to come further into the yard, closer to the house.

"Whoa! Whoa!" The man in the yard was waving his arms and shouting above the roar of the big truck.

Half of Elizabeth's house tilted sharply and came to rest on one end leaving the other end jutting up into the air. The men made several attempts to right it; but the rain had softened the ground. The two back wheels had dropped over a little rise in the contour of the yard and stuck there. The men told Ralph it would have to sit through the weekend until they could get some special equipment.

Elizabeth's heart sank every time she got a glimpse of the backyard. It looked like a huge white elephant taking up the whole yard. *How could they possibly move it without wrecking it and tearing up the whole yard in the process?* The days dragged by dominated by the sight of the half trailer sitting cock-eyed in the yard.

Monday morning, the men returned with what they called a wench truck. Within fifteen minutes, the second half of Elizabeth's new home was being eased into it's place beside the first side. Elizabeth's fears were unfounded. The men left. Their job was done. A new crew was to come and join the two sections together.

The new crew came the next day but they didn't finish. Then they had to go to another job and could only come back to finish on their off time. Elizabeth had expected to move in the day after the house was delivered. She was not prepared for the delays. Ralph still had to arrange for the final hook-ups for water, sewer, electricity, and telephone lines. Each had its own reason for delay.

Elizabeth's life was stuck in a sort of limbo. The longer it took to get her trailer home set up the more she was slipping into a private despair. Elizabeth had no job; she had no home. She had no life of her own. She was simply taking up space in Arlene's life; and she had no power to make things different. The life she had built for herself in Philadelphia had no relevance here nor was it there to go back to.

Elizabeth needed to be patient and to be appreciative of how people were inconveniencing themselves for her. Her real feelings seemed inappropriate and had to be hidden. She believed that she had no right to any emotion except gratitude; and gratitude was not her strongest emotion at this point.

Elizabeth had been promised that the house, when set up, would be no more than two feet off the ground. In reality, that was not possible. No one except Elizabeth could even remember the promise. It made no difference to anyone else but to Elizabeth it was more reason for despair. From her bedroom window in Arlene's house, Elizabeth could see that her house was at least four feet off the ground. A set of metal steps like those that had been beside the sample home on the lot was sitting at her front door. Stairs had been the cause of Elizabeth leaving her life in Philadelphia. Now stairs were blocking her life again.

Little by little, Elizabeth's belongings were moved out of Arlene's dining room and down to the trailer. The trailer still had no water, gas or electricity but Elizabeth knew that she would have no life of her own until she established a home for herself. That meant she had to move in despite the metal steps. Elizabeth could not allow the metal steps to keep her out.

She resigned herself to the system of sitting on the steps to go in and out that she had used when she looked at the sample on the trailer lot. As her belongings were moved, Elizabeth began to spend a few hours a day at the trailer unpacking, sorting and setting up. Often, Arlene's children came along. They never seemed to think that Elizabeth's way of getting in and out was strange. To them, it was just the way Aunt Elizabeth did things.

Nearly a month after Elizabeth came to Beaver Falls, everything in her house was hooked up except the electricity. Ralph figured out a way to run an extension cord from a socket in the kitchen of the trailer to an outlet in his garage. Although this only supplied electricity to the kitchen and one light in the living room, it was enough for Elizabeth. At last, she could spend her first night in her new home.

CHAPTER 27

The early morning sun was streaming in her bedroom window when Elizabeth awoke the first morning in her new home. She had gone to bed at dusk the night before while she could still see to move around without electricity in either her bathroom or her bedroom. It had felt good to sleep in her own bed again. Elizabeth was wide awake but she lay in bed a few minutes longer getting used to her new surroundings.

The room was quite small; even so, her furniture fit nicely. Elizabeth felt a sense of tranquility as she looked around. Through the window on one side of the room, the high hedge that bordered the alley was visible beneath the rays of morning sun. The hedge offered privacy and buffered any sounds from the alley, which was only a few feet away.

Turning over, Elizabeth could look out of the window beside the head of the bed. A light breeze was gently moving the curtains. The branches of an old apple tree that stood between the back of the garage and the trailer swayed slightly in the breeze. Elizabeth was pleased with the way the trailer fit between the old fruit trees at the back of the lot. They shaded the dining room and living room as well as Elizabeth's bedroom; and they lent a sense of permanence to balance the temporary feeling of a trailer home.

Shona seldom bothered Elizabeth when she was sleeping but she always seemed to know immediately when Elizabeth woke-up. Now she was standing beside the bed staring at Elizabeth, willing her to get up and start their day.

"Okay, Shona, I'll get up. I suppose you want to go out." Elizabeth put her feet on the floor and sat up. Shona headed to the hall and waited for Elizabeth with just a hint of impatience.

Elizabeth opened the sliding door for Shona to go out and waited to call her back in. Shona would wander out of the yard if she were left on her own. When the more urgent things were finished, Elizabeth intended to fence an area for Shona. Until then, Elizabeth needed to keep an eye on her when she wasn't tied to one of the trees.

The day stretched out ahead of Elizabeth. The first whole day in her new home. The day she had begun to think would never come. To this point, all of Elizabeth's attention had been focused on the immediate task of getting her home ready to live in. Today she was moving into the future, a future that held only unknowns. Elizabeth believed that she was where God wanted her to be, but what He wanted her to do, and how she would survive, were questions she had refused to dwell on until now.

Elizabeth had lived very frugally for the last two years, and now she had what was left of her small savings, her last paycheck, and her vacation pay. Elizabeth would have to make that money last for as many months as possible. Ralph had helped her get a mortgage that had allowed her to use less of her savings as a down payment on the trailer and he had done some of the lot preparation himself. With Ralph and Arlene's help, Elizabeth had made the move from Philadelphia as economically as possible, but Elizabeth needed an income.

The thought of looking for a job was overwhelming. As long as Elizabeth stayed inside her new home, she could see herself as a competent person, a whole person. Outside the trailer, she was faced with physical obstacles at every turn highlighting her failure to be what she would term a whole person. *How was she going to project the image of wholeness? Or was it too late?*

"I hope you don't mind my just dropping in." Marilyn let herself in the front door carrying the baby in her arms and herding her two and a half-year-old in ahead of her. "I'm leaving the kids with Arlene while I get some groceries. Can I get you anything?"

"I'm just trying to figure out what to start on. Why don't you have a cup of coffee before you go? I'm keeping those old toys right here in the closet. Maybe Kerry will play for a little while."

"Sure, but can I make it tea?" Marilyn searched the sparsely stocked cupboard. "I guess you did all right last night. When do you think the utility company will turn the electricity on?"

"I have my name on a waiting list for a final inspection. They told me they are running about two weeks behind, so I'm not counting on anything for another ten days at least."

Elizabeth was pleased to see Marilyn and the boys. The one thing about the future that Elizabeth was sure of was that she had come to Beaver Falls to spend time with her sisters and to get to know her nieces and nephews. She wanted to be a real part of their lives. Elizabeth needed to be independent but she also longed to belong. Her family was where she should belong.

"Marilyn, you could pick me up a newspaper. I need to look at the classifieds."

"I don't think you'll find much in *The Times*."

"I know but maybe it will give me some ideas." Elizabeth paused. This was probably not the time to really get into this subject, but right now, it was too close to the surface of her mind. "Truthfully, even if I find a job, I don't know how I can commit to it as long as I have to deal with these trailer steps. I can't get in and out in the rain or snow. I don't know what I'd do if I had a job."

"Will told me that he's going to build a concrete front porch for you; but he says the ground has to have time to settle first." Marilyn's tone was apologetic and Elizabeth was immediately sensitive to having somehow made Marilyn feel guilty.

Elizabeth changed the focus of her comments. "I had my employment file from Temple Placement Service sent to Ralph's office. Glenn wrote a reference for me and so did the Dean of Students so I have something to use if I see something I can apply for."

Marilyn was gathering up the toys in preparation for taking the boys to Arlene's when Ralph came in carrying a large coil of heavy-duty electrical cord.

"I can plug this extension cord into a bedroom and run it out to the garage. That should give you lights through the whole place."

"Great! I won't have to go to bed with the birds tonight."

Elizabeth enjoyed the luxury of spending an evening relaxing on the couch with a new Agaitha Christie mystery. Her schedule was her own for the first time in months. Elizabeth was feeling a little more settled than she had felt when she got up that morning.

"Okay, Shona. It's late, we'll go to bed." Elizabeth reluctantly put her book down. Shona was restless, wanting to go out before settling down for the night.

Shona followed Elizabeth to the dining room door where Elizabeth slid the screen open wide. Shona stepped forward and stopped.

"Go on." Shona looked out into the darkness but didn't move. Elizabeth snapped on the outside light. Shona still didn't move.

"GO! ON!" Shona took a step backwards.

"Shona, go on out." Elizabeth tried to lighten her tone of voice. Shona was very sensitive to Elizabeth's disapproval and Elizabeth's irritation was compounding the problem.

"Alright, Shona, you can go out the front door." Shona followed Elizabeth across the rooms to the front door but stopped again at the doorway.

"What is your problem? You've been out there before. You've got to go out. We're going to bed." Shona remained motionless gazing into the darkness.

Elizabeth braced herself against the door post with her left arm and with all the strength she could muster pushed Shona out the door with her other arm. The element of surprise was on Elizabeth's side, and Shona scrambled down the steps and into the yard. In a few minutes, she was back standing at the bottom of the steps looking up with a kind of desperation in her eyes. Elizabeth opened the door and Shona dashed in as though something was after her.

Elizabeth put her head out the door and looked around. She could not see anything that would explain Shona's strange behavior. Elizabeth closed up the house and went to bed. Whatever it was would be gone by morning.

Elizabeth was mistaken. The next morning, Shona still resisted going out. It was the same thing. Shona was eager to go out until she got to the door and then she balked. Each time, it got harder for Elizabeth to force her out the door.

Arlene's youngest daughter, Nora, was a bright spot in Elizabeth's days. Nora had just turned three and was totally delighted to have Elizabeth living next door. The three older children liked having an aunt nearby, but they were often busy with their friends and other activities.

Arlene's youngest was just a year old. He wasn't old enough to come and go on his own like Nora.

"Nora, it's six o'clock. Your mother said to send you home at six to eat supper." Nora had been at the trailer most of the afternoon playing, talking, and being Elizabeth's little helper.

Elizabeth pulled the screen door open for Nora. Nora was too small to make the high step down from the trailer to the top metal step. Nora sat down to slide out onto the steps. Instead of sliding out, she let out a little shriek, scrambled up, and ran back into the room refusing to leave. *First Shona and now Nora--what was going on?*

"Nora, I think you are big enough to go out the front door. Just hold onto the screen door and take a really, really big step down. You can do it." Elizabeth could only reassure the little girl and encourage her.

Obediently, Nora held the door open with one hand and stepped out onto the wide ledge at the front door. As soon as her little bare foot touched the ledge, she yelped again and ran back. This was too much. Elizabeth had to get to the bottom of this.

"Nora, come here." Elizabeth sat down and put her arm around the little girl who was trying so hard to do what she was told to do. "I need to know what is happening, Nora. What is wrong?"

"It goes round and round and round," she whimpered making a circular motion with the hand that had held the screen.

"I'm going to call your house. We'll get someone to come down and help you." The only thing that was clear to Elizabeth was that she couldn't get Nora home without help.

Arlene sent Nora's older brother Joe to carry Nora home. He came and went without a problem. Later, Ralph came to check things out for Elizabeth.

"Apparently, there's a small amount of electrical current running through the frame of the trailer." Ralph speculated.

"I don't think I've felt anything when I've gone out."

"Probably, it's not enough to affect adults or even the older children, but little children and dogs will feel a jolt from it."

"That makes sense. Shona sure hates to step on it."

"I'll get someone here tomorrow to find out where the current is coming from. I can carry Shona out tonight if you want me to."

"Thanks. That would really help. Just come over sometime around 10:30."

Elizabeth was glad to have a reason for Shona's behavior, but the reason made her feel uneasy. Elizabeth felt like she was on a deserted island or living on a powder keg. Ralph was quite casual about the situation and Elizabeth tried to tell herself that his casualness meant that there was no real problem. Never the less, she was relieved when the workman arrived the next morning with a voltage meter.

Elizabeth tried to find things to keep herself busy as Ralph and the workman came in to find the circuit breaker, went back out to check the hook ups, and came in again, busy in their own world leaving Elizabeth out. Elizabeth could see them standing at the corner of the garage deep in conversation. Finally, the workman left and Ralph came into the trailer.

"It's fixed."

"Fixed!" Elizabeth had not expected to hear those words. "What was wrong?"

"We plugged the extension cord in backwards. Essentially, we were sending the ground into the frame of the trailer instead of into the ground."

"I never thought it would be so simple. What a relief."

"Until your electricity is turned on, just be sure that if anyone unplugs these cords they get them put back just like they are now. I'll give the utilities a call and see if I can speed things up at all."

Elizabeth was relieved to find that Shona was willing to go out again without hesitation. Nora was not afraid to come to the trailer again either. Settling in was getting back on track for Elizabeth.

CHAPTER 28

"Hello! Anyone home?"

Elizabeth was sitting at the high counter that divided the kitchen and the living room, facing the front door. She looked up from the letter she was writing to see LouAnne, a friend from her freshman year in college.

"LouAnne! Hi! Come in!" Elizabeth was surprised to see LouAnne and pleased as well.

"I heard you were here." LouAnne burst in with her usual bubbly enthusiasm. "My apartment is just up the street on Darlington across from the school. I decided I'd take an evening walk and stop in and see if you were home."

"I'm glad you did. I thought you were gone for the summer. Do you want to see the place?" Elizabeth slid off the stool and came around the counter to begin a tour. "The trailer really has a lot of space."

LouAnne followed Elizabeth through the rooms, freely poking her head into cupboards and closets as they went along and exclaiming her approval with each new discovery.

"Oh, you're still painting!" LouAnne squealed as she saw Elizabeth's easel set up in the studio workroom with her old palette and oil paints lying nearby.

"Not exactly. I haven't painted for years but I'm going to start again as soon as I get settled."

"Are you going to get a job?" LouAnne had always been very direct.

"I'm looking. Do you have one to offer?"

Elizabeth dreaded that inevitable question. It put her immediately on guard. Elizabeth wanted to be respected as a valid person and she feared that her answers to variations on that question would expose her for what she really was. Her best defense was to give the impression of being self-confident and to be matter of fact in her answers. People usually took her at face value and the conversation would move on to safer topics.

"Not one that pays." LouAnne laughed. "I've got to get going before it gets dark. Do you want to get together for dinner tomorrow evening? We could go to Eat&Park downtown."

"Fine. It would be good to catch up." Elizabeth had missed those kinds of social encounters that had been so much a part of her life in

Philadelphia.

The next day, Elizabeth determined that she had to spend some time looking for a job. The subject might come up again that night at dinner. Elizabeth would rather talk about what she had been in Philadelphia than what she was right now; but that didn't always work out. Even more discouraging was the fact that there was very little more Elizabeth could do to locate a job.

Elizabeth had inquired about openings at both the local small private college where she had spent her freshman year and at the community college. There were no positions open at either place and this was a community where people settled for life. Job turnover would be very slow. Accessibility to the college buildings presented a second major drawback to employment for Elizabeth.

As much as Elizabeth wanted to take action, there was simply nothing she could do. Nora brought the classified section of Arlene's paper and stayed to watch Sesame Street on Elizabeth's TV. Shona was being slightly irritating. She didn't seem to want to leave Elizabeth's side but she didn't seem to want anything either. Her behavior was pressuring Elizabeth. There were no jobs in the classifieds for Elizabeth to check into.

Elizabeth was glad to escape to Eat&Park with LouAnne. The conversation flowed easily. LouAnne talked and talked filling Elizabeth in about life in Beaver Falls. Elizabeth relaxed. It was dusk when they got back to the trailer. LouAnne brought a doggy bag home to Shona.

"Shona, we're home. Look what LouAnne brought you."

Shona looked up from where she was lying but showed no interest in getting up. She was panting heavily and moved sluggishly when she finally responded to Elizabeth's urging and stood up.

"Shona's been acting strangely all day. Do you know anything about dogs?"

"No."

"I'm worried about her. I don't know if there is something wrong or what I should do."

"I don't have any experience with dogs but she doesn't look very perky. The mother of a couple of my first and second graders is always saving animals and nursing them back to health. Do you want me to call her and see what she says?"

"Yes. Please do."

"I'll have to go home and get the school directory. She has an unlisted number."

After LouAnne left, Elizabeth could only wait restlessly. She tried to encourage Shona regretting her impatience with her dog earlier in the day. The ringing phone broke into Elizabeth's growing feeling of isolation and offered her a human connection.

Elizabeth gratefully picked up the phone. It was LouAnne's friend. She asked Elizabeth several questions to verify the details LouAnne had given her.

"I think you should get her to a vet. LouAnne said you're new to the area, so I called my vet. He and I have dealt with each other a lot. He said he would see Shona tomorrow morning at eight before his regular office hours. Is that alright with you?"

"Thank you! I really appreciate your help."

"I gave LouAnne directions. She said she would drive you out there. It will be a bit of a drive but Dr. Kaye is really good."

The front door opened and LouAnne came in. "Is that Mrs. Brown? Let me ask her something."

Elizabeth surrendered the phone and went to reassure Shona that something was being done. LouAnne went home after she and Elizabeth decided on the time they needed to leave the next morning and Elizabeth got ready for bed.

The night was long. At first, Elizabeth thought that she would not be able to sleep. Shona had followed her to the bedroom and settled on the floor beside the bed. Shona's breathing seemed to get more labored as the night went on and was mixed at times with a kind of whine. Elizabeth did fall asleep, but she wakened often. Each time she woke Shona's breathing frightened her but it panicked Elizabeth more the time she awoke and thought she didn't hear Shona breathing at all.

Morning finally came. Shona was not better; in fact, she was beginning to give off an unpleasant odor. Elizabeth forced herself to eat some breakfast while she waited for LouAnne to arrive. They had decided to take Elizabeth's car because of the dog. To save time, Elizabeth took Shona out and got her into the car a few minutes early.

Elizabeth and Shona were both waiting in the car when LouAnne got there. Elizabeth handed LouAnne the keys. She was in no shape emotionally to drive. LouAnne knew the roads, so it made sense for her to take the wheel. On the long drive, Elizabeth kept up a nervous chatter telling LouAnne all about Vronsky and Leda and voicing her current fears for Shona. Silence in the car was unendurable. It allowed Shona's distress to come too close.

LouAnne parked the car in front of the office. Elizabeth handed her the leash. They had already decided that LouAnne would take Shona in for the exam. Elizabeth sat in the car and watched, relieved to see that Shona didn't balk at the door. A few minutes later, the door opened and the doctor came out with Shona on the leash and LouAnne following behind. Elizabeth had not expected this.

Doctor Kaye walked around the car to the open widow beside Elizabeth. Shona stood contentedly at his side, looking at him not at Elizabeth.

"You have a very sick dog," he began. Elizabeth waited for him to go on. "She needs immediate surgery."

Elizabeth's mind and emotions froze. She said nothing waiting for him to finish.

"Your friend told me about your other dog. She said you would be afraid of surgery for Shona. I want to be out front with you. Shona is very sick. I can't guarantee that she will pull through the surgery; but I do know that without it, she will die."

"When will you operate?" Elizabeth spoke more to break her silence than to gain information. "Right away. Shona has a condition called endometriosis and a blocked cervix that has caused the poisons that built up to get circulated through her system. If this continues, she'll go down hill rapidly. The sooner we operate the better chance she has. It is good that you brought her in when you did."

"Okay. Do what you have to. Shona, you be a good girl for me."

"You can call after one o'clock. We should be able to tell you more then. I'll want her to stay over night at least."

LouAnne got back into the car. Dr. Kaye walked back to the clinic with Shona at his side. They disappeared inside. Shona didn't even look back.

"Shona seems to really trust Dr. Kaye." Elizabeth tried to sound casual but in the midst of everything else, she was feeling a little rejected by Shona's walking away without even looking back.

"He has a very gentle manner. Maybe she knows he's going to help her."

Neither LouAnne nor Elizabeth talked much on the way home. There wasn't much to say. Shona would be all right. Elizabeth was sure of that; but no one could really be sure. LouAnne's silence was more comforting to Elizabeth than words would have been.

"Call me. I can drive you out to pick Shona up tomorrow, if you need me." LouAnne handed Elizabeth the car keys and turned to head down the alley toward her apartment.

It was still early. The whole trip had only taken a little more than an hour. Not much time had gone by but a lot had changed. Everything felt different. Elizabeth hated the way she over reacted to everything, but her emotions always took her by surprise. The words 'I want to be out front with you' both frightened her and reassured her. Dr. Kaye had not been overly pessimistic. *Shona would probably be okay, but what if she wasn't? How long had she been sick and Elizabeth hadn't noticed? What would life be like for Elizabeth if she lost this loyal companion?*

Elizabeth kept herself busy in the studio. She felt like it was a stroke of genius when the idea occurred to her. She could get a number of canvases stretched and ready for her to begin to paint. She used unsized canvas. Sizing the canvas meant more steps but less strength was needed. First, she had to staple the canvas loosely onto stretcher frames with her staple gun. Then, brush on rabbit skin glue, and lay the framed canvas on a flat level surface to dry taut before painting on a sealer. Canvas that was already sized had to be stretched taut as it was being tacked or stapled onto the frames. This had been difficult for Elizabeth to do in college, impossible now.

The beauty of doing it today was that she could use floor space to dry the canvases and she wouldn't have to be working around a dog and watching that her canvases didn't get stepped on. Elizabeth had enough supplies for three medium size canvases and four smaller ones. She was encouraged to have accomplished something productive.

Marilyn's timing was perfect. Elizabeth was just cleaning up when Marilyn arrived.

"I thought you might want some company. Have you had lunch yet?"

"No, I haven't but I'm getting hungry." Elizabeth opened her refrigerator to see what she had to supplement the bread and lunchmeat

Marilyn brought with her.

Eating and getting the playpen set up in Elizabeth's bedroom for the baby's nap filled in the time until Elizabeth could call Dr. Kaye's office. As the time drew nearer, Elizabeth found herself watching the clock. She waited until ten after one; then dialed the number Dr. Kaye had given her.

"Shona came through the surgery fine. She's beginning to come out of the anesthetic now."

"That's good news."

"Yes, but Shona's not out of the woods yet. I will say things are looking very positive. Call back in the morning and we'll know when you can pick her up."

Elizabeth sat down on the couch and put her feet up on the coffee table. She could breathe freely for the first time in about sixteen hours. They were still being cautious but Elizabeth knew the crisis had passed. This dog would live. Marilyn returned from taking Kerry over to Arlene's to play with Nora and Elizabeth told her the good news.

"There's something about going through a crisis like this that makes you have to look at other things more head on."

"What do you mean?"

"Marilyn, I don't think there's any chance I can get a job out here. I've been through interviews before and I know I can't fake it now like I did then. I don't have the balance or the stamina I had a few years ago. On top of that, every thing around here is on hills and has steps."

"What are you going to do?"

"I'm going to keep looking, hoping, and praying for a job; but I think I'm going to have to apply for social security disability, too. I hate it, but I have to do it."

There wasn't anything for Marilyn to say. In fact, there wasn't anything more for Elizabeth to say on this topic. Elizabeth had said the words aloud now they were a reality. She was glad it was Marilyn who had heard them. Marilyn would not think less of her.

CHAPTER 29

Elizabeth called Dr. Kaye's office early the next morning.

"Shona is standing beside my desk at this very moment. She's doing great. The doctor said that you can pick her up anytime after two this afternoon."

LouAnne drove Elizabeth out to get Shona. To Elizabeth, the entire countryside looked different today. Yesterday, things had blended together as a slightly blurred background to road signs directing the way to their destination. Today, there were trees, homes, and farm buildings all standing out in three-dimensional fullness. Elizabeth enjoyed the ride through the western Pennsylvania countryside.

Shona was stronger than Elizabeth expected. She climbed into the car and settled down on the back seat as though nothing had happened. Elizabeth and LouAnne stopped for soft ice cream on the way home while Shona dozed contentedly on the seat behind them. Life had slipped back to normal.

Elizabeth had two things she must do. She needed to write to Erma at Carolann Kennels. Elizabeth didn't know how Shona's surgery would affect the contract she had signed since Shona could no longer have a litter of puppies. She had had to pay the veterinary bill with her credit card. If she now needed to purchase Shona from the kennel, Elizabeth would fall even deeper into debt.

The other thing was to find the Social Security Office and find out about applying for disability. Elizabeth looked up the address in the telephone book and set out to locate the office. She wanted to see what would be involved in getting into the office. Actually, it looked pretty easy. The office was on a side street near Beaver Fall's main business district. There was a parking lot across the street less than a block away. Elizabeth could handle that.

Monday morning, Elizabeth got up ready to force herself to take that first step. The weather was good. Elizabeth was nervous as she worked her way down her steps and walked on out to her car. She was always at her shakiest when she was nervous but it gave her confidence that she had seen the location and knew what to expect.

149

The parking lot was nearly full when Elizabeth got there, but she did find an empty space and pulled her car into it. Elizabeth got out, locked the car, and crossed the street. Except for Elizabeth, the sidewalk was empty making her feel embarrassingly obvious as she walked toward the door of the Social Security Office. Elizabeth's attempt to appear both casual and purposeful to hide her embarrassment was thwarted as she tried to swing the heavy glass door open. Elizabeth nearly landed on the sidewalk, thrown off balance because she had shifted her weight to counter-balance the movement of opening a heavy door but the door didn't move. It was locked and Elizabeth was caught off guard.

Quickly regaining her stability, Elizabeth stepped back to read the printing on the door.

Office Hours
Tue Thurs & Fri
10 AM – 4 PM

. A flash of anger went through Elizabeth. The Social Security Office had no Monday hours. Elizabeth had accomplished nothing for all her effort and was left standing foolishly in front of a locked door. There was nothing to do but return to her car and drive home; and it was not over. She would have to go through all this again.

It was Friday before Elizabeth could get herself to try again. The office was open and filled with people. The receptionist looked up briefly as Elizabeth approached her desk.

"Yes?"

"I need some information about Social Security Disability."

"Take a number." The receptionist gestured to a rack of cards with large numbers printed on them and went back to her paper work.

"I just need some information. Isn't there a brochure or something?"

"Take a number and sit down!" The receptionist answered without raising her head. The tone of her voice indicated that Elizabeth was slightly dense or unable to follow directions.

Elizabeth took a numbered card from the rack and located an empty seat in the crowded hallway that served as a waiting room. This was going to be a long wait. Elizabeth wished she had thought ahead and brought a book.

The office was one large room with five desks arranged to allow a straight-backed chair to be placed in front of each desk and space for people to move around and between the desks. Four of the desks and their straight-backed chairs were occupied. As each person would leave the straight-backed chair, the occupant of the desk would call out a number and someone from the hall would move on to the chair in front of that desk. The vacated chair in the hall didn't stay empty for long either.

Elizabeth's turn finally came. She sat down and explained her situation to the man behind the desk. He shuffled through the stacks of papers on his desk and pulled out the form he wanted.

"I'll need your social security card."

Elizabeth slowly searched the contents of her purse looking for the card. She wanted to slow things down. She felt like she was being thrust into a process she wasn't quite ready for. She found her card and handed it to the man in front of her.

"I don't know the regulations. What does it take to qualify for disability? Are you saying that I qualify?"

"I can't tell you if you do or don't! Your case will be evaluated. All I can do is fill out this application."

"What I want to know is what determines whether I qualify or don't qualify."

"You just have to prove that you're totally disabled and can't hold a job." He glanced at the clock on the wall and turned back to his papers. "I have to ask you these questions."

Elizabeth answered the questions and signed the forms. The application process was started. There was nothing more for Elizabeth to do until they contacted her. The next step would be an evaluation by their doctors. Whether or not she qualified for benefits would not be finally decided until six months after her last day of employment. She would not know until January.

Elizabeth sought refuge in her car. She wasn't ready to start the engine. That would be a commitment to move 'into' life, and right now, Elizabeth wanted to move 'back from' life. She had just launched into an effort to prove that she was a totally incapable person in hopes of finding a way to support herself. Elizabeth had spent her entire adult life fighting to keep people from seeing any of her weaknesses. What she was now doing was in conflict with the image she wanted to present and was devastating to

Elizabeth. *Was this her only choice?*

The parking lot was metered and Elizabeth's time had run out. She started the car and drove home. Shona came to the door when she heard the car, wagging her tail, happy to have Elizabeth return. Coming home did draw Elizabeth back into life and the intensity of her feelings began to subside.

While she was eating lunch, the phone rang. Elizabeth picked up the phone and heard a familiar voice on the other end.

"Elizabeth, this is Loretta." Loretta paused long enough for Elizabeth to respond before going on. "I'm back here at Crammer Hall. I ran into LouAnne when I was moving in. She and Janie were playing tennis. Anyway, she told me you'd moved out here."

"It's great to hear from you, Loretta. When can we get together?"

Elizabeth and Loretta had not kept in close contact in the years since they had lived together in Philadelphia, but their friendship had remained solid. She knew, from LouAnne, that Loretta had left Pittsburgh last January to come to Beaver Falls to be in charge of one of the women's residences at the local college.

"I've got meetings tonight and all morning tomorrow, but I'm free from the afternoon on. The girls move in on Monday. The student Resident Assistants are back now for the meetings."

"Why don't you come up as soon as you can tomorrow afternoon. We could have supper together if you have time." Reconnecting with Loretta was very good for Elizabeth particularly at this point in time. Elizabeth and Loretta were quite different; but the differences, though sometimes frustrating, allowed each to contribute to the other's life in unique ways. Elizabeth never had to hide her disability from Loretta because Loretta never seemed to notice any disability. Loretta noticed other things in Elizabeth, and that was what gave their friendship its depth.

Loretta lost no time drawing Elizabeth into her circle of friends. With Loretta around, Elizabeth found it easier to establish relationships that didn't get derailed by that ever-present question, "What do you do for a living?" She was able to sidestep that question and present herself as somebody instead of a nobody. Even without a job, Elizabeth was beginning to build her life again.

Elizabeth's finances were getting more and more restrictive. If the disability income was approved, it would be retroactive and she would be able to catch up. Elizabeth had no plan for what to do if it was denied. One good thing was that Erma had written to say that Elizabeth could keep Shona. There would be no charge. Erma said they were just glad that Shona had a good home. Elizabeth felt grateful to the kennel and thankful to God for this gift and encouragement.

Elizabeth tossed the paperback novel onto the coffee table. She had wasted the whole afternoon reading that book. In fact, she was wasting a lot of time reading these days. Elizabeth knew she was reading to escape, but escape seemed to be all she was up to whenever she was alone. Now it was past dinnertime.

Elizabeth started to stand up. The couch seemed to be too low. She was having a hard time coordinating her balance with her strength. *What was the problem?* She got off and on the couch all the time. There was nothing around to use for leverage. Suddenly, the reality of what was happening overwhelmed her and Elizabeth burst into tears. Feelings of hopelessness washed over her as the tears flowed. Elizabeth was caught by surprise. She never cried. This was out of control.

"Well, Elizabeth, you can sit here and cry all night or you can figure out how to get up and get on with life. Which is it?" The moment of weakness had passed. Elizabeth reined in her emotions and set her mind on what to do. She closed her mind to what she feared she couldn't do.

Elizabeth looked around. She needed something like the back of a chair to give her leverage. The nearest chair was at the desk. The desk was not far away but it was not within reach. The telephone was across the trailer in the kitchen area. Elizabeth made a mental note to call tomorrow and arrange to have a phone put in beside the couch.

The coffee table was the solution Elizabeth was looking for. She could slide onto the coffee table and inch it across the floor to within reach of the chair. Her plan worked. She was on her feet. Before she went to the kitchen to make herself some dinner, Elizabeth moved the coffee table back to its place and determinedly placed the desk chair beside the couch. She had come so close to defeat, but she had figured a way out and she could keep the same thing from happening again. From now on, the chair would always be in reach.

CHAPTER 30

"Have things begun to settle down at the dorm, Loretta? I always hated the roommate hassles the first couple weeks of school."

"I hope so. I just told everyone they have to give it a six weeks trial before I will even talk about changes. Most of them can adjust to each other if they have to."

Elizabeth understood the pressures of Loretta's job. She remembered clearly her own dormitory days. As a result, Elizabeth offered Loretta her extra bedroom as a place for Loretta to stay on her one night a week off and tonight was Loretta's first official night off. This arrangement would work well for both of them. Loretta liked to ask Elizabeth's advice on situations and, for Elizabeth, that provided a way for her to be involved in something beyond her own four walls.

"Since school has started, I'm having a harder time with not having a job. It really feels strange. Everyone else is starting a new school term. I'm not. I feel like I should be; and I have all this information in my head about rules, regulations, and procedures that's totally useless in my life now. It's like the old saying 'All dressed up and nowhere to go'. It's a waste and it's pretty depressing."

"Maybe you could volunteer in the financial aid office."

"No, Loretta, financial aid offices deal with confidential information. They couldn't take volunteers."

"There must be something for you, Elizabeth."

Loretta stubbornly refused to back down and she had unlimited confidence in Elizabeth's abilities. On one level, Loretta's words encouraged Elizabeth, but they also fed her feelings of guilt that she wasn't trying hard enough.

"I've exhausted all my ideas. I want to start painting but I can't seem to get any inspiration. I've usually painted people. I think I need to change my subject matter if I can, but I'm most interested in people."

"I know. That painting you did of the three of us when we lived with Jenn in Philly was a great conversation piece. You captured our personalities. What happened to that painting?"

"I'm not sure. It got lost in one of my moves."

"But it was so big! How could it get lost?"

155

"Someone took it off the stretchers and rolled it up. It was easier to over look that way and it got left somewhere. I still have the stretchers to reuse."

"Maybe you could sell some paintings."

"I don't know. I'm pretty nonfunctional. I start things but can't seem to carry through on any of them. Last week I did make some sketches for Christmas cards. I want to send handmade cards this year, but I haven't figured out a process to mass produce them."

The front door opened and Nora quietly slipped in and slid onto the nearest chair. At the sound of the front door, Shona came out from the bedroom to see what was happening. Loretta immediately started to tease Shona, pretending to throw a dog toy for her to fetch, and Shona trustingly dashed after it.

"Loretta! Shona isn't allowed to play in the house."

"I know. I know." Loretta acknowledged that she heard but faked another toss.

Shona spun around her big tail knocking a book off the coffee table with one big sweep.

"No, Shona. Shona! No. No." Loretta's voice had a teasing lilt. She rose to her feet, hands behind her back giving Shona cause to think the game was still on.

"Loretta! Shona!" Elizabeth grabbed her coffee cup and saucer just in time as Shona's tail swept across the table again. "Take her outside! She's too wound up!"

Elizabeth breathed a sigh of relief mixed with annoyance as Loretta let Shona out the front door bumping the dog with her knee as they went. Shona was a well-behaved dog. Loretta was the disruptive one. Nora sat quietly on her chair looking at Elizabeth with solemn eyes. She knew that Loretta had broken the rules of Aunt Elizabeth's house and that was a very serious matter. Nora didn't know what to expect when adults broke the rules.

The beginning of this school year was hard on Nora, too. 'The guys', as Nora called her older brother and sisters, were gone all day and busy with activities and homework after school. The baby took up a lot of her mother's time. Nora was at loose ends; and she and Elizabeth had become sort of a team. Elizabeth often took Nora with her to visit Marilyn so that the cousins could play while Elizabeth and Marilyn talked, cooked, or worked on their sewing projects together.

Other days, Nora was Elizabeth's little helper in the trailer. Nora liked to do real jobs and worked diligently at every task. She helped Elizabeth with the laundry putting clothes into the washer and taking them out of the dryer. Elizabeth would wash the kitchen floor with a sponge mop while Nora, on her hands and knees, used an old toothbrush to loosen dirt sticking in the grooves of the pattern on the floor tile. Elizabeth had always been drawn to children and the time with Nora gave a special meaning to her days.

Tonight, Nora was following her usual pattern of spending the time between supper and bedtime at Aunt Elizabeth's. They sat in comfortable silence until Loretta and Shona returned followed by Nora's older brother, Joe.

"Mom wants you to come home now, Nora."

Joe delivered his message and left. The little girl slipped off her chair and followed her brother out. Shona headed for her water dish then retired to the back of the house again. Loretta dropped onto the end of the couch.

"Shona wore me out!"

"I guess you wore her out, too."

With that comment, Elizabeth closed the subject of playing with Shona. Loretta and Elizabeth would always clash over Loretta's behavior with Shona. This night off was to be a way for Loretta to relax and unwind. Their conversation drifted onto more interesting topics, and by the end of the evening, Elizabeth had let go of her frustration with Loretta.

As fall moved into winter, the weather became unstable and Elizabeth found fewer and fewer days pleasant enough for her to leave the trailer. Loretta had always been a link with people for Elizabeth; and now she continued to bring people to Elizabeth. Through Loretta's efforts, the trailer became both a center for people to get together and a place to come when they needed to talk something through.

Gradually, Elizabeth's life in Philadelphia was fading and a new life was emerging. Years ago when, as a teenager, Elizabeth had come face to face with the facts of muscular dystrophy, she had resolved that her only value was not in what she was but in what she could give to 'the whole people' around her. Now for the first time in her adult life, Elizabeth could not avoid facing that reality. Her new life must move in that direction but it would not be without internal struggle.

In January, the official notification came that Elizabeth's application for social security disability was approved. The monthly checks would begin in February. Elizabeth could almost feel a physical weight lift when she read the notice. She could begin to look ahead again and make plans.

The unanswerable question, *What will you do if the application is denied?* no longer lingered threateningly in the background, but her relief was tempered by the recognition that she had been officially judged to be unemployable. Never before would Elizabeth have accepted that judgement. Elizabeth took some comfort from reminding herself that this is God's plan. He had provided for her and for that, Elizabeth truly was grateful.

Elizabeth would not be able to live extravagantly, but now she knew she could pay her monthly bills and whittle away at her debts. By spring, the retroactive money would be in her hands. Elizabeth began a priority list. It felt so freeing to be thinking about what she could do rather than disciplining herself to be content with what she had.

Top on the priority list was a front porch. Elizabeth sketched out a plan for her brother-in-law, Will, to work with. Will agreed to build Elizabeth a concrete porch with wrought iron railings and two sets of wooden steps. One set of steps was at the end of the porch facing Arlene's house and the second set was at the opposite end nearer to Elizabeth's parking space.

Work began as soon as the ground thawed. Elizabeth had a few days when she was completely confined to the trailer, but it was worth the inconvenience. After ten months, Elizabeth could finally walk in and out of her home. She could even choose to go out on a rainy day if she wanted to.

Elizabeth was discovering that life in Beaver Falls would always be defined by the school calendar. Many of her friends and acquaintances were involved with either the newly formed Christian Grade School or the college. Time had gone by fairly quickly. The spring semester was now over and Loretta was talking about leaving for most of the summer.

"I told the dean yesterday that I would take the first summer school session. There will only be a handful of upperclassmen. The college just wants someone to be responsible for the building."

"After that, are you going back to the Catskills?"

"Yes. The folks are back for the summer so I want to spend time with them." Loretta took a sip of coffee and winced.

When Loretta and Elizabeth were together, they followed Loretta's Norwegian heritage and had their evening coffee with sweets regardless of the season. It was a muggy spring evening but they were enjoying their coffee none-the-less.

"I'll be glad to get this tooth taken care of. I have an appointment with Nick next week."

"You drive all the way to Pittsburgh to the dentist?"

"Yea, I started going to Nick when I was living up there. When I called him to make this appointment, he suggested that I ask you if you wanted to ride along and see his office."

"See his office! He's conniving to get me to the office to see if he can talk me into having my teeth checked. He knows how I avoid dentists."

"Well, he did say there was a space open after my appointment. He suggested we all have lunch together at Nolans, around the corner, afterwards. I'm supposed to call him back."

"I haven't seen Nick for at least a year and a half. It's time to touch base with him again. Tell him I know what he was doing, and I will have my teeth cleaned and a check-up. I know it's been too long."

Doctors and dentists had not been on Elizabeth's priority list but now she needed to think about that. She had always depended on Dr. Bendle for everything when she was in Philadelphia. Elizabeth needed to think about replacing her with someone in Pittsburgh. Nick had taken care of the question of a dentist even before she had thought about it.

CHAPTER 31

The little bit of shade the tree had offered was shrinking fast, and the Kansas sun was too intense to endure without shade. Elizabeth and Madge gathered up the remainder of the lunch paraphernalia and repacked the car. The shade from the small tree had not reached the car and the sun beating down on the car had turned the interior into an oven. Madge poured some water into Shona's dish and coaxed her to drink a little more before getting her into the car again.

Elizabeth and Madge were on their way to Colorado. Madge would be visiting a friend then flying back to Pittsburgh. Elizabeth's mother had rented her home in Iowa and moved to Colorado. She was working with her sister, Elizabeth's aunt, in a personal care home her sister owned. Elizabeth was going to spend several weeks with her mother then the two of them would drive back to Pennsylvania together.

Madge got behind the wheel. It was her turn to drive. Inside the car, the heat was stifling. They rolled down the windows and headed back to the interstate. When they got back onto the highway, the speed of the car helped to get air moving through the open windows moderating the affect of the heat. They rode in silence for a while. Madge and Elizabeth were just beginning to get to know each other and were not completely comfortable with each other yet.

"Elizabeth, the temperature gauge is registering in the red."

"That's been a problem with this car ever since we overloaded it coming back from Iowa one year. Try slowing down. Usually, if you slow down, the temperature will go down some."

Madge followed Elizabeth's suggestion and the needle slipped back down to high normal. After a few minutes, it began to creep up again and Madge slowed her speed even more. The slower the car moved the more they could feel the heat of the day. They rode on each silently watching the temperature gauge. An air of tension was building.

"I don't think I can go any slower and stay on the interstate, but I'm afraid the engine will overheat unless I slow down more."

"I think you're right, and the slower we go, the more unbearable this heat gets. I'm getting worried about Shona. Do you feel the car shake from her panting?"

"Yes. She doesn't look good. What should we do?"

They continued on in silence for a while. Then Elizabeth had an idea.

"What would you think of stopping now at a motel and getting Shona into air conditioning? We could sleep until nine or ten and get up and drive when it's cooler."

"Drive all night, I don't think so. That isn't really safe."

"I don't see a problem, Madge. When I was growing up, my folks did a lot of our traveling at night."

"I'd be very uneasy."

"I don't see that we have much choice. Shona can't take much more, and we aren't getting anywhere fast at this speed. Can you think of another solution?"

"Oh! I don't like this." Both Elizabeth and Madge fell silent each stressed in their own ways. Shona shook the car with her panting and sweat trickled down their faces.

Madge broke the silence. "Okay. Let's look for a motel. I'm not sure I can sleep, but the air conditioning will feel good."

They did sleep, all three of them. It was nearly midnight when they ventured out again. Elizabeth stepped out of the cool light of the air-conditioned room into a gray wall of heat. The wind was blowing making leaves rustle like paper. It was the sound and feel of a Kansas night as she had experienced it as a child on summer vacations. Memories flooded back. Memories of the long lost innocence of childhood when life was simple and experiences were adventures.

The other rooms of the motel were dark, everyone was settled in for the night. Elizabeth and Madge worked as quietly as possible as they went in and out loading the car again and making final preparations for leaving. Shona was growing more and more anxious as the room was emptied. She seemed relieved when it was finally her turn to leave the cool comfort of their room.

Elizabeth drove out of the deserted parking lot, turned onto the deserted road, and then merged onto the deserted interstate. Both Madge and Elizabeth were gripped by a strangely lonely feeling as the darkness closed in around the car. A sense of solitude followed and each related to it in her own way. Elizabeth enjoyed solitude, whereas, solitude made Madge uneasy.

Elizabeth felt herself becoming slightly impatient with Madge's fears.

If Elizabeth acted on every fear she had, she would never do anything. Elizabeth had made many trips at night. This was actually working well. The air was warm but without the sun, the car was running fine. They could keep their speed up and make good time. Shona was sleeping peacefully on the back seat.

Elizabeth glanced at the gas gauge and noted it was only a quarter full. "I'd better get off at the next service exit and get some gas."

"There's one coming up in a couple miles," Madge responded.

"Here's the exit ramp. Which side is the gas station on?"

"It's over there." Madge pointed across the road. "The sign is off. No, the whole station is dark."

Elizabeth pulled the car back onto the interstate, her confidence shaken. Madge's concerns had not been completely baseless. Elizabeth had forgotten about the gasoline shortage and the changes it brought. Even in Beaver Falls, very few stations stayed open after six. *How could she have forgotten that?* And now they were in the middle of Kansas, surrounded by farmland far from city traffic. *Was it possible that all the gas stations along the interstate would be closed?*

The night seemed to get darker as they sped down the road passing other exits with darkened stations. There were few other cars on the road, perhaps to avoid the very situation they now faced. Elizabeth said nothing. She did not want Madge to panic from sensing her own rising stress, as the needle on the gas gauge was steadily moving toward empty. They were not in desperate need of gas yet but they soon would be.

"There is supposed to be fuel ahead. See if you can tell if it's open." Elizabeth tried to sound casual.

"It looks like the lights are on."

"Good. If we can fill up here, we probably won't need to stop again until breakfast. Everyone should be open by then."

Madge was right. The lights were on; the service plaza was open. The station had a five-gallon per customer limit on gas sales but it was waived for night customers. As the attendant filled the tank, Elizabeth began to relax again but she would take to heart the lesson she had just learned.

The remainder of the trip was without incident. Elizabeth left Madge with her friend and drove the last hundred miles alone. She was surprised at the tension she felt alone in the car, far from anything familiar, with mountains rising up around her, but Elizabeth was also taking a step back into the independent person that she had been. And it felt good.

Elizabeth's life was on hold again. It seemed like the previous year had been a year of waiting--waiting to move into the trailer, waiting for a way to walk in and out of her house, waiting for an income, just waiting to get started. Now those questions had been resolved but she was a thousand miles away and her life again on hold.

The weeks in Colorado stretched out longer than she had planned. The timing was dictated by her mother's schedule; but then, there was no reason that Elizabeth needed to get back, no job, no personal ties. She had come to Colorado to be a daughter, to be part of her mother's daily life for a little while, but it was harder than Elizabeth had expected to live patiently in that role. She was anxious to get back to the life she was building.

Elizabeth tried to make this time productive. She brought art supplies intending to go home with sketches of Colorado scenes to use as the basis for paintings, but she could never decide what to sketch. Instead, while she spent time with her mother at work, Elizabeth made charcoal drawings of the elderly people at the personal care home and ended up giving them away to the residents. Much of the time, she worked on a crewel embroidery wall hanging. It grew daily, marking the time.

In late August, Elizabeth's mother was finally free to take her two-week vacation; and they set out on the long trip to Pennsylvania. Elizabeth had to do all the driving; so, anxious as she was to get home, they were forced to break the trip into short days. Elizabeth remembered the gas shortage and remained vigilant. The trip went smoothly.

Just before Elizabeth left Beaver Falls for Colorado, she had arranged with a college student to build a wooden deck across the back of the trailer. The deck was finished when she returned home. Elizabeth was very pleased. The deck was great; it expanded her living area. Now she could sit outside. On one end of the deck she could sit under the shade of an apple tree and on the other end she could sit in the sun. Her house was complete.

Elizabeth's time in Colorado had served the important purpose of breaking the pattern of lifestyle she had fallen into before her front porch was built. When she returned, fall activities were getting underway, and her friends were settling into their regular schedules after the summer break. Elizabeth felt freer this year to go out and join in activities outside her home, but with this change, she encountered a new stress.

In Colorado, Elizabeth had not had any image to protect. In Beaver Falls, it was different. Elizabeth was painfully aware that people's perception of her would be affected by what they saw. It was harder for her to hide her weaknesses when she went out than it was when she was in her own home. She had to try to learn a new set of ostrich ways.

The weekly church service was the first place Elizabeth regularly appeared in public. Elizabeth had figured out ways to make this manageable. She had carefully chosen the church for its teaching but also for its building and for its people. Loretta and several of Elizabeth's friends were members so this was a decision Elizabeth was comfortable with. Elizabeth was happy to have a church home again.

Elizabeth drove down the alley beside the church and parked in the grass near the back door. She was in good time. Elizabeth always got to the church early to allow herself time to get out of her car, into the building, and locate a seat before people began to arrive. It was especially important tonight because they were having a guest speaker and people from all around the Pittsburgh area had been invited. Elizabeth expected to see friends she seldom had opportunity to see. She wanted them to see her at her best. She dreaded the awkwardness of first-time-in-years encounters.

Loretta sat with Elizabeth during the service. As soon as the service was finished, Loretta gathered up her things.

"I have to help in the kitchen. Are you coming downstairs for refreshments? There's a lot of people here you probably want to talk to."

"I don't think so, Loretta. I'll just talk to people up here for a little while. The stairs are really a problem and my car is up here in the back." The church was built on a steep hill. Elizabeth was always careful to park near which ever door she wanted to use. She parked beside the front door when she planned to be in the social area and in the back when she needed to be in the worship area of the building.

"Well, if you decide to come down, I'll drive your car around to the front when you're ready to leave. I need to get going."

Elizabeth, automatically slipping into ostrich mode, turned to assume a casual position and remained seated on the pew. As people recognized her, they came over to speak to her. Elizabeth didn't have to move. If there was no one speaking to her, she busied herself with imaginary tasks so that she could legitimately remain seated while the room cleared out. She paused as she searched her purse for a pen (that she didn't need) to say hello to Nick who had come with a group from Pittsburgh.

"How was your trip to Colorado?" he asked.

"Long, but good. I didn't succeed in getting those landscape sketches done that I told you I was going to do."

"That's too bad. Couldn't you find any scenes you liked?"

"I think there was too much, too panoramic. I seem to need boundaries."

"Shall we get some refreshments?"

"Yes. You go on. I've got a couple things to do then I'll be down."

Elizabeth had answered Nick too quickly. Now she was committed and would somehow have to get downstairs without people noticing her unstable gait. Elizabeth knew that it would be hard enough just to stand up after sitting for so long. Nick moved on toward the stairs and several other people stopped to say a quick 'hello' to Elizabeth on their way to get refreshments downstairs. Out of the corner of her eye, she could see that the room, at last, was empty except for two people talking in the doorway in the back, but they were engrossed in their conversation. She could get up now.

Elizabeth prepared to try to stand up. She gripped the back of the pew in front of her with her left hand and put her right hand in just the right place on the back of the pew she was sitting to give her leverage. She knew that this system would work but she also knew it would not be graceful. Her first clumsy attempt failed.

"Can I help?" It was Nick. Where had he come from? Elizabeth thought she had successfully dismissed him. She tried again.

"No, thank you. You can go on; I'll be down."

"I'll just wait." He stepped into the aisle and stood waiting.

Elizabeth hesitated. She was skilled at what she called the ostrich approach but it was not working now. Nick was not being side tracked. He was not going to leave her to her secret struggle. Elizabeth had no choice but to get to her feet in Nick's presence. She braced herself for the awkwardness between them that she had learned to expect at times like this and pulled herself to her feet.

"These stairs might be easiest." Nick's manner didn't change as he matter-of-factly led the way to a back staircase. The steps were less intimidating than the longer open stairs of the front entrance; but at the top of the steps, Elizabeth stopped realizing that she was too stiff and too shaky to risk taking the first step.

"Oh, Nick, I think I had better just go home. I don't think I can manage this."

"I'll get a couple of my friends and we can carry you down on a chair." Nick's response was quick and decisive. "I'll be right back."

Nick returned with his friends and carrying a straight-backed wooden chair with arms. Elizabeth tried not to let her insecurity show. The chair wobbled a little as they descended the steps but they all arrived safely at the bottom. Nick's friends went back to their interrupted conversations. Nick waited while Elizabeth got out of the chair. Nick and Elizabeth walked around the corner into the main room as though nothing unusual had just happened.

Elizabeth picked up some cookies. Nick got some punch and chatted for a few more minutes questioning her in ways that prodded her to stop procrastinating and start to work in her painting studio. The cloak of the ostrich had slipped off for a few minutes but no harm had come. It slipped easily back in place and Elizabeth felt safe again.

CHAPTER 32

Elizabeth searched through her oil paints until she found the tube of raw umber. She squeezed a small dab of the paint onto her palette, dipped her brush in turpentine, and diluted an edge of the small mound of paint with her brush. Then picking up the photograph, she sketched the scene onto the canvas with her brush. Elizabeth rolled her stool away from the easel and sat studying what she had done. She was pleased with the sketch; it was a good start.

The sound of her front door opening and slamming shut again alerted Elizabeth that some one had come into her house.

"It's early in the day," Elizabeth thought. "It must be Nora."

"Aunt Elizabeth. Aunt Elizabeth! Aunt Elizabeth!" The little girl's voice began to rise in distress.

"I'm back in the studio, Nora."

"I thought no one was here!" Nora appeared at the studio door. Her face showed relief followed by a surge of interest. "What are you doing?"

"I'm going to make this picture into a painting." Elizabeth handed Nora the snapshot Jenn had sent to Elizabeth.

The picture was of Jenn's little daughter sitting in a tree with her older brother, half hidden, a few branches higher. Jenn commissioned this painting, remembering Elizabeth's painting that hung in the apartment they shared in Philadelphia. Elizabeth hoped she could live up to Jenn's expectations. Elizabeth had lost contact with Jenn for several years after Jenn left Philadelphia. Now that Elizabeth lived in Beaver Falls, she and Loretta had had occasion to visit Jenn and her family in New York State. Elizabeth was pleased to be able to renew the friendship.

"Aunt Elizabeth! She's just my age!"

"Yes, her name is Nikki."

"Can I play with her?"

"She lives a long ways away; but if this painting works out, her mother will come down to get it. I think she will bring Nikki, and you can see her then."

"I think, first we will be shy of each other; then we'll get along pretty well."

The telephone was ringing. Elizabeth left Nora, still engrossed in the

169

photograph, and went into the other room to answer it. The woman on the phone was calling from the Muscular Dystrophy Association to inform Elizabeth that her first appointment with their clinic in Pittsburgh was scheduled for next week.

Elizabeth had very mixed feelings about this news. Her memories of the annual clinic visits during her childhood were basically negative. The visits were always demoralizing experiences. As an adult, Elizabeth had never had the inclination or the time to pursue this avenue of possible help, but life was different now and Elizabeth had initiated this appointment. She called MDA and asked to have her name officially registered with the local chapter. This was a major step for Elizabeth, and she was apprehensive of every aspect of this decision.

Elizabeth's apprehension grew as the day of the appointment neared. The local chapter offered to supply a volunteer to drive her to the clinic and that seemed to be the best option for Elizabeth. She didn't know how to find her way around Pittsburgh, so she couldn't drive to the hospital by herself. Also, Elizabeth wanted to separate this part of her life as much as possible from her 'real life', and did not want to involve anyone who knew her.

The day of the appointment came quickly. Mr. Jones, the volunteer, picked her up very early that morning to be sure they got to the hospital by 8:30 a.m. Elizabeth had not met Mr. Jones before he arrived that morning, and he was not at all what she had expected. Mr. Jones appeared to be well into his seventies, a thin wiry man driving a very large car. He hovered nervously trying to help where no help was needed and made Elizabeth even more tense. During the long drive to the hospital, Mr. Jones plied Elizabeth with personal questions. His questions had the feel of gossipy curiosity not genuine interest. Annoyed, Elizabeth kept her answers pleasantly vague, sidestepping the intent of the question whenever possible. Elizabeth didn't know why it seemed so important to her to maintain a sense of privacy.

When they got to the hospital, Mr. Jones drove to the emergency entrance. He got out of the car and went inside returning with a wheelchair. Elizabeth was taken back. She had never used a wheelchair before. *Was this the routine of a clinic visit? Did she need to comply?* Confused, Elizabeth got out of the car and sat in the chair. She felt like she was relinquishing all control of the situation; and as she did, she seemed to revert to that passive child alone in the hospital in Iowa City.

Mr. Jones knew exactly where to go, expertly negotiating the maze of hospital corridors. Elizabeth was lost. They finally entered a large waiting room ringed with doors opening into small examining rooms. Elizabeth sat in the wheelchair while Mr. Jones presented her paperwork to the woman behind a desk that was located at one end of the long room. He picked up a couple of magazines, handed one to Elizabeth, and sat down in a chair beside her. After a few minutes, a nurse came out of the room behind the desk with a record file in her hand.

"Elizabeth McKievey," she announced in a loud voice.

Elizabeth closed her magazine and raised her head. The nurse walked over to her. "Elizabeth?"

"Yes." Elizabeth laid the magazine down as the nurse wheeled her into the laboratory room.

"How are you doing?"

"Fine, thank you."

"Can you stand up and get on the scales?"

"Sure." But Elizabeth found that it wasn't as simple as she expected it to be. "I guess I need to be able to use that counter for leverage. The wheelchair doesn't give me the right angle."

The nurse finished her routine and drew an excessive quantity of blood then wheeled Elizabeth back to her place in the waiting room beside Mr. Jones. Elizabeth did not know what to expect next. They waited as the room began to fill.

"Elizabeth McKievey." A youngish looking man wearing a white coat was standing in the doorway of a room a few yards away.

"Yes."

"In here please."

He went back into the room. Elizabeth's wheelchair was not in a position where she could get out of it to follow him. She hesitated for a moment unsure of what to do. Mr. Jones looked up questioningly, then got up and pushed her to the door.

"Right over here." Mr. Jones pushed her to the spot indicated and turned to walk out the door. "No, you can stay. Sit down."

Mr. Jones sat down in the chair beside the desk and waited. The young man introduced himself. Elizabeth heard him say 'Dr.' but his name didn't register. She was too caught-up in trying to make sense of what was happening. It didn't seem quite right. The doctor closed the door and sat down at the desk. He began to ask Elizabeth questions about herself, her whole history, medical and personal. Mr. Jones was listening intently, taking it all in. Elizabeth had no choice but to give out all the information she had previously withheld.

When the doctor finished questioning Elizabeth, he turned to Mr. Jones and asked, "Do you have anything to add?"

"No. I just met her this morning."

"What! You're not her father!?"

"No." Elizabeth interjected. "He's just the driver."

"Then what are you doing in here? Please wait outside!"

"You told me to stay." Mr. Jones answered innocently as he stood up to leave.

Elizabeth was overcome with feelings of humiliation. Her silence had contributed to this mess. Usually, she was in control but this was uncharted water for her. Both of these men knew the procedure of the clinic. She didn't. Elizabeth told herself that all Mr. Jones had observed was a medical history; but, still, she felt compromised in some way and she felt stupid.

The doctor said nothing more about the mix up. After he examined Elizabeth, he explained that this visit was the first in a process that would take a couple of months. There would be tests and evaluations to confirm the diagnosis of Elizabeth's original doctors. In the years since her original diagnosis, new procedures had been developed which would now be used to verify the diagnosis and to establish her case file. This was not what Elizabeth wanted. Perhaps, it was what she needed. At any rate, it was what she had started.

On the ride home, Elizabeth and Mr. Jones exchanged a little small talk between longer silences. Mr. Jones's curiosity had been satisfied, and Elizabeth was trying to blank out the whole clinic experience while at the same time she braced herself for more trips to the hospital. They parted at her door knowing that they would be seeing a lot more of each other in the coming weeks.

Nora waited until Mr. Jones car drove away before coming in search of Elizabeth. Nora's presence helped restore Elizabeth's sense of self. Nora wanted to do the little jobs that made up their daily routine together. She wanted to talk about the painting of Nikki and why it wasn't quite finished yet. Elizabeth's mind began to focus again on her life in the trailer. After Nora went home, Elizabeth went back to the studio to spend a few minutes painting. While she was answering Nora's questions, she had noticed a detail she wanted to work on. Elizabeth seemed to work best this way, short periods of time between longer stretches of observation and contemplation.

Elizabeth had been painting for several months. She had finally moved from talking about painting to actually painting. The breakthrough happened after Elizabeth had clarified something for herself when she told Nick that she needed boundaries when it came to painting landscapes. Outdoors she was overwhelmed by the vastness before her. Elizabeth thought she wanted to paint landscapes, but she didn't know where to start or where to stop. As an artist, Elizabeth felt apologetic for this failing and especially for her solution.

Elizabeth decided to use, as the basis of her paintings, landscapes that already had boundaries. She began to paint from photographs and magazine pictures. Elizabeth was still unsure of her ability as a landscape artist, but her friends encouraged her by asking to buy the paintings. Elizabeth sold them pretty much at cost and used the money to replenish her supplies.

The photo Jenn asked her to paint was fun to try. It was a combination of people and nature, a welcome break from what she had been working on. Elizabeth was pleased with her progress on the painting and for the way it drew her back to the easel at moments like this. She didn't have much time to work tonight. Loretta was due any time for her night off, away from dorm responsibilities.

Elizabeth was just beginning to clean her brushes when Shona, who was outside in her little fenced yard, started barking announcing Loretta's arrival.

"That's really coming along!" Loretta dropped her bag in her bedroom and came on into the studio.

"Thanks. I'm pleased with it. I hope Jenn will be."

Elizabeth finished cleaning up and the two friends went out to the living room.

"Oh, good. You already made the coffee. Let me pour us a cup. I've got a situation in the dorm that's getting to be a mess. I want to get your thoughts."

Elizabeth settled into her place on the end of the couch slipping comfortably into her role of sounding board/ advisor/counselor. Her emotional turmoil caused by the trip to the clinic earlier in the day was safely tucked away. People wanted her strength not her weakness. Later, today's events would come out as another comic experience in Elizabeth's life.

CHAPTER 33

The trips to the MDA Clinic with Mr. Jones were finally finished. The outcome was a reaffirmation of Elizabeth's original diagnosis. Her strength in various muscle groups had been tested and documented. Her body chemistry had been analyzed and recorded. There was a thick case file now with Elizabeth's name on it detailing all the ways that physically Elizabeth was inadequate. There was no cure. There was no treatment. There was only categorizing and labeling, and Elizabeth felt categorized and labeled.

Elizabeth had not expected any other end result; but not expecting another result did not exclude a secret, yet undefined, hope for something better. Now the process was over and all hope was dashed. Elizabeth was thrown back into the struggle of how to live with the person she was; and again, it seemed like God was sending her mixed signals. God had provided a home and an income for her. He had given her a good mind and creative abilities. *It seemed like He was taking care of her and had a purpose for her life; if so, then why had He allowed this physical disability to squash the person she could have become? What did God expect of her?*

Elizabeth wished she hadn't called MDA and opened the door again of this Pandora's box, but she had. Now she had to figure out a way to get the lid back on. From a human perspective, Elizabeth reasoned, this would be defined as a self-image problem. What was her self-image? Elizabeth decided that she actually had two separate self-images. One self-image related to who she was as a personality. It, Elizabeth thought, was positive and strong. But there was another Elizabeth, a physical being. The self-image rooted in that part of Elizabeth was growing ever more negative and was now threatening to overwhelm the positive image. Elizabeth resolved that by keeping these two images separate, she could block out the negative and be able to go forward.

Elizabeth, again, focused her mind and her time and energy on things that she told herself were means of using the gifts God had given her. Elizabeth was pleased that people were beginning to recognize her abilities. She took on the volunteer job of doing the bookkeeping for the Christian Grade School where her friends were teachers. She agreed to be the chairman of the Christian Education Committee at her church and she tried to make her home a hospitable center. Although she was not a creative cook, cooking had always been a creative activity for Elizabeth. The creative part for Elizabeth was in planning and preparing meals especially meals for guests or for holidays.

This afternoon, she was preparing dinner for Nick. She wasn't planning anything very elaborate. Nick had come to Beaver Falls for a meeting; and since he was in the area, he was coming over afterward to talk to Elizabeth about commissioning a painting for his church.

The morning had been hectic. Elizabeth was up bright and early waiting for the cement mixer truck to arrive. Will, Marilyn's husband, had enlisted a couple of his friends to help him make a partial driveway for Elizabeth so that she could park her car beside the front porch. Once the concrete was poured, it had to be smoothed continuously until it was set. Will was experienced in cement work. The project was entirely in his hands. It required no input from Elizabeth yet it seemed to take up her whole morning watching, checking on the progress, and just generally staying alert.

Elizabeth had forewarned Nick to park his car in the alley, walk around the garage, and come through Arlene's yard to reach Elizabeth's front door since the driveway construction was blocking the regular entrance to the trailer. By the time Nick arrived, all activity was over. The men had gone home. The cement was set and left to dry. Elizabeth had managed to settle down and get things together for the meal. The rolls were ready to come out of the oven when Shona announced Nick's arrival.

Conversation flowed easily through the meal. Elizabeth was glad to see that Nick was enjoying the dishes she had prepared, even though it was a simple meal.

"These rolls are really good. Are they whole wheat?"

"Yes, thank you." Elizabeth was pleased. Nick's comment focused on her specialty. "I used my mother's recipe for potato dough, but I substituted wheat flour for some of the white flour and added wheat germ. I guess they aren't technically whole wheat."

"Do you bake much?"

"Actually, I have been baking bread a lot recently. It's new for me and surprisingly time consuming. I find that I'm having to choose between baking bread and painting. Bread seems to be winning."

"I guess that brings us to our agenda." Nick turned the talk toward the purpose for his visit. "We're redecorating the library at the church. The committee asked me to contact you about painting something for us to hang in the library. They'd like an original oil rather than a commercial reproduction."

"What kind of a painting do they want?"

"I think that would be up to you."

"I don't know, Nick." Elizabeth dreaded trying to live up to the expectation of other people. "Are they thinking of a landscape? I'm not a landscape painter. You've seen my landscapes. They're okay, but not great. My style is too heavy. Personally, I like a landscape that kind of flows."

"No one was specific about the subject. I don't think they are set on a landscape. I like the way you use thick paint. What are you working on now?"

"I'm trying some still life paintings. I'll show you what they are like. Shall we go back to the studio first and have dessert afterward?"

"Fine. Can I put this food in the refrigerator?"

"Yes, thanks." Elizabeth pulled herself to her feet feeling awkward and self-conscious, even though Nick was busy clearing the table.

The painting Elizabeth was just starting was on the easel and drew their attention immediately. Elizabeth pointed out the still life set-up on the top of her sewing machine cabinet across the room.

"I'm doing bottles right now. I'm just kind of using what I have around the house. I do like bottles. They have interesting shapes and I like trying to catch the reflection of light on them. The set-up, though, is kind of boring."

"You have some ivy in the kitchen, don't you?" Nick had made a quick assessment of the set-up and the shapes Elizabeth had blocked in on the canvas in front of them.

Elizabeth nodded as Nick left the room. He returned in a few minutes carrying the pot of ivy and added it to the arrangement of bottles on the cabinet. Nick stepped back, then went over to rearrange the leaves, and stepped back again to study the effect.

"It needs something else." Nick was talking more to himself than to Elizabeth. He went back out to the living room and came back with several small items in his hands.

By the time they returned to the table for dessert, the still life set-up had taken on life. Elizabeth could hardly wait to work on the painting again, but that would have to wait until morning. Now they needed to finish their discussion about the painting for the church library.

"I think a still life painting would be fine. Do you have an idea for it? I doubt that they will want bottles." There was a hint of subtle humor in Nick's voice.

"Of course not!" Elizabeth's reaction to Nick's teasing about the bottles was spontaneous. Slightly embarrassed by her loss of control, she went on. "Maybe something like a lamp with some old books. What size of a painting are they thinking of?"

"I think the size you are working on now would be good. It's a large room so it needs something that won't look lost on the wall. I have a kind of fancy old Coleman oil lamp with a glass shade. I could bring it down and build a still life around it."

Elizabeth agreed that Nick could give the committee a tentative 'yes' from her and present them with the idea of the lamp and books still life. Elizabeth hoped they would approve, but she was relieved when Nick said it would be a couple of weeks before he got back to her. She could put off facing her insecurities. Elizabeth felt honored that they wanted one of her paintings, but what if she couldn't produce a quality painting for them?

Beaver Falls was having an unusually pleasant fall, and Elizabeth was taking advantage of the nice days to visit Marilyn and her boys. Nora loved to visit her cousins. As often as possible, she went along with Elizabeth. On good days, Elizabeth enjoyed the long drive through the country, but not today. She had gotten behind a slow moving tractor and it was making them late.

"Well, Nora, I think the guys will have to wait for us today." Arlene's car was broken down and Elizabeth had promised to pick up the children after school for her.

Elizabeth was driving with one eye on the road and one eye on the clock on the dashboard. They just might make it if the tractor would stop at the next farm. To her relief, that was exactly what happened. Elizabeth resumed normal speed again, but they had lost valuable minutes. She took the back way to College Hill hoping to save a few minutes by avoiding the traffic lights. The children would not be looking for her car so she had wanted to get there a little early.

Elizabeth was not early. As she had feared, she and Nora were a few minutes late and the building already looked deserted. The school was held in the basement of a church building. The door into the basement was closed and no one was in sight. Elizabeth knew the rules. Teachers never left children outside, unsupervised. Elizabeth guessed that they had taken her nieces and nephew back inside with them while they cleaned up their rooms.

Elizabeth parked her car at the curb across from the basement entrance. She had to decide what to do. There was no point in honking the horn. The heavy door would block out street noise. The door was down a set of steps putting it out of Elizabeth's reach. She would have to send Nora.

"Nora." Nora was in the back seat standing behind Elizabeth. Their eyes met in the rearview mirror. "The guys are inside. I need for you to go in and tell them we're here."

Nora stood motionless. Her eyes fixed on Elizabeth's eyes in the mirror. Elizabeth waited.

"Aunt Elizabeth," she faltered and started again. "Aunt Elizabeth, some jobs are too big for little girls!"

Nora was right, this was a job for the adult, but Elizabeth could not do it. She saw fear rising in Nora's eyes. It would take all the courage Nora could muster to do what Elizabeth was asking of her.

"I know, Nora, but you can do this job." Elizabeth hoped to instill confidence through her tone of voice. "I'm going to be right here, watching you. You just go down the steps and open the door. If you don't see the guys, just ask Miss Martin, she'll find them for you."

"But what if I can't open the door?"

"You try. I'll be watching. If you can't open the door, come on back to the car, and we'll talk about it."

Elizabeth wished she could offer Nora more than simply her presence; but, right now, that was all she had to offer. Nora slowly got out of the car and crossed the street. The church building loomed over her. The closer she got to the building the smaller her little figure looked as the quiet little voice echoed in Elizabeth's head. *Aunt Elizabeth, some jobs are too big for little girls.* Elizabeth was aware of how much she loved that little girl.

Nora started down the steps. At that moment, two girls ran out of the house next door, across the lawn and down the steps ahead of Nora. They pulled the door open and held it for Nora before they went into the building. The door burst open again. The guys rushed out and over to the car in a flurry of papers and school bags. Nora followed more slowly, still a little overwhelmed. Elizabeth wondered how many of life's greatest accomplishments go unnoticed by the world around us. *We summon all our courage and life just goes on.* Elizabeth hoped she remembered to tell Nora that she had noticed and that she was proud of her.

Elizabeth needed to get home and make the icing for the carrot cake. Nick was bringing the lamp for the painting for his church. Nick was making several stops on his way to her house, so they had decided to forego dinner and just have coffee and desert after the still life was set-up.

The coffee was brewing and Elizabeth had just put Shona out when Nick arrived. Elizabeth was glad she had thought of putting Shona out. Nick had his hands full and didn't need to have a large dog bounding around as he carried things in. The lamp was larger than she has envisioned. It would be an interesting object to paint.

Elizabeth had decided to use an old Bible with slightly tattered edges. She had gotten it out and put it in the studio in the afternoon. Nick went right to work reassembling the lamp and setting it up on the sewing machine cabinet that Elizabeth used for her still life set-ups. Nick had also brought a pothos plant and some collectable items he thought he might use.

Elizabeth watched while he repositioned the Bible and the plant. It looked good. Nick was satisfied with the way it was going. He took a small flowered vase out of his box and carefully placed it in the arrangement. Elizabeth's heart sank. It was a beautiful little antique vase with an intricate design. She would never be able to paint that.

"Okay. I think that's it." Nick was pleased with the result of his work and waited for Elizabeth's response.

"It's a good set-up." She was aware that she was not giving it the enthusiasm it deserved, but her lack of confidence in her ability got in the way. "I'll see what I can do with it."

There was nothing more to do in the studio. They turned out the lights and went back down the hall to the living room. Elizabeth's mind was still on the little vase. *It added so much, but could she paint it?* Distracted, Elizabeth didn't notice a small piece of gravel on the carpet. Her foot twisted as she stepped on the stone. Off balance, her leg twisted under her and Elizabeth found herself sitting on the floor. Nick hurried over to her and reached down to help.

"Leave me alone!" Elizabeth was too humiliated to realize what she had said. Her mind was a turmoil. She had to figure out how to get back to her feet without humiliating herself further. "Get me that footstool. It's beside the bookshelf."

Nick brought the stool and handed it to Elizabeth. She could not do this gracefully, but it was the only way she knew to get herself up off the floor. Slowly, she dragged herself onto the stool. From there, she was able to move onto a nearby chair and from there to the couch. Once Elizabeth was safely on the couch, Nick took charge of serving the coffee and desert. Elizabeth was grateful for the time to try to compose herself again.

"Nick, I apologize. I'm really sorry." Elizabeth couldn't put it behind her yet.

"For what?"

"For being do clumsy and making such a spectacle of myself."

"I never think of you as clumsy." Nick was thoughtful. "I just think 'Elizabeth does the best she can'."

Nicks words had impact. Elizabeth still felt humiliated and exposed; but Nick had given her something to ponder, a new way to look at things after she could get some distance from tonight's disaster.

CHAPTER 34

The activities of the day were done, and Elizabeth settled into her corner of the couch. From her vantage point, Elizabeth could see the entire living area of the trailer. Dusk was creeping into the kitchen and dining room opposite the couch leaving Elizabeth at the center of a small island of light cast by the lamp on the end table. Elizabeth surveyed her home. She was pleased with its simple homeyness. It was peaceful and orderly. Here and there on walls or windowsills were little evidences of her personality and her life. Elizabeth was filled with a sense of quiet contentment. She opened her book ready to be drawn back into the story.

Darkness was complete when the phone rang bringing her back to the present. Elizabeth put down her book. The story was engrossing, but she was glad for a break.

"Hi." Nick was at the other end of the line. "I'm calling for an update on the painting. I need a report for the committee meeting tomorrow night."

"Okay. Well," Elizabeth paused, "I think it's coming along. I have been working on it."

"Good. I wasn't sure after the last time we talked."

"I HAVE to keep painting now that I started. I have no choice! That was a tricky thing you did, putting the plant in it. That plant keeps growing, and it keeps turning toward the window for daylight! Every time I come back to the painting, the leaves are in a different position. I can't keep up with it!"

Nick was laughing. He had an infectious laugh that bubbled out like a pot boiling over. Elizabeth could never be quite sure if he was laughing with her, at her, or about her, but it drew her into the humor whichever it was.

"I was also calling about a week-end conference at the end of November up at the Christian Study Center. I thought you and some others from Beaver Falls might be interested in going. Maybe the painting will be finished by then, or you could just close the studio drapes for the week-end!"

"What is the conference on?" Elizabeth ignored Nick's last comment. Nick was always slipping in those little tongue-in-cheek statements.

"That's why I thought several of you might be interested. The topic is 'Interpersonal and Ethical Perspectives'. Dorm work and teaching would bring up a lot of those issues and, of course, you're the 'consultant to the counselors'." Nick couldn't resist another tongue-in-cheek remark. He grinned and went on. "I've registered to go."

"Where exactly is the study center?"

"It's in the mountains about fifteen minutes from turnpike exit 9. I've been there several times. We could meet near a Pittsburgh exit and I could lead the way." Nick didn't give Elizabeth time to reply. He hurried on, "When I called the study center, I asked about accommodations for you. They have a couple of bedrooms in the building where the lectures are given. If you want to come, you could stay in one of those rooms. Meals are in another building but there's parking at both buildings. We could just drive you to meals. I think it would work out."

"It sounds interesting. Let me talk to Loretta and some others and see who might want to go." Nick had taken away a lot of the unknowns for Elizabeth, before they could become obstacles. It did sound workable.

"I'll send you a brochure. If you want to go, we probably ought to reserve your space as soon as possible. I'd be glad to call for you."

"Thanks, Nick. I'll let you know by the end of next week."

Elizabeth hung up the phone and returned to her book. She would look at the brochure before she gave this idea serious consideration; but, already, thoughts of who she might get to go along came filtering into her mind.

By the weekend of the conference, the painting for the church library was finished and drying. Elizabeth had worked diligently on it. The little vase had taken shape for her. It, along with the plant, balanced the heavier lines of the lamp and the Bible. Elizabeth was pleased with the final product, and when Nick came down to see the painting after it was finished, he seemed pleased with it, too. He said he was sure the committee would like it.

Nick helped her set up a new still life with a new plant in it and, again, he put in an item more ornate than Elizabeth would ever have risked trying to paint. Elizabeth decided not to start the new painting until after she got back from the conference.

Friday evening, traffic was heavy and the route to the study center turned out to be long and complicated. Elizabeth was glad they were following Nick rather than trying to follow directions. Elizabeth, Loretta,

Bonnie, and Lynn rode together in Bonnie's car. They all felt completely lost by the time Nick turned his car into the driveway of what appeared to be an attractive ranch style home. On one side of the house was a parking lot filled with cars. A sign reading 'Lecture House' pointed to the front door. They parked both cars and got out leaving their bags inside. It was too late for registration, but they were just in time for the evening lecture.

Elizabeth found an empty seat near the back of the room where she could be an observer as she adjusted to her surroundings. She liked what she saw. The room was attractively furnished with a large fireplace as the focal point near the lectern. On the mantle was a wood sculpture in the shape of a cross. Elizabeth admired the artistry of the sculpture and the choice of paintings hanging on the walls. Rows of folding chairs filled in the floor space not taken up by two small sofas and two matching chairs.

The room was nearly full. It was a very mixed group made up of men and women with a wide variety of personal styles and an equal variety of ages. Some were introduced as staff members or as spouses of staff members but most of the people were there for the conference. Elizabeth opened up her notebook ready to take notes. She was glad she had come.

After the meeting, they got their room assignments. Bonnie and Elizabeth stayed in the Lecture House. Elizabeth's other friends were staying in the Guest Lodge on the property. No one felt much like socializing. It had been a long day. Elizabeth and Bonnie unpacked and went to bed.

Saturday dawned a crisp cold gray November day. The morning went quickly. One lecture in particular captured Elizabeth's attention. The speaker was Harry Wilson. His topic was interpersonal perspectives. He talked about six areas of human nature or human need. Elizabeth wasn't sure how he was designating them, but he listed the areas as religious, relational, vocational, sexual, physical, and core aspirations.

Elizabeth underlined two lines in the handout Harry had provided and put a star in the margin for added emphases. She read the statements again. *No single area is to be ignored, and one area is not to crowd out the others by taking more than its share of time and energy. To the extent that a person is lacking in one or more of these areas, he/she will experience some degree of psychological and physical disintegration.* This thought was something she wanted to come back to. *Was it correct? How did she fit?*

Elizabeth welcomed the change of pace when it was time to go to Cedar Lodge for lunch. The food was good and the atmosphere was casual and friendly. When they broke for lunch, Elizabeth had thought that the sun was about to break through; but now she wasn't sure. The sky was colorless and the wind was gusting. Dry leaves swirled across the ground. There was a hint of snow in the air as they started back to the Lecture House.

Inside Lecture House, someone had built a crackling fire in the big fireplace. Elizabeth joined the group warming their hands in front of the fire. The few minutes outside between the car and the front door had chilled her to the bone.

"Looks like we're going to get that snow."

"How much are they predicting?"

"I heard twelve to eighteen inches with blizzard like conditions."

"They are saying it will be ending around midnight. The roads should be cleared by the time the conference is over tomorrow."

Elizabeth listened to the conversations around her. A blizzard in this cozy lodge with a fire crackling in the fireplace sounded almost inviting but could she cope. Dinner tonight was to be at different staff homes. She couldn't just ask for a tray from Cedar Lodge. Actually, Elizabeth told herself, she could get by. She had packed instant coffee, breakfast bars, and fruit. If the blizzard came, she would just stay at the Lecture House while the others went out to eat.

By the time the afternoon seminars ended, the entire landscape was transformed. Snow had been falling steadily through the afternoon. Winds had plastered snow against tree trunks and windows and had built little cliffs where the ground had appeared to be level. Elizabeth stood beside the window marveling at the scene before her.

"Where are you scheduled to go for dinner?" Nick was preparing to go out and help the men shovel the snow in the parking lot.

"I don't know, but I'm not going out in this. I have some fruit and breakfast bars."

"You'll miss the fellowship if you don't go to dinner. When I finish shoveling, I'll find out where they scheduled you."

Elizabeth selected a book from the bookcase and found a comfortable chair where she could watch the snow swirl past the picture window. She was content to be on the sideline as people bundled up to go outside and came in stomping and shaking snow off at the door. Bonnie came in from cleaning off her car and joined Elizabeth.

"This reminds me of home. Winters in Buffalo were long, with endless snow. Nick said to tell you that they've reassigned you to the Andersons. They're close, right beside Cedar Lodge."

"Bonnie, I don't want to go out in this at all!"

"Don't worry. We'll get you there. Just wear the warmest clothes you brought. You did bring your snow boots didn't you?"

"Yes, but not for a storm like this. I'd rather stay in."

Elizabeth's protestations fell on deaf ears. An hour later, she emerged from her room dressed in a heavy wool sweater and wool slacks. Unstylish, heavy snow boots topped off her uncoordinated outfit. Nick, Bonnie, Loretta, and Lynn were all waiting for her. Nick had arranged to eat dinner at the Andersons, too. Bonnie, Loretta, and Lynn would be going to another home a little further away.

"Where are your gloves?" Nick asked as they helped her into her jacket.

"I didn't bring any. I don't go out in this kind of weather. I really don't think I should go."

"I'll look in the lost and found."

Nick was as determined that she was going as Elizabeth was that she was not going. Anxiousness was making Elizabeth feel weak-kneed. She sat down on the nearest chair. Nick rummaged through a box on the shelf of the hall closet and came back with his hands full.

"Try these." Nick handed Elizabeth a pair of gloves. They were a little large but they would work.

Bonnie took the long wool scarf out of Nick's hand and wound it around Elizabeth's neck covering her chin and mouth.

"You look like you're ready for a sleigh ride!" Lynn teased.

"Wait. One more thing." Nick rushed back to the lost and found and retrieved an oversize stocking cap.

Returning, Nick pulled the cap snuggly over Elizabeth's head covering her ears and forehead. Everyone burst out laughing as Elizabeth had turned into a pile of warm clothes with only her eyes and nose barely visible. Nick proclaimed her ready to go and went out to move his car as close to the door as he could get it.

With Bonnie and Loretta steadying her on either side, they stepped out into the blast of icy wind. Elizabeth would have been blown off her feet if her friends had not been hanging onto her. She was grateful that it was a short walk to the safety of Nick's car. Bonnie and Loretta made their way on over to Bonnie's car. Lynn had gone out ahead and had the engine warming for them. They waved cheerfully as Bonnie guided her car carefully out of the parking lot ahead of Nick.

The drive to the Anderson home was short. Nick stopped the car near the steps to the front porch and left it running while he went inside to find help. As she waited in the car, Elizabeth observed with relief that the house blocked the main blasts of wind.

Nick wasn't gone long. He returned with their host carrying a captain's chair and two other men. All Elizabeth had to do was get out of the car and sit down on the chair. Her heavy snow boots anchored her feet to the ground as she stood up and unsteadily moved to the chair. Even without the wind, the air was bitterly cold. Once seated, Elizabeth concentrated on not sliding off the chair and let the men do the work. They paused in the foyer to brush off snow and hang the damp coats and scarves on hooks along the wall, then carried Elizabeth on her chair over to the dinner table. Elizabeth was spared the awkwardness of struggling to get out of the chair to come to the table but it was not without a price. For Elizabeth, the price was the discomfort of having her weakness displayed so obviously while the other guests talked in the living room until dinner was called.

Dinner was served. Everyone's plate was filled, when Stan Anderson suggested they introduce themselves and tell a little about themselves. Elizabeth had not faced this dreaded situation for a couple of years, but the old feelings surfaced immediately. Once more, her inadequacies were revealed. When it was Elizabeth's turn, she had little to say and that intensified her feeling of nothingness. The conversation at the table moved on. Elizabeth found it lively and interesting, but she remained an observer. The evening ended early because of the weather.

Elizabeth was uneasy about going back out into the storm but the return trip went smoothly. The fire was still flickering in the fireplace at Lecture House. After Nick left, Elizabeth sat watching the fire, the events of the day pushing her thoughts and feelings into turmoil. Other conferees filtered in. Someone put another log on the fire and stoked the coals.

Harry Wilson brought a carload of people back in his four- wheel drive. They all gravitated to the fire continuing the conversation they had begun in the car. Elizabeth became part of the circle before the fire. The conversation fit with questions Harry's lecture had stirred up in Elizabeth.

"It seems unrealistic that anyone could balance all six areas you talked about." Elizabeth spoke up for the first time. "People don't have that much control of their lives."

"I didn't say all areas had to be in balance. I said we have to be working in all areas and not ignoring some and putting all our energy into one or two areas. That's what I meant by balance."

"What about vocational? Some people just can't get a job."

"Okay. A vocation is not a job. You have a vocation even if you don't have employment. Vocation is more of a calling. Something you are, whether you are employed or not."

The idea was new to Elizabeth. She had never thought about having a vocation.

Harry stood up. "I've got to get going. Elizabeth, maybe you would be interested in doing an independent study some time. Think about it. Good night everyone."

The fire was burning down and people began to go their separate ways. Elizabeth felt spent. She just wanted to crawl into bed under the covers and shut out the world. Elizabeth found Bonnie already back in their room reading in bed. She was no more interested in conversation than Elizabeth was. Talk could wait until morning.

CHAPTER 35

Cooking was therapeutic for Elizabeth as well as being a creative activity. Her kitchen was arranged so that the kitchen range and the work counter formed an L-shape with a double sink at the bend of the L. Elizabeth could move one of the high barstool type chairs to the kitchen sink, sit on it, and use a kick-stool to support her feet. From that position, Elizabeth had access to the stove and the oven, the counter, drawers, sink, and garbage disposal. Once she gathered pans and ingredients, Elizabeth could do most of the work of cooking and clean up while sitting at the sink; and while she worked, she had time to think.

As Elizabeth pushed the onions she was chopping into the skillet for sautéing, her mind was rerunning thoughts from last weekend's conference. *What did people being 'made in the image of God' mean in Elizabeth's situation?* She had always believed it was true but had never questioned how to relate to that on a practical level. Now it seemed that one thing it meant was that Elizabeth had to view herself as a single unit, one image. She needed to integrate her physical self with her personal self, the negative with the positive; and Elizabeth was not sure she could deal with that.

She put her thoughts on hold as the front door opened, and Joe leaped over the doorsill and onto the living room carpet, swinging the door closed behind him all in one motion. Joe was thirteen and just beginning a long awaited growing spurt.

"Oh! Oh! Ah! Ah! Oh!" Joe was pounding his bare feet on the carpet. He dropped to his knees to scratch Shona's ears. "Hi Shona. How's your day going? You're such a good dog."

"Joe there's snow on the ground! Why are you barefoot? You'll freeze your feet!" There was no way to get from Joe's back door to Elizabeth's front door without crossing the yard covered with four inches of snow.

"I know. I just wanted to see if I could do it." Joe jumped up, touched the ceiling, and circled around into the kitchen. "Mom wants to know if she can borrow a stick of margarine."

"Sure. Look in the refrigerator." Elizabeth turned down the flame under the skillet and stirred the onions.

"What are you cooking, Aunt Elizabeth? It smells good. Are you having company?"

191

"Yes. I'm making a casserole. My friend, Nick, is coming down to pick up the lamp painting."

"Oh, yeah, that's a neat painting. I like it." Joe located the box of margarine and slid an individually wrapped quarter into his hand. "Well, I better get back. Mom's waiting for this."

"Don't go back barefoot. Someone will bring your shoes over." Elizabeth's words were heard as a challenge or not heard at all. Elizabeth shook her head in a mixture of disbelief and resignation as she watched Joe, jacketless and shoeless, dash across the yard.

Elizabeth turned her attention back to the casserole she was working on. She was looking forward to Nick's visit and talking with him about the conference. Nick often asked thought-provoking questions. Elizabeth could use some help in sorting out her thoughts.

The table was almost set. Elizabeth carefully turned the plates so that the fruit design in the center of each plate would face the person sitting at that place. The food for their meal was ready for Nick to put on the table when he arrived. Elizabeth's guests always had to take over the final chores of putting a meal on the table. When her guests arrived, Elizabeth would change from cook to kitchen manager.

Shona's barking announced Nick's arrival. Elizabeth turned off the oven and the burners on the stove and let Nick take over. She wished she could do it herself but there was no way she could carry hot dishes to the table.

After dinner, Nick took over again. He put the food away while Elizabeth settled in the living room. As usual, they decided to enjoy their dessert and coffee in the living room.

"You said the conference stirred up some questions for you." Nick reopened the conversation they had begun over dinner. "Like what?"

"There were a bunch of things. One thing was the question of being a valid person without having a job. Usually, I can use my ostrich approach, but last weekend it was impossible."

"I don't understand the 'ostrich approach'. I think you've mentioned it before."

"The best way for me to deal with my disability is to act like an ostrich. The ostrich hides his head in the sand when danger approaches; and if it comes too close, he has a powerful kick. I learned years ago that when I let people know the facts of my disability they shut doors or withdraw. If I act like the ostrich and hide it or sidestep direct questions, I can do okay. I'm pretty skillful at being the ostrich." Elizabeth spoke lightly, but they both knew there was an underlying seriousness.

"Elizabeth, do you really think that's the right way to handle it?" Nick chided her.

"Actually, I do." Elizabeth was serious. "It's the only way I can keep from being rejected or written off. I've learned that by painful experience."

"Did you feel like people rejected you or wrote you off at the conference?"

"It was mixed. At dinner when I had to say I didn't have a job, I did. Later, when I was talking to Harry Wilson, I didn't; but then, I was more in the ostrich mode. Did I tell you Harry suggested that I do an independent study?"

"No, you didn't. What did you tell him?

"We left it open, part of the ostrich; but I'm not really considering it. I don't think I could manage regular trips to the study center. Besides, Harry is intimidating. He thinks I'm more intellectual than I am. I'd hate to have him find out!"

"An independent study sounds like a good idea to me." There was no hint of teasing in Nick's tone. His voice was firm. "I just don't think the ostrich is the right way for a Christian to deal with disability!"

Elizabeth did not respond. Nick's words and tone jolted her. Obviously, Nick could not understand. He had not lived her life. He didn't know the times she had wrestled with God over this matter.

"In fact, why don't you do an independent study on that. You could study what Scripture says about disability." Nick pressed his point deeper.

"I'll think about it." Elizabeth was closing the door on further discussion at the moment, but she knew she would think about it whether she wanted to or not.

Nick let the matter drop. They had one last evaluation of the painting for the church, and Nick took his leave. He had a heavy schedule the next day.

Elizabeth got up the next morning ready to start painting again. She selected a small canvas and began to sketch the still life Nick had helped her set up before the conference. This painting was to be for another friend. Specifically, for a room her friend was redecorating. Elizabeth's paintings were beginning to be a blend of her artistic ability and her interest in people. Her unique style was beginning to develop.

That evening, the couch looked particularly inviting. It had been a productive day, but Elizabeth was anxious to finish the dishes and settle down for the night. She emptied the dishwater, rinsed out the sink, slid down off the high stool, and pulled it back to its place at the high counter. Finally, she could relax.

Elizabeth had just put her feet up on the coffee table when Arlene came in the front door. Arlene rarely came over after supper. Surprised, Elizabeth sat up to say hello, but Arlene ignored her. She walked directly to the telephone and picked up the receiver.

"I need to use your phone," she said her voice devoid of emotion. "There's a fire on the third floor; and apparently, the phone got knocked off the hook up there."

Arlene was calmly matter of fact. Elizabeth was not sure she had heard correctly. She said nothing while Arlene opened the phone book, located a number and began to dial.

"I want to report a fire. 703 Dogwood Road. Third floor. No. Okay." Arlene put down the phone and turned around. "I've got to get back."

"Send the kids down here." Elizabeth wanted to help, but there was nothing else she could do.

"Joe and Jeanne aren't home." Arlene was at the door. She seemed uncertain. "The fire's just on the third floor."

"Okay. Send the kids down. They need to be out of the way."

"All right."

After Arlene left, Elizabeth went to the row of windows that made up one wall of her living room and looked across the yard at the big brick house. Everything looked normal. The back door opened and two small figures began to make their way across the dark yard as the sound of the fire siren pierced the night air. A third little figure came out and down the porch steps. Elizabeth returned to the couch. Her knees felt weak and she needed to appear strong. Fire had been a reoccurring subject of Elizabeth's nightmares.

Elizabeth waited. Vickie came in followed by Nora. Vickie had come without a coat. Nora was shivering despite the blanket she had wrapped around her shoulders. Neither girl spoke. Elizabeth waited again but no one came.

"Where's Ben? I saw him come out. He should be here." Ben at six was the youngest of Arlene's five children.

Nora and Vickie looked at each other questioningly and moved to the window. Nora pulled the blanket around her tighter.

"I don't see him." Vicki's eyes searched the yard. "There he is. He's just coming out of the house now."

In a few minutes, Ben came in the front door wearing his coat and his boots. He stopped inside the door to take his boots off and hang his coat on the closet doorknob. Ben, too, was silent.

"What took you so long, Ben. I was getting worried." Elizabeth broke the silence again.

"I was taking my cars out of the house."

"All of them? Where did you put them?" Elizabeth was surprised at the little boy's presence of mind and methodical reaction to an emergency situation.

"I put them under the back porch by the steps." Ben went directly to the windows where he could watch his house. "The firemen are going in," he announced flatly.

Ben remained at the windows while the girls moved aimlessly around the room. Each was lost in their own thoughts--thoughts that converged in the same fear.

"Who discovered the fire?" Elizabeth thought it might help to talk, and she still was at a loss to know what was actually happening.

Nora spoke up. "I was sitting in the big chair doing my homework. I looked up and it looked like smoke floating down from upstairs." She stood up and walked to the windows the blanket still wrapped around her.

"Did you see the fire?" Elizabeth pushed on.

"No, just smoke."

"Dad said he'd take care of it. He took a bucket and went upstairs. Mom wanted to call the fire department."

"Did your dad go up to the third floor?" Elizabeth knew how casual Ralph was about fire.

"Yes." Vickie volunteered. "When he opened the door to the third floor there was a huge cloud of smoke. He took a bucket of water up."

"Where was your dad when you left?"

No one answered at first. Then Ben assumed leadership. "We don't know."

"No one saw him come back down?"

They shook their heads in answer.

"Are you worried?" Elizabeth knew the answer to that but she voiced the question anyway.

Again, the only response was a nodding of heads. The children needed reassurance but Elizabeth could not give it to them. She didn't know what the situation actually was.

"Should we pray about it?" Elizabeth offered.

"We'd better!" Ben turned abruptly away from the window and dropped into the nearest chair.

The girls nodded. Elizabeth's prayer was short. She asked for safety for Ralph, protection for their house, and peace of mind for them as they waited. As soon as Elizabeth finished, Ben resumed his vigil at the windows. It was impossible to tell how much time had gone by. Minutes seemed like hours.

"There he is." Ben announced in a flat steady voice. "I can see him through the window. He's in the dining room."

Vickie and Nora hurried to the windows. Relief showed on every face. The vision of their father disappearing into a cloud of smoke was replaced with the familiar image of Ralph engrossed in conversation, this time with one of the firemen.

"The firemen are leaving. Let's go home." Ben was still assuming the role of leader. He reached for his coat and boots. Vickie and Nora followed.

Elizabeth said, "Good-bye," and let them leave. Her home had served as a refuge through a crisis; but now they needed to be with their parents in their own home. At this moment, Elizabeth was an outsider. Her mind was a turmoil of questions about the fire, but she knew she had to be patient. Tomorrow, Arlene would tell her all about it. Tonight, her questions would be an intrusion. Oddly, Elizabeth felt overwhelmingly lonely.

CHAPTER 36

Elizabeth was finishing a late breakfast when she saw Arlene crossing the yard with a mug of coffee in her hand. The events of the night before were on Elizabeth's mind. She was glad to see Arlene coming over.

"Good morning!" Elizabeth's greeting was a little too cheerful.

"Is it?" Arlene snapped as she closed the door behind her, crossed the living room, and chose a chair with a clear view of the sidewalk leading up to the back door of her house. "I have to watch for the insurance adjuster. Ralph's gone already. He had to be at the office early today. The adjuster's supposed to come sometime before noon."

"What happened last night?"

"Oh, it started as another chimney fire. You know how Ralph loves to build a roaring fire in the fireplace." Elizabeth also knew how uneasy those roaring fires made Arlene. "Apparently, some flames got through a crack in the chimney where it goes through the third floor. That big wooden wardrobe sits right beside the chimney to block the storage area from our bedroom area. Enough flames got out to catch the back of the wardrobe on fire."

"Oh, Arlene, that's scary. Was there a lot of damage?"

"Everything is a mess over there, but there's very little fire damage. Mostly smoke damage."

"What about water damage?"

"Ralph had the fire pretty much out by the time the firemen got there. He refused to allow them to use the hoses inside. He had a hard time convincing them, but he was adamant. So, we were spared the water damage that would have caused."

"The kids were pretty worried about Ralph going onto the third floor."

'Well! So was I! The smoke was really thick and heavy. It's a wonder he wasn't overcome, but you know Ralph! There was no stopping him." Arlene jumped up. "There's the adjuster. I've got to go."

Typical of Arlene's visits Elizabeth was left with a feeling of being stopped in mid sentence. The visit didn't answer all of Elizabeth's questions; but, at least, she had learned the basics. Elizabeth could wait to hear the whole fire story. Over the next several weeks, Arlene sat in Elizabeth's living room often, detailing her frustration with the cleanup and the endless paper work for their insurance claim.

As time went on, Elizabeth listened and sympathized with Arlene's plight; but her mind was preoccupied with something else. Elizabeth's life had hit another bump in the road, and she had to figure out how to manage the ramifications.

It was no longer safe for Elizabeth to sit on the high stool at the sink. She could not be sure she could get off without falling. Elizabeth had fallen once. Her leg just buckled before she could adjust her balance. Elizabeth could not risk using the stool anymore. She had to develop another system to get the kitchen work done or limit her cooking which would change her whole life style.

Elizabeth was managing but only managing. She consciously paced her strength, standing at the stove, counter, or the kitchen sink to work for short periods of time and sitting at the dining room table for jobs like chopping vegetables and making sandwiches. Elizabeth was not satisfied that this was the only solution. What she needed was someone to design a stool that would raise and lower hydraulically for her to use. Then she could go back to sitting at the sink to do her work.

Ideas like that kept Elizabeth hopeful; and, at the same time, they discouraged her by the monumental task of following through on them. Leafing through a magazine one afternoon, Elizabeth saw an advertisement for a simple three-wheel scooter with a seat. It was actually a battery-operated wheelchair, but what caught Elizabeth's attention was the statement: *Accessory to elevate seat to a maximum of 7 inches available.* Maybe this was something she could adapt. Elizabeth decided that it could not hurt to ask for information about the seat elevating option. A letter would be relatively anonymous. Elizabeth carefully drafted a letter asking for specific information.

The company did not answer letters. They sent salesmen. The man had called out of the blue at an inconvenient time. Elizabeth did not want to answer his questions over the phone about her physical condition and her interest in the wheelchair while her friends were sitting in the room. It was easier just to make an appointment for him to come to her house. Elizabeth dreaded his coming. She hated to meet strangers who could only observe her physical disability without knowing her personal strengths. She didn't need a wheelchair. What she needed was to be able to sit at her sink to do her work.

Mr. Skulimoski, the salesman, was due in a half an hour. Elizabeth hoped that her friend, Betsy, would get there before he did. Elizabeth was counting on Betsy to be a buffer between herself and Mr. Skulimoski. Betsy was a nurse and the wife of an elder in Elizabeth's church. Elizabeth trusted Betsy enough to seek out her counsel in this significantly personal part of her life.

Betsy and Mr. Skulimoski arrived at the same time. Elizabeth heard them introducing themselves to each other as they walked toward her front porch. Knowing that Betsy would usher him in, Elizabeth remained seated in her corner of the couch. She was relieved that her unsteady walk and tenuous balance was not the first impression Mr. Skulimoski would have of her.

Mr. Skulimoski was a kind, fatherly man who was completely sold on his product. His wife used one of these chairs and he was anxious to share his first hand knowledge. Elizabeth waited a little impatiently while he brought the chair into the trailer, showed them how it came apart to fit into the trunk of a car, and demonstrated the operation of the chair. Finally, he was ready to hear Elizabeth's questions.

"I was interested in the feature for raising the height of the seat. Is it hydraulic?" Elizabeth turned the focus to her real of interest.

"That's something new. It isn't hydraulic. It operates like a car jack. The kind that has a scissors type action. It's covered by a soft plastic cover that expands and folds down sort of like an accordion."

"What would that look like?" Elizabeth was skeptical.

"It looks like a big black box that sits under the seat. I might have a picture out in the car. Let me go look."

While Mr. Skulimoski went to his car, Betsy moved from the chair to the couch where Elizabeth was sitting.

"Well, Elizabeth, what do you think?"

"I don't know. The seat swivels, so I probably could back it up to the sink and turn around to work but...." The sound of the screen door opening stopped her.

"This is what I was thinking of. It doesn't show it very clearly." Mr. Skulimoski hurried back in carrying a folded newsletter in his hand. He handed it to Elizabeth. "You can keep the newsletter."

While Elizabeth studied the darkened photo in the newsletter, Betsy refocused the discussion. "What about the cost?"

Mr. Skulimoski took out his note pad and began to jot down figures. He asked Elizabeth for preferences in type of seat and other options, looked on his charts, corrected his figures, and came up with a total of just over a thousand dollars. The seat raising mechanism would add another four hundred and ninety-five dollars. Elizabeth was not ready to even think about spending that much money.

"I'll keep this in mind. I don't need a wheelchair. I'm not sure I would use it enough to be worth that kind of money."

"You might be surprised at how much you would use it."

Mr. Skulimoski began to use low-key sales pressure. "I delivered a chair last month to a man who keeps it in his car and just uses it when he goes out shopping and so forth. I got the most enthusiastic thank-you note from him saying how it has changed his whole outlook on life."

"I need to think about this. Thank you for coming." Elizabeth could not take pressure, even low key pressure. She wanted space now. She wanted Mr. Skulimoski to leave. She couldn't think with that chair sitting in her living room.

"Let me just write this up for you to think about. Then you can call me if you decide to order a chair and the paper work will be all done."

"Okay."

"Now, if you decide to order, it takes about six weeks for delivery. The company assembles each chair according to the individual order."

"Fine." Elizabeth did not want to encourage further conversation with Mr. Skulimoski.

Betsy held the front door open while Mr. Skulimoski maneuvered the wheelchair through the door to disassemble it on the porch. When they were alone, Betsy returned to their previous conversation.

"That's quite a machine. What do you think?"

"Like I said, I think it would work; but I can't justify spending that kind of money just to sit at the sink."

"Maybe you would use it for other things, like he said. You could go to the mall or even the grocery store with it. You said you don't go shopping because there is too much walking."

"That thought crossed my mind. In some ways I'd like to go ahead and get one, but Betsy, I don't have any savings. I'd have to use my credit card but the maximum is only a thousand dollars. With my income how could I justify that extravagance when I don't really need it?"

"I think you should pursue it. Would you mind if I talk to the Deacon Board at the church and see if they have any money to lend you out of the Mercy Fund?"

"I guess not. I would only need about six hundred dollars."

After Betsy left, Elizabeth went back to the studio to try to work on her latest painting. She needed get some distance from the tension of the afternoon, but she was too distracted to paint. Elizabeth was on the verge of making a decision that would have major ramifications. The chair, if she bought it, could be a major help; but, even though it looked like a large scooter, the fact remained that it was a wheelchair. Elizabeth didn't want to invite a wheelchair into her home, into her routine of daily living. Life seldom offers choices that don't involve some sort of trade-off. Elizabeth was not sure she was willing to take this trade-off.

Elizabeth had made up her mind by the time Betsy got back to her with an answer from the Deacon Board. They were willing to loan her the money she needed to purchase the chair, and Elizabeth was now willing to accept the wheelchair as part of the solution to maintaining her present lifestyle. Elizabeth called Mr. Skulimoski.

"Elizabeth, I'm sure you've made the best decision and you'll be very happy with it." Mr. Skulimoski was enthusiastic.

"I think it will be a help." Elizabeth was not ready to share his enthusiasm.

"I will call the order in. That way we'll get a head start on the six weeks it takes for delivery. Then, if you will send me a check for the first payment I'll send it on with the paper work to the home office, and we'll be all set. Do you still have my card?"

"Yes, I do. I'll get the check in the mail. Thanks for your help."

Elizabeth replaced the receiver on the phone. The wheels had been set in motion. Now she had to let Betsy know. Betsy was the contact with the Deacon Board.

The next afternoon, Betsy brought the check. Elizabeth had not expected such a quick response.

"The Deacons asked me to tell you that this is not a loan. It is a gift from the church." Betsy handed Elizabeth a check for twelve hundred dollars.

"I only asked for six hundred." Elizabeth's words revealed the confusion in her mind. "I mean this is so generous. That nearly pays for

201

the whole chair. It was supposed to be a loan."

"Well, this is what the Deacons decided to do. They want to do this for you."

"I'm really grateful and I'm touched by their generosity."

Elizabeth didn't know what to say or even what to think. This gift would make life much easier for her in more than one way. God had provided for her again through the members of her church; and again, He was providing something for Elizabeth that she wasn't quite ready to accept.

CHAPTER 37

Arlene saw the UPS truck stop in front of the garage. She watched while the driver unloaded two big boxes, slid them onto a dolly, and started around to Elizabeth's trailer. Dinner for her family was in the oven. She glanced at the clock on her kitchen wall. There was time to go over to Elizabeth's and try to uncrate the wheelchair.

The two boxes took up most of the floor space in Elizabeth's living room. Mr. Skulimoski had intended to deliver the chair himself, but he was recovering from emergency surgery. The surgery came up after Elizabeth placed her order for the wheelchair. Rather than delay delivery, he arranged for the factory to ship the chair directly to Elizabeth. Elizabeth preferred it this way. Mr. Skulimoski would have expected her to show excitement at the chair's arrival; and this way, Elizabeth would not have to pretend to be enthusiastic. She was free to feel whatever she felt without apology.

Arlene had no expectations. She came over to do a job that needed to be done.

"I guess this is what you've been waiting for. Which box should I open first?" Arlene always dispensed with preliminaries and got directly to the point.

"I don't know. Just get everything out and we'll go from there. I hope I remember how it went together."

The cartons were a challenge. Arlene had to find a screwdriver to pry loose the staples holding the heavy cardboard together. Additional cardboard held the contents firmly in place. Arlene pulled out a large packet of papers and handed it to Elizabeth. Among other things, it contained a manual for the wheelchair detailing how to assemble the chair for use.

"Okay, now we are in good shape. Is the base wedged in there too tight?"

"I may have to tear the box apart."

"Go ahead. We won't need it again."

The chair was assembled and the connections seemed to work. Arlene and Elizabeth were surveying the result of their combined effort, when Ben came in the door looking for Arlene.

"Oh! Neat!" Ben's mission was immediately forgotten. "Can I ride it?"

"No!" Arlene's response was quick and intense. "This is a wheelchair! It's for Aunt Elizabeth to use."

"It isn't ready to use yet, Ben. We have to charge the battery first," Elizabeth interjected, as Ben, still in awe, walked over to inspect the chair.

"My dinner is ready to come out of the oven. I'll plug this charger in." Arlene was anxious to be on her way. "Ben, help me take these boxes to the garage. Elizabeth, do you want me to send a plate over for your dinner tonight?"

"Thanks. I'd like that."

After Arlene and Ben left, Elizabeth remained on the couch observing her new wheelchair. She wished it wasn't sitting there so publicly in her living room. The different reactions of Arlene and Ben to the chair mimicked the conflicting reactions Elizabeth herself was experiencing.

The sight of the chair was cause for hopeful anticipation, but it repulsed her at the same time.

Elizabeth let the battery charge all evening. When she was ready to go to bed, she disconnected the charger; and for the first time, Elizabeth sat down on the chair. She tested the controls located on the handlebars. The left side moved the chair backwards and the right side moved it forward. It wasn't too hard. Slowly, Elizabeth backed the chair up then moved forward toward the kitchen. She maneuvered the chair around in the small kitchen and backed up to the sink. This was the real test. Elizabeth located the switch and raised the seat. The maximum height was lower than she had been used to, but it would be workable.

In the next few weeks, Elizabeth adjusted quickly to the lower height. She was pleased to be able to freely work in the kitchen again. When she was not working in the kitchen, Elizabeth kept the chair parked in the kitchen where it was both convenient to use and out of view from the living room. True to Mr. Skulimoski's prediction, Elizabeth did find the chair useful in other ways. She could use it to carry things from place to place in the house that she could not manage while walking. The chair was working out.

Shona was outside racing along the fence barking frantically. Elizabeth glanced at the clock on the kitchen stove. It was too early for Nick to arrive. From her seat at the sink, Elizabeth could see through the open front door to the corner of the garage. A UPS driver came into view walking briskly along the garage carrying a large box and keeping as much distance as possible from Shona. Elizabeth dried her hands, swiveled the seat so that she faced the controls, and maneuvered the wheelchair around the kitchen counter and into the living room. She reached the door at the same time as the UPS driver.

"Package."

"Thanks. Put it on the floor right here, please." Elizabeth backed away from the screen door and indicated a place where the box would be out of the way.

"Sign right here." He handed her the clipboard and a pen.

"Sorry about the dog."

"It's okay. Have a good day." He hurried off the porch and down the driveway still keeping as much distance as possible from Shona who was escorting him off the property.

The box could wait until tomorrow. It was her order of art supplies, and the timing was good. Elizabeth was ready to start a new painting. Nick was bringing an antique mantle clock with him tonight to set up a new still life. A mutual friend had commissioned a painting with the clock as the central figure in it. Elizabeth sold her paintings to friends and acquaintances for just enough to keep her in art supplies. It suited Elizabeth. The cost was within the budgets of her buyers and not so high as to allow Elizabeth to worry that the price was greater than the painting's value.

Elizabeth returned to the kitchen. The next time Shona barked it would be Nick, and Elizabeth still had things to do before dinner would be ready to serve. This would be the first time Nick had visited since the wheelchair had arrived. Elizabeth was anxious to be ready to park the chair and get out of it as soon as Nick came in. She slid the muffin tin of cloverleaf rolls into the oven just as she heard Shona begin to bark. Usually, the rolls would have been ready to come out of the oven when Nick arrived. The UPS delivery had slowed things down, but Elizabeth was content to have gotten the rolls in the oven before turning the kitchen over to Nick.

Elizabeth parked the chair and the evening took on the comfortable familiarity of eating a leisurely meal, adjourning to the studio for a painting critique, followed by conversation with dessert in the living room.

"I take it the chair is working out all right even though you had reservations?" Nick had finished serving the coffee and the desert and was ready to settle down.

"I guess the answer is 'yes'."

"You don't sound convinced yet." Nick made his comment sound like an exaggerated understatement.

"Change is hard!" Elizabeth could not ignore Nick's words. His good-natured chiding compelled her to try to justify herself. "The seat doesn't go quite high enough and it drives me crazy that it won't go side ways. I'm used to rolling around on the office chair in the studio."

Nick did not respond. He left his question open knowing Elizabeth would think about it later and re-examine her reaction. Instead, he refocused the conversation.

"Have you thought about building a ramp so you could get off the front porch with it?"

"Marilyn said that Will can build one later this summer. I can't really get anywhere, though, except to the car. The wheelchair doesn't work on gravel. The rest of the driveway is gravel."

"You're just using it in the house?"

"Just in the kitchen, mostly." Elizabeth felt herself resisting Nick's questions. She didn't know why because she wanted to bounce her thoughts off him. "I did go to the mall once with Marilyn and the boys, and I had an interesting experience. I went to the mall last fall. That time, someone pushed me around in a regular style wheelchair. I hated the way people notice you when you are in a wheelchair, so I just sat back and told myself, 'this is an empty wheelchair that someone is pushing around the mall'. When I went with Marilyn this time, we were coming from the entrance toward the stores and a group of teenagers were coming toward us. I started to do the same thing; but when I sat back, I took my hands off the controls and the chair rolled to a stop. It was kind of a shock. I can't be passive in this chair."

"Was pretending to not be in the chair like the ostrich?"

"That's exactly what it was." Elizabeth knew Nick's point of view; but with Nick, she always plunged in anyway. Now she would have to get herself out again. Instead, she dug herself in deeper. "I've got to revise the ostrich to fit life with this motorized chair."

"I'm still not convinced of the ostrich, Elizabeth. Have you thought about doing the independent study? This might be a good time to start it."

"Oh, Nick! I knew I should have bitten my tongue."

"Well, I just might be right! It's happened before!" Nick had made his point and knew it. Before Elizabeth could respond, Nick broke into laughter.

Elizabeth gave in. "I will write to Harry Wilson and see what is involved in an independent study."

"Good!"

Elizabeth was not sure it was 'good' in her definition of good. She did not want to focus her time and her intellect on disability. She did not want to have to deal with what she would learn. In high school, Elizabeth had naively chosen to write her term paper on muscular dystrophy and had been devastated. Her trust in God got her through that time, and her ostrich insight made life livable. *Did she dare search the Scripture to see how God viewed disabilities? Would history repeat itself? If Nick was right, she would lose the ostrich, then what?* Now the stakes were higher. Her disability was impacting her life more, but that was the reason it was time for her to reevaluate things. Elizabeth wondered if she could live with what she discovered.

CHAPTER 38

Elizabeth moved restlessly around the trailer. She was waiting; and waiting always made her anxious. Harry Wilson said he would be there by 3:30. It was a little after 4:00 and there was no sign of him yet. Elizabeth hoped her directions were clear.

As she had promised Nick, Elizabeth had written to Harry asking for more information about an independent study. The timing seemed right. Elizabeth had been surprised when Harry called to suggest that he meet her on her own 'turf'. He had business in Beaver Falls at the college the next week and could easily stop to see her after his business was finished. Elizabeth was a little put off by his style of using popular slang, but she welcomed the opportunity to talk with him in her own surroundings where she felt more confident. Now, her confidence was fading as the minutes ticked by.

"Helloo!" Harry appeared at the screen door as Elizabeth turned back from putting Shona out through the sliding door.

"Hi, I didn't see you coming."

"I came around the wrong side of the garage. Sorry I'm late. The meeting ran late." Harry dropped his books and papers on the coffee table and relaxed into the overstuffed chair near by. "I'm due in Pittsburgh by 6:30, so why don't we jump right in."

"Fine." Elizabeth was glad to let Harry do the talking.

"You wrote that you are interested in pursuing an independent study. What I have in mind is to work from the framework for a balanced life that I talked about at the conference you attended. Does that sound interesting to you?"

"Yes, in general but specifically what does that mean?"

"That depends on the individual. We would assess each area and see where you would want to start." Harry paused as the phone began to ring.

For a moment, Elizabeth thought she would ignore it. The insistent ringing drew her hand to the telephone. She picked up the receiver. "Hello."

"Elizabeth, this is Lynn. Do you have a few minutes for me to run something by you?"

"Actually, Lynn I'm tied up right now. Could I call you back?"

"Sure. I'll be home all evening."

Elizabeth returned the receiver to its cradle, and Harry picked up where he had stopped.

"I would expect you to come up to the study center to meet together for a couple of hours about every other week. We would have to schedule times when conferences were not taking place. Is that something you could work with?"

"I think I can work it out. At least as long as the weather is good." Elizabeth hated to appear dense; but to her, Harry's answers left everything vague. "I think I'd like to try it and see how it goes."

Harry was ready to get on his way to Pittsburgh. He pulled some forms out of his pile of books and papers and handed Elizabeth some inventories for her to fill out to bring to their first official meeting. They settled on Thursday of the following week for Elizabeth's first trip to the study center. Harry walked briskly out of the trailer and down the driveway amid a barrage of barking. Shona had missed Harry's arrival and was making up for it as she escorted him to his car.

Elizabeth sat in her place on the couch mildly confused, wondering if she knew what she had just agreed to and wondering what to do now. Elizabeth didn't know whether to get supper and then call Lynn or to call Lynn and then get supper, and she didn't know why this was such a major decision. Her action made the decision for her. Elizabeth picked up the receiver and dialed Lynn's number.

"Lynn, this is Elizabeth. Is this a good time for you to talk?"

"Yes, it is. I'm still working on this project. Are you ready to hear about it?"

"Yes."

"I'm developing a special unit for my class this fall. I'm trying to integrate subject matter and people experiences. One afternoon, we are going to a home for the elderly to write letters for them. Another day, my class will spend a morning with the kindergartners reading to them. I want my class to understand that all people have value."

"I like your plan."

"Good, because I was hoping you would be willing to be part of the unit."

"How?"

"I would like to have you come in one afternoon in your wheelchair and teach an art class. I think it would be very good for my class to interact with you on that level and not always be the helpers. What do you think?"

"I'm not sure. When do you need to know?"

"Well, I need to get my lesson plans done in the next couple of days; but if you think you might do it, I can go ahead and schedule it in as 'pending'."

"Do it. I don't have any negative reaction. I'm just need to think about it. It's been a lot of years since I taught any art classes and never fifth and sixth graders."

"I have a really good class this year. I think you'll like them. I'll tentatively put you in for four weeks from tomorrow. Okay?"

Elizabeth hung up the phone. Strangely, she felt energized. This was a challenge but also something she had a measure of control in. The independent study with Harry was a challenge, but it overwhelmed her. It seemed to be beyond her control. Elizabeth was glad to be pulled back into familiar territory. Lynn's plan was what Elizabeth needed right now. If she could come up with an idea for the art class, she would do it.

The idea came fairly quickly, and Elizabeth was pleased with it. She would have the class work on a still life picture. First, she would have a drawing lesson, followed by an experience in color. Perhaps the children would use colored chalks. She would have to ask Lynn if there were pastel chalks in the art supply cupboard. In the mean time, Elizabeth would paint the same still life with oil paint and take her painting along for the class to see an example of a still life painting.

Elizabeth had made good progress on the painting by the time she went to her first appointment with Harry at the study center. Bonnie was interested in checking out the study center library and arranged her schedule so she could drive Elizabeth to her appointment. Elizabeth was glad to have Bonnie's company and her help. When they got to the study center, Bonnie went in search of Harry. Elizabeth waited in the car. She had brought the wheelchair. Walking outside of her house was just too difficult. Using the wheelchair would reveal less weakness than walking would, and Elizabeth did not want Harry to write her off just yet.

Harry and Elizabeth met together for an hour; then they joined Bonnie for lunch at Cedar Lodge. After lunch, they separated again agreeing to meet at the car ready to leave at 2:30. By 2:30, Elizabeth was ready to leave. The day had gone well but Elizabeth was glad to get back into the comfortable security of her own car. Bonnie took the wheel again. As they traveled the winding country roads, they made small talk watching for the landmarks that would guide them back to the turnpike. When Bonnie merged the car onto the turnpike, they both relaxed.

"Well, how was your time with Harry?"

"It was good. Although, I may have gotten more than I bargained for. I have to start an exercise program. He's really into physical fitness."

"What kind of an exercise program?"

"To start with I'm supposed to start using my exercise bike again. He had a bike there, and we worked out a way I could use it sitting on the wheelchair. We took the seat off the one Harry had, and I backed up to the bike, turned my seat around to face the bike's handlebars, and raised the seat of my wheelchair. Then we had to devise a way to keep my feet on the pedals. We more or less tied them on. It works."

"That sounds pretty creative."

"And it doesn't stop there. He's planning to devise a weight pulley system for me to use. I already do the range of motion exercises on the bed. I'll be spending all day exercising!" Elizabeth's mildly sarcastic words hid her real feeling of hope that she could rebuild some physical strength. At least now, she had a plan and some guidance.

"Bonnie, what would you say your vocation is?"

"Teaching, I guess. Why?"

"I've always thought in terms of employment, a job, not a vocation. I haven't had a job for a long time, but Harry says they are different. He says that your vocation is your God given calling in life and it doesn't change with your circumstances."

"I remember him talking about that at the conference we went to. What's your vocation?"

"I don't know, and I'm supposed to figure it out before I come back in two weeks."

"Maybe your vocation is 'artist'."

"No. I'm not comfortable with that at all." Elizabeth was silent for a while, then went on. "Harry was pushing counselor from the inventories I filled out, but that's not it either. The thought of that pressures me and kind of scares me."

"I don't know, Elizabeth. I think it would fit. You do a lot of unofficial counseling. Maybe you just need to get used to it."

Elizabeth let the topic drop, but over the next week, she wrestled with the question of a vocation. But she got no closer to an answer. *Did she really have a calling? Did everyone really have a God given calling in the way Harry defined it?* She had to resolve this before she saw Harry again.

The day for Elizabeth's art lesson with Lynn's class came quickly. Elizabeth's painting was barely dry enough to take. She had arranged a simple set-up using some early American type items she had sitting around her living room with a plant added for variety. Nick would have found a way to give the arrangement a spark, but Elizabeth squelched the urge to call him to come down and fix it. Instead, she reasoned that these uncomplicated shapes would be best for the classroom.

Elizabeth arrived at the school during lunchtime while Lynn's classroom was empty. She wanted to have the still life arranged and her painting set on an easel before the students returned. She made it with time to spare. The bell rang and the first group of boys seemed to tumble through the door joking and poking at each other. The girls came more or less in pairs, and the loners of both sexes straggled in last. Elizabeth wondered if she would be able to connect with these young people.

Lynn settled the class down and introduced Elizabeth as her friend, a member of the School Board, and an artist. Then she asked Elizabeth to tell the class about herself. Lynn hoped to stimulate some interaction between her class and Elizabeth on the subject of disability. Lynn had prepared the class in their morning lessons. Following Lynn's instructions Elizabeth talked for a few minutes then asked for questions. She braced herself. Children often asked awkward questions and Elizabeth needed to answer all their questions honestly.

One of the boys was the first to raise his hand. Elizabeth nodded an acknowledgement.

"How does that cart work? He leaned forward eager to see her answer.

"The controls are here. This side goes forward and this side goes backward." Elizabeth demonstrated as she talked.

The next hand came up. "How fast does it go?"

"This one goes four miles per hour. Some can go five or six miles an hour, but I chose the slower one."

"What does the motor run on?"

Elizabeth looked questioningly at Lynn. The discussion was not going as planned and Elizabeth needed help.

"We'll let Miss McKievey answer this last question and then pass out the paper for our art class." Lynn rescued Elizabeth and redirected her class.

The rest of the afternoon went pretty much as Elizabeth had planned it. She enjoyed moving from student to student giving advice and encouragement as needed. The students worked diligently on their pictures. All in all, for Elizabeth, the afternoon was a success.

Later, as Elizabeth sat at her place in the kitchen chopping vegetables for the western omelet she was making for her supper, her mind was reviewing the events of the afternoon. They had not talked about disability at all yet they had accomplished the objective – to see the person beyond the disability. The uniqueness of the wheelchair had taken the children's attention and the disability had lost its importance.

"It was," Elizabeth thought, "like the wheelchair was a bridge that let the children meet me on common ground."

The word 'bridge' struck a cord. *That was it,* she thought. That was her calling. Elizabeth's calling was to be a bridge. That might not fit Harry's definition of vocation, but it fit Elizabeth. This was something she could work with.

CHAPTER 39

Elizabeth picked up the receiver and dialed Arlene's number. The phone only rang twice. Arlene was waiting for Elizabeth's call.

"Hello."

"Hi. I'm ready to leave. Are you free to come down?"

"Yes. Just let me take Ralph's coffee up and I'll be right over."

"Okay. I'll go on out and get in the car." Elizabeth hung up the phone and made her way to the kitchen where the wheelchair was parked. She could finally ride it out to the car now that Will had finished making a ramp from the porch to the concrete slab where her car was parked.

Arlene got to the car by the time Elizabeth was settled in the driver's seat. She pulled the wheelchair around to the back of Elizabeth's small station wagon, dismantled it, and loaded it into the cargo area. Arlene closed the back hatch and came around to Elizabeth's open window.

"All set. I'll close your front door. What time will you be back?"

"Thanks!" Elizabeth did a quick calculation. "I should be back here by three. My meeting with Harry should be finished by one o'clock, and the trip takes about two hours. I think three is about right."

"Okay. Just stop in front of the garage where I can see you and honk. I'll watch for you. Have a good day." Arlene hurried back across the yard.

Elizabeth slipped the key in the ignition and started the engine. She let the engine idle while she organized things on the seat beside her. She had her notebook, the books she needed, change for the turnpike tolls, and green grapes and crackers (*not that she would be hungry but eating helped reduce her stress*). Elizabeth was making the trip to the study center alone for the first time and it was a big step for her. Over the last few years because of her difficulty walking, Elizabeth had also limited her driving, so much so, that now the thought of a two-hour drive on her own was unnerving.

Mentally, Elizabeth divided the trip into three parts. The first part, from her trailer to the turnpike, was familiar; but it was city driving and, thus, not without stress. Elizabeth was a skillful driver but her skill required an elevated alertness and an intuitive ability to predict what another driver was about to do. She was always aware that she could not rely totally on her physical responses.

Once Elizabeth got through the turnpike tollbooth *(having managed the tricky business of rolling down her window and reaching for the ticket)*, she merged her car into the light traffic and relaxed. Elizabeth felt a sense of freedom as the car picked up speed and the road opened up before her. There was a rhythm in the traffic flow that Elizabeth was comfortable with. She settled in, reached for a grape to relieve her dry mouth, and enjoyed the next hour.

The final stretch was the part that had concerned Elizabeth the most. As she drove away from the tollbooth, her tension returned. From here on, she had to travel a two-lane highway and then a very narrow country road. Two things worried Elizabeth. One was making a wrong turn and getting lost. The other was getting either behind or in front of a logging truck in the mountainous terrain. Elizabeth glanced at the clock on the dashboard. She was a little behind schedule.

Elizabeth drove to the top of the hill and turned left off the turnpike access road. The turn took her across the turnpike and headed her toward the mountain. Nothing looked quite right and Elizabeth was beginning to doubt that she was on the right road. Then, to her relief, she recognized a structure back in the trees and a logging road entrance. A sense of familiarity began to grow and Elizabeth's tension slowly dissolved into a kind of focused alertness.

The study center looked deserted when she drove onto the grounds. Harry was to meet her in the parking lot and help her. There was no sign of Harry. Elizabeth parked her car and turned off the engine, glad for a few minutes to unwind. She had made it. She was actually here in the study center parking lot. This trip was a test, a small step back to the independent person Elizabeth had been in her Philadelphia days. Today she had driven, completely on her own, two hours away from everything that was security for her. Elizabeth's life was a strange mixture of dependence and independence, and she was just beginning to think that one might not have to cancel the other out.

Ten minutes went by. Elizabeth was wondering if she had gotten the date mixed up when she saw Harry came out of Cedar Lodge. He waved and headed toward her car.

"Hello." Harry stopped at Elizabeth's open car door. "Let me get the wheelchair unloaded. Then I'll ask you how the trip went."

They had to pay close attention to the mechanics of getting from the car to Guest House because the planned sidewalks were not built yet. Elizabeth was learning that there were rules for using this style of wheelchair outside. Failure to respect the rules could land her on the ground. Harry stabilized the chair for her, and they reached the building without trouble.

"To answer your question, the trip really went smoothly despite my nervousness." They were settled in Harry's temporary office, and Elizabeth could finally concentrate on conversation.

"I didn't think you'd have any trouble. What were you nervous about?"

"Everything!"

"Oh." Harry didn't know how to take Elizabeth at times.

"You drive around Beaver Falls by yourself don't you?"

"Not as much as I used to. There isn't much point. I can't be very independent when I have to have someone there coming and going to load the wheelchair. I hate always interrupting Arlene to come down and help."

"Does she complain?"

"No; but I know it isn't always convenient. Her life is pretty hectic with five children."

"Maybe you and Arlene could work out a plan for what times she would commit to being there to help you." Harry liked negotiations, contracts, and scheduled relationships.

"This morning I had an idea." Elizabeth took a different direction. She knew that Harry's suggestion would be of no practical help, and she didn't want to get side tracked into arguing about it. "My idea is financially out of the question, though."

"What is your idea?"

"I was thinking that if I had two of these wheelchairs, I could just keep one in the car all the time. Then I think I could at least go and come from my own house alone. The trouble is that these scooter style electric chairs are really expensive. I can't even consider it."

"Now wait. That sounds like a good idea. Don't just discount it. There might be a way. What about second hand chair?"

"I don't think so. This is a new company. I don't think it's been in operation long enough to have used chairs available."

"It would be worth checking out at least. I'll make that one of your assignments for the next time we meet. Check around and see what the possibilities are."

217

Harry moved on to other topics, asking for a report on her exercise program and her assigned reading. Their time went quickly. Shortly after one o'clock, Elizabeth was once more settled in her car ready for the drive home. The tension she had felt when she started out in the morning had been replaced by a wary confidence. She had done it once. She could do it again and this time, Elizabeth was driving away from the unknown into the known. The trip home was uneventful. Arlene was waiting. Everything had gone well.

Elizabeth went to work on her assignment the next day. She called Mr. Skulimoski. He didn't seem to think it was an unreasonable request. In fact, he knew of a second hand chair for sale, and it would cost a third of what Elizabeth's new chair had cost. Mr. Skulimoski said that he would check to see if it was still available.

Everything happened quickly. Elizabeth worked out a new budget that included payments for the second hand chair. Her finances would be tight for a while, but she could do it. The chair was still available. Elizabeth decided to buy it and also update the seat lift on her original chair. The company had designed a hydraulic lift unit that did away with the unsightly black box with its maintenance problems. The additional cost would lengthen her financial strain but Elizabeth decided it would be worth it.

Elizabeth's impossible idea became a reality even before she reported back to Harry. In fact, her report next week would include an evaluation of its success. Elizabeth was meeting Nick tonight at a restaurant halfway between her trailer and his home. It had been a day of anticipation and preparation. Elizabeth was ready to leave early. She didn't know how long everything would take, and she didn't want to feel pressured.

Elizabeth had gone over and over all the details in her mind and even given herself a trial run. She paused at the door to go over her mental checklist one more time. She had the cordless phone so she could call Arlene if she needed help. She had the wire clothes hanger she had stretched into a long hook. The last item was the porch light. Elizabeth snapped on the light and let herself out the door. With the clothes hanger hook, she pulled the front door close enough for her to get it shut.

Everything went smoothly. Elizabeth managed to push the wheelchair away from the car at the right angle for her to get the car door shut. She climbed across the gearshift into the driver's seat and sat for a few minutes memorizing the location of the wheelchair. Success, when she returned, would depend on Elizabeth's ability to park her car in precisely the same spot it was in now. Satisfied, she started the car, backed out of her driveway, and headed off to meet Nick.

"You haven't told me how the independent study is coming." Nick had just returned from his second trip to the salad bar. He handed Elizabeth a cornmeal muffin.

Elizabeth waited for the waitress to finish refilling her coffee cup before responding. "What do you mean? That's what we've been talking about."

"We haven't talked about what you're finding that the Bible says about disability. I thought that was what you were going to be studying."

"I've been waiting for Harry to get to that. I keep thinking that we'll get through the preliminaries and get focused, but it doesn't seem to happen. I can't figure Harry out."

"Maybe you should just go ahead and start on your own." Nick had a way of tenaciously sticking to a subject until he was finished with it.

"Truthfully, I don't know how to start. All I can think of are the examples of healing, and healing isn't the point of what you're suggesting."

"Why don't you start with the Book of Job."

"Job?" Elizabeth didn't quite see a connection between Job and the topic of disability. "I guess it would be a place to start at least. Harry doesn't actually seem very interested in having me pursue that topic. He keeps trying to steer me toward counseling."

"I'll be interested in what you find in Job." Nick's mind was set, and Elizabeth had learned what that meant.

It was late when Elizabeth turned her car into her driveway. The wheelchair was sitting where she had left it a few hours earlier. Elizabeth carefully guided her car onto the stretch of concrete and shifted into park. She sat for a few seconds studying the back of the wheelchair. She needed to back up a little bit. A few inches would make a critical difference. Satisfied, Elizabeth turned off the engine, climbed back into the passenger seat, and opened the door. She had done well. Using the wire hanger hook, she pulled the chair within reach and maneuvered it into position beside the car.

Elizabeth slid out of the car onto the chair, got her things out of the car, and shut the door. She sat for a few minutes beside the car feeling a deep sense of satisfaction and joy. The moon was shining brightly. Elizabeth was overwhelmed with a sense of gratitude toward God. She felt alive again.

CHAPTER 40

Nancy and Elizabeth pooled their money and came up with enough to cover the bill and leave a reasonable tip for the waitress. The young girl had been very patient while they lingered over a late breakfast. Nancy and Elizabeth were making this a leisurely morning. They had come an hour's drive to have breakfast at a well-known Pennsylvania Dutch restaurant in Ohio. From here, they would head to a nearby mall that, they were told, had a large art supply and craft store. Nancy had to be home before her son's school bus dropped him off so they needed to start paying attention to the time. They gathered up their things and left the coziness of the inner room where they had been seated.

"It snowed!!" Nancy was the first to get a view through a window. "I can't believe it! We haven't been here that long."

Elizabeth moved forward to where she, too, could see through the window. There was no mistake. The ground was covered, and snow stood two inches high on the wooden fence rails. There had been no warning--no sign of snow when they arrived.

"Was this forecast? It's really coming down out there."

Elizabeth did not want to believe what she was seeing.

"I'm sure it wasn't forecast. It must be just a fluke of nature. It may not even snow in Beaver Falls. What shall we do?"

"We better go right home. They've shoveled and salted in front of the door. You bring the car over here. I don't think this wheelchair can go through snow."

Nancy's hands were red with cold by the time she got the windshield cleared and the wheelchair loaded. She needed to sit and let the heater warm them before tackling the drive home. Elizabeth had not driven in snow for several years. Nancy was very insecure about driving in snow, but she had more recent experience than Elizabeth and thus was the best choice for this drive.

Nancy drove slowly out of the parking lot onto the main highway and into the path the snowplow had provided. The car skidded when Nancy braked to a stop at the traffic light. Elizabeth held her breath fearing the worst, but the car stopped. Cautiously, Nancy turned onto the state road that would take them back through the Ohio countryside to Beaver Falls.

221

Ahead was whiteness, with only the narrow path of the plowed snow breaking the perfect blanket of whiteness covering everything.

"If it weren't for the plow, I couldn't tell where the road is."

"I know. This is really bad. This is going to be a long drive home!" Elizabeth could feel Nancy's stress building, but was battling her own too much to be of help to Nancy.

"Look! The road ahead isn't plowed!"

"It looks like the plow made that turn-around off to the left and just went back. Now what?"

"We have to go back. We can't go on if it isn't plowed. Let's go on up to Youngstown and get on the turnpike. The turnpike should be okay."

Nancy guided the car through the turn-around and back to the intersection. Snow was already building up again on the road making driving treacherous. The nearer to Youngstown they got, the more traffic they encountered adding another hazard to the drive.

"One mile to the turnpike entrance." Elizabeth was reading the signs while Nancy concentrated on driving. "It should be right up here."

"It's closed!"

"I don't believe this. Just keep going. There are several turnpike entrances around Youngstown. We'll have to try another one."

"We're getting further away from home instead of closer."

"I know, but we should be okay once we get on the turnpike. I just hope it isn't snowing at home."

The next entrance was open. They both breathed a sigh of relief as they drove up to the tollbooth. The tollbooth operator handed Nancy a ticket and warned her to be cautious. He said that road conditions were poor, and his warning proved to be accurate. They had used up a lot of time just getting to the turnpike. Now it was necessary to drive well below the speed limit. They were further delayed because they had to retrace the miles they had traveled in the wrong direction to get to the turnpike. Nancy was beginning to worry that she might not be home in time to meet Brett's school bus. Elizabeth was beginning to hope that Arlene had thought of checking to see if the wheelchair was outside.

The snow did not let up as they got closer to home. It was still coming down as they drove into Elizabeth's driveway. Elizabeth's wheelchair was sitting where they had left it on the concrete pad. Five inches of snow stood on the seat, on the pads of the armrests, on the cover of the motor, and on the base of the scooter. Lesser amounts stood on the handlebar controls, the wires of the basket, and the rim of the front bumper. Elizabeth didn't want to believe her eyes.

"Nancy, I think you'd better call Arlene and see if she can come and get me into the trailer. You won't be home in time for Brett if you have to deal with this mess."

"I can't believe this snow. I'll probably have to shovel a path for Brett's wheelchair." Nancy was silent trying to collect her thoughts, "Okay. What is Arlene's number?"

"It's on the front of my address book beside the living room phone."

Nancy made the phone call, then tackled the job of cleaning the snow off her van parked in front of Arlene's garage. She was ready to leave by the time Arlene came carrying a broom and a snow shovel. Arlene swept, shoveled, and pushed until she got Elizabeth into the trailer.

Although it was early in the season, Elizabeth saw this experience as a sign that it was time to go into winter mode. Winter mode meant that she stayed at home most of the time and always had someone with her when she did go out. Elizabeth and Harry agreed to put the independent study on hold until spring. Nick said that this would be a good time to start the real study into disability and reasserted his suggestion to start with the Old Testament Book of Job. Although Elizabeth still had misgivings about opening herself up to that subject, she knew that Nick was right.

The Book of Job was confusing. The whole book was a running dialogue between Job, his various friends, and finally God. Elizabeth had a difficult time keeping track of who was speaking and when the speaker changed. She made notes in the form of an outline to try to understand what she was reading. The book didn't exactly deal with disability except that Job's illnesses disabled him; and Elizabeth noted that Job wrestled with God over the same issues as she did.

While she worked on figuring out what dialogue belonged to which character, a more significant understanding dawned on Elizabeth. The reason she could not get started finding out what God teaches specifically about disabled people is that He doesn't. God does not divide people into categories. Whatever God teaches about people applies to all people. As simple as that idea was, it astounded Elizabeth. From the time she had first learned the facts about muscular dystrophy when she was fifteen, she had thought that God had assigned her to an inferior category of people.

Elizabeth had, for years, been fighting the pressure to resign herself to being less than a whole person, someone whose life had no value. Sometimes the fight was with other people, sometimes with herself and sometimes with God, but seldom was there any rest from the vigilance she had needed to keep.

Elizabeth's study now began to take shape and direction. Her misgivings no longer held her back, but Elizabeth was not a disciplined scholar. Her progress was sporadic and slow. It was too easy for Elizabeth to get side tracked by a bookkeeping problem, a new painting, or the people in her life. When the weather cleared and she started the trips to the study center again, Elizabeth regretted her lack of discipline. She feared Harry's opinion of her would go down, but Harry didn't seem to have had the same expectations that she had for herself.

Elizabeth was on one hand relieved but on the other hand unnerved and confused. Harry seemed to have his own agenda that he was fitting Elizabeth into. Elizabeth was not sure she could make herself fit. Harry's next assignment for Elizabeth was to lecture to his next group of conferees. Elizabeth was not comfortable with this assignment. Harry didn't listen to her objections. He only said, "Who will teach us about disability if you don't? Doesn't that fit with your idea of being a bridge?" Elizabeth had no answer to Harry's questions.

The long drive home gave Elizabeth time to think, but her mind was frozen in a cycle of insecurity. Elizabeth decided that it would be good to talk this over with Nick. He could help her sort things out; besides, it was time for him to critique the painting she was currently working on. She turned her mind to the familiar task of planning a menu.

Nick was an easy dinner guest. Everything didn't have to be perfect for him to enjoy the meal. Elizabeth felt free to try a new recipe or fallback on old favorites. Tonight, she had done both. The asparagus/ham casserole was a new recipe, but the cheesecake for desert was in the category of 'tried and true'. Elizabeth was glad she had made the cheesecake, as the casserole had not lived up to her expectations.

Between dinner and dessert, Nick and Elizabeth went back to the studio to evaluate the latest still life painting.

"I'm thinking this painting is finished, but there is something about it that just doesn't work." Elizabeth always felt a little uneasy when her work was being discussed. "I do really like the way the leaves of the angel wing begonia turned out."

"Uh huh." Nick agreed absently as he studied the canvas on the easel. "That patch of blue in the upper right is distracting to me. It draws the focus away from the plant."

"Really?" It was Elizabeth's turn to study the painting. "I see what you mean. I was trying to pick up the blue in the leaves, but it draws attention instead."

"You could balance it with the same blue down here. Maybe just muting it would work, but I don't think so."

"That might be the whole problem. I'll work on it and see what happens." Elizabeth felt a little stupid for not seeing the obvious herself. Nick had a good eye for what made a painting work. "Thanks, Nick. I'm ready for cheesecake. Are you?"

They returned to the living room--Elizabeth to the task of moving onto the couch as gracefully as she could manage, and Nick to the task of serving the coffee and dessert.

"Your cheesecake turned out really good. It's firmer than usual isn't it?"

"Yes, it is. I tried baking it a little longer this time. I think I like it better this way."

"It's very good." Nick stirred milk into his coffee and took a sip before going on. "What did Harry say about your winter progress on your study?"

"He didn't really discuss my ideas with me. He listened but didn't really give me feedback. He just moved on to talking about what he wants me to do next. He wants me to give a lecture at a conference at the study center next month. It will be a small group, but the idea really intimidates me."

"Did you tell Harry that?"

"I tried, but he doesn't hear. He thinks I'm something I'm not. People come to the study center to hear speakers with a reputation, not to hear me. I'm not a public speaker. People don't usually relate very well to me until they get to know me. I don't want to embarrass myself."

"Elizabeth, I think you are just going to have to prepare a lecture. Then if you don't think you can speak before the group, tell Harry and be firm. Did he give you a title for the lecture?"

"No. He's leaving that up to me. I'm just supposed to talk about something related to disability. I wish he had given me some direction. I don't even know where to start."

Nick got up and refilled their coffee cups. He cut himself another sliver of cheesecake. Elizabeth was still toying distractedly with her first piece.

"A title that just pops into my mind is 'Bridging the Disability Gap'." Nick sat down again and adjusted the amount of milk in his coffee. "Now you have a title, it gives you a place to start. Think about it!"

"Okay." Elizabeth gave a noncommittal acknowledgement of Nick's suggestion. She was not quite ready to give up her resistance to the lecture assignment, but Nick had offered his advice and closed the door on the subject for this evening.

Nick's title did release the lock on Elizabeth's mind. She finally got down to work making an outline for a lecture. Her ideas began to flow. First, she explained what she meant by a disability gap, then discussed the common element what she termed 'personhood', and ended with suggestions of ways to interact that emphasized the similarity and thus bridged the gap.

Elizabeth was basically pleased with her completed outline. She typed a final version and mailed a carbon copy to Nick for his evaluation. Nick returned it a few days later with notes penciled in the margins, some were tongue-in-cheek comments calculated to get a rise out of her and some were helpful questions or suggestions. Either way, Elizabeth could tell from Nick's comments where she was communicating clearly and where she was not.

Elizabeth had made it over the first hurdle. She had been able to organize her ideas into a lecture. The next hurdle was going to convince herself that she could actually give the lecture. Elizabeth had a week before her scheduled trip to the study center. Once or twice each day, she would take the typed papers and practice aloud. Sometimes the words would fall into place so easily that her confidence would soar. Other times, she would talk herself into a corner with no way out but to start over.

Elizabeth was as prepared as she could be; but no matter how well prepared she was, success was beyond her control.

CHAPTER 41

The early morning air had the cool freshness of a new morning with the promise of a hot summer day ahead. Elizabeth was glad to be out early before the neighborhood woke up and the hustle and bustle of ordinary life set in. She was leaving home early to give herself plenty of travel time and to give herself extra time at the study center to get organized.

Elizabeth had made the drive often enough that this part of today's trip was routine. What was not routine was the purpose of today's trip; and, for that reason, Elizabeth was tense as she drove away from her trailer and headed to the turnpike entrance outside the city limits. As usual, Elizabeth's tension gave way to a sense of freedom as she settled into the rhythm of turnpike driving.

She had an hour of easy driving ahead of her, time enough to talk through the lecture one more time. Elizabeth had already practiced it so much that she was sick of it, but she was still unsure of herself. Elizabeth resigned herself to one final practice, this time from memory. The introduction was getting too long as she searched for the right wording. Frustrated, Elizabeth decided to go on; but she could not get past the introduction. Her mind was a blank. She was dependent on her outline. Elizabeth anxiously dug through the pile of things on the seat beside her and came up with the outline.

The miles flew by as Elizabeth fumbled her way through the lecture. Much of the time she drove holding the typed pages against the steering wheel where she could easily see what came next. Elizabeth arrived at the study center somewhat less confident than she had been when she left home.

She was pleased with her timing. Harry was able to help her into Lecture House while everyone was gone for a coffee break. Elizabeth had time to gain as much composure as possible before she became the focus of attention.

People began to filter in. Elizabeth could overhear snatches of conversation as they located their seats. Two women came in chatting together. One of the women gathered up her notebooks and turned toward the front of the room.

"I'm going to move to the front row." She explained to her companion.

"I get frustrated trying to hear the speakers at times. I'm almost deaf. So I try to sit close enough to hear; and, if I can't, I'll at least be close enough to lip read."

"Let me get my things. I'll come up and sit with you."

That fragment of conversation struck a blow to Elizabeth's fragile confidence. No one could read Elizabeth's lips. It was part of the pattern of her muscular dystrophy that her facial muscles lacked normal movement. This woman had unknowingly highlighted Elizabeth's greatest fear in public speaking; and, now, she was going to be sitting within arm's reach watching Elizabeth's face through the entire lecture. Elizabeth did not know how she could give her lecture without being affected by this woman's response when she began to speak.

Before Elizabeth had time to regain her inner composure, Harry assembled the group, introduced Elizabeth, and sat down. Elizabeth clung to the typed pages of her outline. She would have to rely on the detail of the outline to get her through this lecture. Elizabeth stumbled over her first few sentences, and then she began to settle down. She was encouraged when several people began to take notes. She sensed that the audience was truly listening and that she was communicating. Elizabeth resolutely avoided looking at the woman in front of her and kept eye contact with a few people scattered through the small group who seemed to be especially interested in what she was saying.

Elizabeth talked for a half-hour. It was a little short of her assigned time, but she was at the end of her outline. In her practices, the lecture had taken longer, and she had been afraid she would talk too long. Now, she hadn't talked long enough; but she was ready to turn the floor back to Harry. She put her papers down and indicated to Harry that she was finished.

"We have about fifteen minutes for questions. Does anyone have any questions for Elizabeth?" Harry stayed where he was seated leaving the focus on Elizabeth.

Elizabeth's expression did not betray the dismay that swept through her. This had not been part of the assignment. Harry was portraying her as an expert, a resource person.

She was not what these people thought she was. Once more, she was in over her head, and it was too late to get out gracefully. Several hands went up immediately.

The fifteen minutes went quickly. Elizabeth found answers coming into her mind. They just seemed to flow. She found herself enjoying the challenge and was even able to interject a little humor at points. These people were seriously interested, and their interest drew Elizabeth out of her self-conscious insecurity and into a real desire to give them helpful answers.

"Let's have one more question then break for lunch." Harry was on his feet now, ready to take charge.

"I don't have a question, but I wanted to say 'thank you'." The woman seated in front of Elizabeth was speaking. "I'm pretty deaf, and when you first started, I was worried that I wouldn't understand anything. But you were very clear. I was able to hear everything. I really appreciate what you had to say."

The group began to clap their hands in agreement with her comments. Their response was unexpected and made Elizabeth feel awkward and unsure of herself, yet gratified at the same time.

"Lunch is in a half hour. We'll meet back here at one thirty." Harry dismissed the group and turned to Elizabeth. "Wow! That was great!"

"You're surprised? What did you expect?" Elizabeth was confused. She could never figure Harry out. She thought Harry had expected her to be a professional speaker, and she was trying to live up to his expectations.

"I knew you would do a good job, but I didn't know it would be that good! Do you want some lunch?"

"No, thank you. I have crackers and cheese to eat in the car. My mother is flying out from Colorado for a visit. I need to get home and get her room ready before she arrives."

Harry was not going to help Elizabeth sort through her feelings. His mind was already occupied with the next item on his agenda for the day. Elizabeth didn't really care. She needed some space. She was glad to get back in her car where she could be alone to examine this experience. She drove to a spot near the turnpike entrance and parked her car under a tree. Elizabeth's emotions were in turmoil. She didn't know what she was feeling. She had expected to drive home feeling relieved that this was behind her and that she had survived. No she had not survived. She had succeeded. Elizabeth didn't know how to process success.

Elizabeth reached for her thermos of coffee, poured herself a cup, and took out the crackers and cheese she had brought with her. The crackers and cheese tasted good. As she ate, Elizabeth relaxed, and as she relaxed, she wished she was not alone. Elizabeth was beginning to feel that this was a moment of personal triumph and she longed for someone to share it with.

The sun was high in the sky diminishing the amount of shade offered by the tree where she had parked her car. Elizabeth put the leftover crackers back into the bag and twisted the cup back onto the top of her thermos. If she left now, she would have time to write to Nick. He would be interested to know how her lecture went and there would be no time to get together with him. Elizabeth's mother was coming to stay in the trailer with her for the next two weeks, and Elizabeth would be responsible for arranging her mother's time and transportation. Marilyn and Arlene had family schedules to work around. Elizabeth's time was freer.

At the end of the two weeks, Elizabeth and her mother would leave for western Kansas and the McKievey family reunion. Elizabeth would be doing all the driving because her mother had recently had cataract surgery and wasn't allowed to drive yet. They planned to take three days, driving six hours a day. Elizabeth was pretty sure she could drive for six hours without getting out of the car to stretch her muscles and take a bathroom break, but that would stretch her physical tolerance to the limit.

From Kansas, her mother would take a bus back to her home in Colorado. Elizabeth was going from Kansas to a National Church Conference in Minnesota. She had arranged to travel with a Kansas family who would do the driving for her. Elizabeth's responsibility ended once they got to Kansas, and Elizabeth was looking forward to others taking over from there.

Shona was Elizabeth's faithful travel companion, but not this time. This was not a trip a dog could share. Shona was staying home under the care of Nora and Ben. Elizabeth knew Shona would be well taken care of, but she still felt a tug of sadness as she backed the car out of the driveway. Shona understood what suitcases meant, and she had stuck irritatingly close to Elizabeth all morning. Now she stood at the door watching with an expression of hurt abandonment in her eyes. There was nothing Elizabeth could do but keep going and leave it to Nora to console her dog.

Elizabeth wondered why she always chose to go to Kansas in late July or August, always the height of summer. The first day of their trip was unbearably hot. Despite the heat, it went quite well. They covered a lot of miles in six hours and Elizabeth was not too tired. Her mother managed to use the hydraulic lift and get the wheelchair out of the car at the motel. They both went to bed that night with a sense of satisfaction. The day had been one of the best mother daughter experiences they had ever shared. Elizabeth had felt an openness and trust that wasn't always evident between them. It had been like two friends traveling together.

Rain began during the night and they awoke to a gray, overcast day. They had packed food for breakfast so that they could get on the road early and have fewer stops. Elizabeth was more concerned about her stamina for driving three days straight than her mother knew, but she felt good as they quietly left the motel in the early morning while other patrons slept. Six hours went quickly. The day was still cloudy keeping the stifling heat at bay. It was early afternoon, and Elizabeth still felt good. They decided to drive on until Elizabeth needed to stop.

Elizabeth got up the morning of the third day feeling confident. The day before she had driven eight hours. That would shorten today's drive. She could do it. Later, Elizabeth was glad she had started the day with confidence. The first two days were interstate driving. On the third day, they left the interstate for state roads as they angled southwest. Off the interstate, the Kansas wind seemed more of a factor to Elizabeth. Her confidence was diminished by a growing concern as they drove through the Kansas farmland.

Still, they made good time arriving at their destination a little after noon. They had chosen to take a motel room not knowing if any of the relative's homes could accommodate Elizabeth's needs. Elizabeth's mother arranged for a room then went in to see if the room was actually workable.

"I don't know, Elizabeth. You had better come in and see if the bathroom will work."

"It looks like we'll need the small ramp for the doorstep, too. Why didn't they just make it flat!" Elizabeth's freedom to go in and out was severely limited by that one little step, and she felt a brief surge of anger.

Her mother didn't respond. She just went about her task of unloading the wheelchair and then to set up the ramp at the doorway.

"What do you think?" She asked as Elizabeth surveyed the tiny bathroom.

"If I can get through the door, I could manage. I'd better see if that's possible. The door's pretty narrow." Elizabeth maneuvered her wheelchair until she managed to just squeeze through the narrow door. Getting out was no easier than getting in. "Well it's possible."

"Shall we take the room? I think there might be another motel outside of town. It might be more modern, but probably not much."

"No, let's stay here. It's in the family." The motel was owned and operated by Elizabeth's cousin on her mother's side.

"I'll get the bags and go back and tell them we're staying."

Elizabeth was glad to be out of the car. The last stretch had been stressful. Elizabeth hadn't wanted to say anything that would worry her mother, so she had kept quiet as the stress increased.

"We have several hours before the McKievey picnic starts at six-thirty." Elizabeth's mother dropped the last of the bags on the bed. "Why don't we eat a little something, and then go see if Uncle Raymond is home. I never let him know we were coming, but he'll know that the McKievey reunion is this weekend."

Uncle Raymond was her mother's brother. A widower, he was a major landowner outside of town. Uncle Raymond was currently using his farm to feed cattle, a very odorous business but very lucrative as well.

"Okay, where am I going?" Elizabeth was again settled in the driver's seat of her car. "Do you know the way?"

"Well I ought to! I grew up around here!"

Elizabeth had not meant to insult her mother. "I'm glad you do. I have no idea how to get there. Which way shall I start out?"

They drove out of town in the direction they had come earlier. A few miles out of town, they turned off the highway onto a local road. Once Elizabeth was off the main road, she felt more confident about her driving. She could slow down and drive at her own pace. Her mother was pointing out different farms and noting changes here and there. She was touching base with her past and there was no need to hurry.

Uncle Raymond's house was not much different than Elizabeth remembered from childhood vacations. Elizabeth stopped her car beside the front gate and turned off the motor. The house was tightly closed up with an air conditioner running to keep the air from the cattle lots outside. Elizabeth's mother got out of the car and went to the door. There was no way to tell if anyone was home, but Elizabeth was pleased to see the door open. Uncle Raymond stepped out into the little entryway and greeted his sister.

Sitting in the car, Elizabeth was too far away to hear the conversation between her mother and her uncle, but she could interpret the gestures. Uncle Raymond motioned for her mother to come into the house. Her mother pointed to the car. Then they both came out to inspect the steps before coming over to the car.

"Hello there." Uncle Raymond came around to Elizabeth's open car window. "We thought you'd be coming. We've got a letter addressed to you in there."

"To me?" Elizabeth could not have been more surprised. Who would even know where she was?

"Yes. Come on in. Get out of that hot car. I'll rig up some kind of a ramp." Elizabeth's mother unloaded the wheelchair while Uncle Raymond and his son-in-law gathered boards for a makeshift ramp. Inside, Uncle Raymond took a bulky legal size envelope from a stack on the shelf beside the telephone. He handed it to Elizabeth.

Elizabeth immediately recognized Nick's handwriting. It was somehow comforting to have a tangible evidence of her ordinary life when she was feeling so far from anything familiar. Elizabeth tore the envelope open and pulled out the small handwritten page. It never ceased to surprise her how much Nick could fit on a small scrap of paper.

"Dear Elizabeth,

I hope this catches up with you before you leave for Minnesota. I was talking to Karl Smyth who is in charge of the adult program at the conference. I told him that you have a good lecture on disability. He said that you should talk to him when you get there. Karl said they might have an afternoon time slot in unscheduled time when you could present your lecture to anyone interested in disability."

Oh, Nick! I can't do that! Elizabeth thought to herself, horrified at the prospect. *I don't even know if I could reconstruct my outline at this point.*

"I'm enclosing a photocopy of the outline you sent me. I thought you probably wouldn't have packed a copy. I'll be anxious to hear how it went when you get back home."

There was a little more general news. Elizabeth pulled out the bulky contents of the envelope. It was her outline. Nick had effectively blocked off every avenue of retreat. The challenge was hers. Elizabeth was stuck in a swirl of emotions in a world of her own while family chatter went on around her. *What was she going to do?*

CHAPTER 42

Elizabeth was glad to be home again, back to her normal routines, to her own bed, and to Shona. Her travels had taken her across three thousand miles, and she had grown weary of adjusting to strange surroundings. It was good to relax in the corner of her couch again.

Looking back, Elizabeth was grateful to Nick for setting the wheels in motion for her to speak at the National Church Conference. Karl Smyth had given her a time slot and designated it a seminar on disability. More people came than Elizabeth had expected. Some of the people were Elizabeth's friends who came to offer her personal support; others were people who actually came to hear what Elizabeth had to say about disability. Elizabeth thought the response was positive. She was beginning to realize that, while this was not a popular topic, it was one that people did relate to once they got into it. Even so, Elizabeth herself was not comfortable dealing with the topic of disability publicly. She felt exposed.

She had been anxious before the seminar, sure that she had nothing of interest to say. Then, as she interacted with the audience, Elizabeth was again drawn to the challenge of communicating, of impacting their thinking. Elizabeth couldn't believe how energized it made her feel. It was out of character for her to enjoy speaking. *What did this mean? Was this God's calling for her life? Why was it all so confusing?* Elizabeth hated being the focus of attention. She was not adept at the social graces. She was not sophisticated, and she dreaded the feeling of being in over her head. *If this was God's plan, why had He not given her a personality that was compatible?*

To add to her confusion, Elizabeth came home from Minnesota to disappointing news. Harry was taking a six-month leave of absence from the study center to investigate a new project in Mississippi. Whatever was next for Elizabeth, Harry would not be guiding her. Elizabeth felt like her horizons were shrinking again just as they had begun to expand.

"What am I going to do with the rest of my life?" Elizabeth directed her question at Lynn. They were spending a rare morning together getting caught up with each other.

"Isn't that a little melodramatic?" Lynn liked to deal with substance. "I'm not sure exactly what you mean."

"I guess it is, but that's what I'm feeling. I was making a life here in the trailer that is good, but I was also trying to learn not to want more. That's what I thought God expected of me. Now I'm not so sure. Harry Wilson says we should always be growing in our vocation, and it's made me question whether I'm living up to my vocation and calling. I'm wondering what my calling really is."

"When you were meeting with Harry, did you identify your vocation?"

"Not exactly. I never totally understood Harry's thinking, but I did decide that I'm supposed to be a bridge. I'm comfortable with that. Everything I do just living can be seen as a bridge. Is that enough, or am I supposed to be doing more?"

"I think what you did at the national conference last summer would fit into that bridge idea. You really got people thinking. Why don't you do more of that?"

"How? I wouldn't have done that if Nick hadn't set it up. There just aren't opportunities, and I almost need a captive audience. People don't think they will be interested. Nick says I need an public relations agent."

"I have an idea. Could you expand what you did at the conference and make it into a series of classes?"

"I'm not sure. Give me a minute to think about it. Are you ready for more coffee?" While Lynn went to the kitchen for the coffeepot, Elizabeth tried to visualize the different sections of her outline. Lynn poured their coffee in silence and settled back into the armchair. Elizabeth picked up the conversation where they had left off. "I could probably stretch it into four classes. What are you thinking?"

"Well, this doesn't answer the question of the rest of your life but in the spring we were planning to have a class in the church school hour on aging. Nathan would teach it, and he doesn't really want to do the whole quarter. I was thinking we could split the quarter. You could have the first four weeks, and Nathan could finish the quarter. What do you think?"

"I could probably do it. Is it the quarter that starts in April? That would give me time to prepare, and the weather should be okay."

"We could do that. We could make it the third quarter."

"Go ahead and bring it up to the Christian Education Committee."

Lynn called Elizabeth the following week to report that the committee had approved her idea. They were titling Elizabeth's part of the series of classes 'A Biblical View of Disability'. Elizabeth's next step was now clear and keeping busy with the preparation allowed her to avoid deeper questions that seemed to have no answer.

After the insight that came to her when she had studied the Book of Job and discovered that God did not separate disabled people into a category of their own, Elizabeth had set aside her plan to study what the Bible teaches about disability. Now to fulfil this new assignment to present a Biblical view of disability, she would have to follow through on the study she had only begun. Nick could not hide his glee when he heard that Elizabeth was being directed back to his original suggestion.

This time, though, Elizabeth was not dragging her feet, afraid of what she might learn about God's attitude toward her. This time it would be a matter of studying how God relates to people and of thinking about how to apply those concepts to disabled people. Elizabeth was ready to clarify some of those things for herself.

As the day of the first class neared, Elizabeth became aware of another dynamic going on within her. These people who would be in the class were her church family. Elizabeth had maintained a measure of safety in these relationships by her ostrich style. This class was going to be a step away from her ostrich style, and Elizabeth was anxious to assure that they understand what she wanted them to understand from what she would be saying.

Elizabeth planned carefully for the first class. This class would set the pace for the whole series. She wanted to be as relaxed and confident as possible. Elizabeth decided that one thing that would help would be to attend the early worship service. The church had two services with the church school between the two services. If she went to the early worship service, she would be in the building and not be rushing in just before the class. Elizabeth often attended the early service. It would not be anything out of the ordinary.

Spring weather had been perfect this year, and the morning of the first class was no exception. Elizabeth closed the front door behind her. She was giving herself a little extra time to drive to the church. She wanted to be sure she got to the church in plenty of time for one of her helpers to see that she was there and come out to get the wheelchair out of the car and help her into the building.

Elizabeth had climbed into the car and was pushing the wheelchair away from the car door when she looked up to see a huge black cloud covering the sky behind Arlene's house and moving in their direction. The weather forecast had been for possible scattered showers. Could she possibly risk leaving the wheelchair unprotected? If it did rain, Elizabeth would come home to find the seat of the wheelchair full of water and the cloth seat pad so soaked that it would take days to dry out. There was really no choice. She would have to get back onto the wheelchair, go into the trailer, and get the plastic chaise lounge cover she used as a rain tent for the wheelchair. Elizabeth was glad she had allowed herself extra time.

Getting the bulky plastic over the front wheel bumper and over the controls and still being able to maneuver the chair was difficult. Elizabeth got the job done and was back in the car. She pulled the cover down over the seat securing it as well as possible, pushed the chair away from the car, and climbed across into the drivers seat before she allowed herself to look at the clock.

Elizabeth still had ten minutes. She might make it. She had just as well try. If she didn't, she didn't. While the engine warmed up, Elizabeth studied the location of the wheelchair so she would know where to park when she came home. She shifted into reverse and backed out. The drive wouldn't take long if she didn't get the traffic light on red. The light was red, but it changed quickly. She was still all right.

Elizabeth turned into the alley that ran downhill along side of the large stone structure, which was her church building. The Deacons had built a concrete ramp to one of the two doors that opened on the high side of the hill. The doors opened into the entryways on either side of the pulpit area at the front of the church sanctuary. They were actually in front of the seated people. Usually, Elizabeth hated that, but in this instance, it would be a help because someone would see her drive up.

As she drove down the alley, Elizabeth saw that the heavy wooden door was shut. She guided the car between the two old oak trees, drove onto the lawn, and parked in her usual place. Moments later, the chimes in the college belfry across the street signaled the hour. Despite everything, she had made it in time, and she was shut out! *Elizabeth was enraged!*

The rage took her by surprise and consumed her. Angry thoughts swirled around in her head. She was not late. *Why wasn't someone watching for her? Why should she always have to get places early? Everyone else could slip in late, but for her it wasn't even enough to be on time! Who shut the door anyway? On nice days like this, it was always left open! Now she would just get into the church in time for her class, no time to calm down and get organized! How was she going to present a positive view of disability after being shut out because of disability!*

Where was God, anyway? God was in control of everything. He let the black cloud come when it did. In fact, He could have made sure someone thought of watching for her. *Why did she always have to be alone? Why was it so impossible for anyone to ever want to share her life? Why did she always have to prove her worth by keeping the burden of her life away from others? Well, she failed today!*

"Get hold of yourself." Elizabeth spoke aloud to try to break out of the cycle. "You've got an hour. Do something constructive."

The outline for the class was on the seat beside her. Elizabeth picked it up to review it and tossed it down in disgust. Words, meaningless words! Her mind picked up the tirade where she had stopped it a minute earlier.

"No! No! You have to calm down." Elizabeth had no idea how to calm herself but she knew she could not teach a class in her present state of mind. Her eyes fell on her Bible on the seat.

Elizabeth picked the Bible up. She opened it to the Book of Psalms and began to read at random. Her mind would not focus, but she read on, forcing her angry words to give place to other words. What she was reading had no meaning, had no impact; but reading the Psalms was distancing her from the raw emotion she had been caught up in. Elizabeth read on.

Unexpectedly, the words at the end of Psalm 73 caught her attention. 'The nearness of God is my good.' Yes! The words brought Elizabeth a flash of memory of the night when she, as a young child, realized that God was a real presence and had cling to that.

'I have made the Lord God my refuge.' Yes! That is what got her through some difficult times in Philadelphia and since.

'That I may tell of all Thy works.' No. Elizabeth felt jolted. She felt convicted. She had been sitting in her car telling God how He had failed her with no thought of His good works in her life.

Elizabeth's mind was turned to recalling God's faithfulness to her. Her anger was gone. The chimes at the college announced the new hour. People were beginning to arrive for the church school classes. Joan and Doug Johnston waved to her and cut across the lawn to her car.

"Good morning!"

"I wasn't sure at first if you were in the car or not." Doug opened the car door. "Can I get the wheelchair out for you?"

"Yes, thank you. I'm ready to go in."

The class was not Elizabeth's most successful. She was not completely at ease. The people gave her their complete attention but not the audience response that would have helped her forget her own awkwardness. They did enter into the discussion time and seemed generally positive. Elizabeth had not realized that this would be as sensitive a time for them as it was for her. Her experience this morning had somehow altered her goals for the series of classes, but it was still too fresh for Elizabeth to sort everything out.

CHAPTER 43

Elizabeth's series of classes were finished. They had gone well. In fact, someone from another church nearby asked her to give the same series of classes in their church. However, even that was finished now; and Elizabeth felt like it had been another false start. Her life settled back into the familiar routine with cooking and painting being Elizabeth's creative outlets. Beaver Falls, in her circles, was a transient area; and a number of her friends had moved on. New acquaintances were becoming friends and filling the empty spots. Yet, Elizabeth missed the comfortable companionship of her old friends.

Loretta had left Beaver Falls to work in Scotland for two years. Now, she was back in the states but had relocated in Philadelphia. Elizabeth was pleasantly surprised when she answered the phone to hear Loretta's voice.

"Elizabeth? This is me, Loretta."

"Loretta. It's good to hear from you. Are you in town?"

"No. No. I'm in Philly. I stayed home from work today with one of my headaches and decided it would be a good time to give you a call. What are you doing these days?"

"Actually, nothing to talk about. How do you like working for a woman's college?"

"I'm enjoying it and learning lots. Some of these students are so mixed up in their thinking, but I won't get into that now. I wanted to ask, 'Are you doing any speaking these days?'"

"No. I've pretty much hit a dead end in that."

"I'm in charge of the spring woman's retreat out here. I don't know how I let myself get talked into it. You know me; I'm no organizer. Anyway, I suggested you as the speaker."

"Oh, Loretta, I don't know."

"You would speak on Friday evening and on Saturday morning. We thought we would have a panel discussion after lunch on Saturday." Loretta brushed aside Elizabeth's reservations. "We're meeting at the Glenn Cove Conference Grounds. It would really be great if you were there. We'd have a chance to get some time together."

"I'm assuming that you want me to talk on the subject of disability."

"More or less. It's not set in stone, but that is the direction the committee was thinking."

"How much time do I have to think about it?"

"The committee's meeting again at the end of the month. I should have an answer for them by then, if I can."

"Okay. I'll get back to you. Can you find out if the conference facilities are accessible?"

Loretta had offered Elizabeth an opportunity to reopen a door that Elizabeth thought was closed. It was disconcerting in a way. Elizabeth had finally gotten past all her questioning of God to the point of accepting the fact that this was just another closed door. Then the door opened a crack again, and Elizabeth was being drawn through it.

As Elizabeth thought about the conference, ideas flooded her mind. She would take a different approach. The first evening, she would talk about being a bridge. Elizabeth would tell about her own journey to understand what the Scripture teaches about disabled persons. With that background, she would go on the next day to the more practical issues of how to relate to each other. She could do it. Loretta was very encouraging when Elizabeth told her what she would plan to do. It was settled. Elizabeth just had to get the outlines of her talks written.

The outline for the first of two talks Elizabeth was to give had been painfully slow to take shape. It had seemed quite possible when she said "yes", but now she doubted herself. It was only the pressure of the days slipping away that kept Elizabeth at her typewriter not wanting the day to come and find her unprepared, floundering in front of an audience.

Elizabeth's style of typing was slow and methodical. With one finger searching out one letter at a time, her thoughts took shape on the page before her. She was revealing a lot about herself in this talk. That is what Elizabeth hoped would make it work as a vehicle for teaching, but letting herself be so vulnerable was hard.

Elizabeth rolled the final page out of the typewriter and read what she had written. The concluding words of this outline had surprised her. They just seemed to flow out, tying all her ideas together. The words that Elizabeth had typed out onto the paper had come from her mind. Now, as she read the outline, it was the reality of their meaning that caught her by surprise. Suddenly, her life made sense in a way it never had before. Events that had been stored away in her memory as difficult or unhappy experiences came out as part of her journey. Pieced together, they each had value, each was necessary as part of God's shaping of who she was. Pain is not wasted, nor is it unimportant. Everything fit.

Elizabeth had no idea why this had not been clear to her before. In fact, it had. She had even voiced it before, but there is a moment when a person moves from knowledge to belief. For Elizabeth, this was that moment. If this outline spoke to no one else, it spoke to Elizabeth and it answered years of 'why'.

The second outline was much easier to prepare. Elizabeth could use a lot of what she had done before in the church school classes. She knew from discussions after other lectures what questions were usually most troubling to people. Still, it was difficult for Elizabeth to keep herself at the typewriter; but she did finish before the deadline.

For the most part, Elizabeth enjoyed the conference. There were friends at the conference that she had not seen for a long time, however being identified as the main speaker kept her from blending in and enjoying some of the informal times. Elizabeth's focus had been on her talks, and they both succeeded in the ways that she had hoped they would. That was most important to Elizabeth.

Once more, the door had opened briefly and then swung shut again. This time, Elizabeth was more willing to allow things to take their own course. In fact, she was somewhat relieved to be free for a while of the stress that came with developing lectures and speaking in public. Life resumed its usual routine, a 'dailyness' punctuated by a crisis now and then.

Shannon, one of her new friends, was sitting in her living room asking Elizabeth's advice on one of those crises that had just arisen last night. Shannon worked as a resident adviser at the college.

"Then you think I should just let it go?" Shannon asked.

"Right now, I think you should. There may be a time when you can address it and you will have more impact then than you will now." Elizabeth had listened patiently *(and with some interest)* to a long, detailed account of a college prank gone wrong.

"Well, I just think they've got to learn." Shannon was too close to it to get any real perspective on the incident.

"Go ahead and confront them if you think it's best. I do think that will just accelerate the conflict and be counter productive in the end."

"Oh! Look at the time! I've got a meeting. Thanks for listening."

Shannon hurried out the door. She had stayed longer than she had intended because she did value Elizabeth's counsel on the conflict she was embroiled in. The abruptness of Shannon's departure left Elizabeth a little disoriented.

Elizabeth remained sitting in her place on the end of her couch. Without invitation, thoughts of loneliness filtered into her mind and the familiar struggle with loneliness began. She had many friends. People liked Elizabeth and often came to talk, to share, to be encouraged. When she was with someone in a one-to-one situation, Elizabeth's mind was fully engaged in trying to understand and respond to the other person in a meaningful way. It meant a lot to Elizabeth to have in-depth conversations and to know that what she said counted.

Strangely, though, it often left Elizabeth, as now, struggling with loneliness. *Why?* Elizabeth asked herself, asked God. *Why am I so likeable and yet not likeable enough for anyone to care enough to want to share my life?* She knew the answer to that, but her disability was on the outside. There was a real person on the inside. *Why didn't people see the real Elizabeth? Why didn't that count?*

In a flash of insight, Elizabeth understood. She understood that for someone to share her life they had to be willing to be identified with her. Sharing was easy but identity was not. Elizabeth knew that she herself had resisted that identity with other disabled persons. *How could she expect more from someone else?*

As her mind began to grapple with this, Elizabeth's thoughts turned into prayer. Elizabeth thanked God for this understanding which could only have come from Him; and she felt freed from some of the pain of the rejections she had experienced. With silent tears rolling down her cheeks, she forgave those who she had only been able to excuse before.

As Elizabeth's heart and mind were turned toward God, words came into her mind, words that had to have come from God. Words that said, "But I want to identify with you. It's my own choice. I'm not ashamed to have people look at you and see me. I've given you my name." Elizabeth was overwhelmed. Tears were flowing freely now. For that moment, all loneliness was gone. All the feelings of failure and inadequacy vanished. For that moment, Elizabeth was filled with a sense of peace and purpose. She belonged.

* * * * *

At the sound of the front door, Elizabeth roused herself from her memories. Her half-full mug of coffee was stone cold. Early dusk was just beginning to creep into the dining room where she sat.

"What are you doing, Aunt Elizabeth?" Nora came in carrying a few items Arlene had picked up for Elizabeth at the grocery store.

"I was just thinking, and I sort of lost track of the time. Would you flip on the light, please? Thanks."

"Mom said she made stuffed peppers for supper. She said to ask you if you want her to send a plate over tonight. Have you eaten already?" Even as a teenager, Nora still made herself available to Elizabeth if she was needed.

"No. I haven't even thought about supper. Stuffed peppers would be great."

"Okay. I'll be back."

The activity in the house brought Shona to the door. Elizabeth moved to the door and slid the screen open so that Shona could come inside.

"I guess you're getting hungry, too. Huh, Shona?" Elizabeth was following the dog as she headed for her empty bowls. "Get back. I'll get you some food."

Elizabeth was glad that she didn't have to think about cooking. She was still too involved in her memories. Nora returned with a plate of food. It was just like Nora to bring Elizabeth's food before she ate her own meal.

"I hope you like it. Can I get you anything else?"

"No. This is great. Tell your mother 'thanks'."

Elizabeth was hungrier than she had realized. She ate quickly. Then she treated herself to another mug of coffee and the last of the carrot cake. The faded papers lay beside her place at the table. Elizabeth's thoughts turned back to the words she had written so long ago. Elizabeth was still pondering the imagery in the narrative she had written. She had described her life as a series of bright flames that flared briefly and turned quickly to dying embers. It was a fatalistic point of view born out of her flawed thinking that she was not a whole person and her life had no value. In those days, Elizabeth had been more surprised by the flames than by the embers. The embers she expected, but the flames stirred up feelings and hopes that Elizabeth thought she had no right to feel.

Elizabeth tried to sort through the parade of memories that had been stirred up this afternoon. In a way, that younger Elizabeth had been right. There were a lot of times her life seemed to flame up with bright promise only to die down again leaving only the coals of promise. What she had not understood then was that the coals, the embers were sometimes as valuable as the flames.

No, there was something else that described her life more accurately. Elizabeth's memories had made that clear. There was an ancient custom in the Middle East. When something significant happened in a place, the people would place a large stone at that location as a reminder. They called them 'standing-stones'.

In the Old Testament, God's people wandered in the desert for forty years and in that desert, they left a number of standing-stones. When the people saw a standing-stone, they were reminded of God and His faithfulness. The stories of His dealings with them were passed down from generation to generation, and retold whenever they passed a standing-stone.

As Elizabeth finished her coffee, she was envisioning a standing-stone set up at every flash of flame and dying ember in her memory. She gathered up the faded pages of her old narrative. Elizabeth was ready to put them back into their file. Someday, she would write another narrative. A narrative that would characterize her life as she now saw it. That would characterize it as a trail of standing stones. Standing stones that merged and fit together, making Elizabeth herself a standing stone."

THE END